J. M.

J. M. O'Neill was born in Limerick City and in the early 1950s worked as a bank official in Ireland, England, Nigeria and Ghana (then the Gold Coast). Returning to the UK, he joined the building construction ranks, becoming an agent and supervising work in many parts of London, the Thames riverside, and the Home Counties. Subsequently he established, in 1967, the Sugawn Theatre and Sugawn Kitchen (a well-known venue for folk music) in Islington.

In 1980 he settled in Hornsey, North London, to devote himself to writing. His plays include *Now You See Him, Now You Don't, Diehards* and *God is Dead on the Ball's Pond Road*. He is also the author of two other novels, OPEN CUT and DUFFY IS DEAD, both published in Sceptre.

Praise for CANON BANG BANG

'Like George V. Higgins of Boston, O'Neill excels at deadpan dialogue and keeps his descriptive powers confined to essential detail . . . Go out and buy it now. J. M. O'Neill is one of the greats'

*Irish Times 'Pick of the Year'*

'A pyrotechnic display of sheer and original mental agility'

*The Sunday Press, Dublin*

'At the simplest level it sets the "sea-divided Gael" in an entirely new focus, casting a searching and unsentimental light on the world of the first and second generation London Irish and their relationship with the wider community. This, however, is only one facet of a book which seems at times to be trying to burst the exactly-calculated confines of its refreshingly modest length. Don't miss it'

*Bernard Share in The Irish Times*

J. M. O'Neill

# CANON BANG BANG

**British Library C.I.P.**

O'Neill, J. M. (Jerry M.)
    Canon Bang Bang.
    I. Title
    823'.914[F]

    ISBN 0-340-54266-7

Printed and bound in Great Britain for Hodder and Stoughton Paperbacks, a division of Hodder and Stoughton Ltd., Mill Road, Dunton Green, Sevenoaks, Kent TN13 2YA. (Editorial Office: 47 Bedford Square, London WC1B 3DP) by Clays Ltd., St Ives plc.

# CANON
## BANG BANG

# Thursday

This was an October morning. Paul Vincent Herlihy, private person, had dressed: a long black flowing cassock, black shoes, a white clerical collar showing at the neck. His bedroom windows were heavily curtained: beyond them, wind gusted and trees and shrubs must be tangled in the sudden confusions; then, in respite, it faded to hoarseness like a distant ebb of tide on gravel.

Grey morning light would be paling outside and, at low water, the river ugly and its littered fissured mud banks. He had arranged his bed. On a bedside table a lamp burned and there was a book: a hand-bound volume of thick manuscript sheets in a coarse leather covering of some animal hide that had been home-tanned, shaped, tenterhooked, and laced with flat slender thongs about a cardboard binder more than a century and three quarters before.

There was an oaken desk and chair facing a curtained window; a blotter, an elaborate inkwell, no longer functional, an open invoice file, letters – 'Mr. P. V. Herlihy', 'Fr. Herlihy', 'The Reverend Canon Paul Vincent Herlihy': a place of business.

He turned a fresh page of a desk diary: Thursday, 29th October 1988.

He had arranged an easel and drawing-board close to his desk. It displayed a ground plan, seemingly uncluttered, uncomplicated, a draughtsman's copy – houses, streets, the River. Framed in the lower right-hand corner was the legend: 'Dory's Jetty. Paul Vincent Herlihy Esq'.

He stood about five feet ten, spare, greying a little, perhaps fifty. An untroubled face. Then suddenly he brought the leather-bound folio from the bedside to his desk, poised an angle light above it and sat. He began again to read

1

the previous night's pages: heavy parchment leaves, careful quilled script, Indian ink that had blackened with age . . .

'*1806. December 1st. London. Dory's Jetty. Three days since on the Dory Spray I returned from the town of Cork on the southern coast of His Majesty's possession, Ireland and its endowments, and in my illness have prepared to indite some brief memorandum of the events, fearful events, that were the culmination of our voyage.*

*November 4th. We left Thames headlands in calm water with valuable cargo stowed. This for our English Lords or their Agents, who are engaged in clearing, indeed the extirpation, of the almost sub-human peasant species indigenous to this Kingdom of Ireland, itself such a bounteous land. Our gracious Majesty, as is custom, rewards great Nobility, his most faithful, with such generous tracts of demesne as may reflect his gratitude. There are some who have chosen to reside over there but a great number, indispensable to our domestic wellbeing, despatch their Agents – men of honour and integrity – who, while retaining a labouring quota, are in the process of weeding the ground so that in not many decades it will be an extension of our England, hardly a jewel, but a modest fragment at least, in the Crown.*

*We Dorys have entered contract to make this voyage once the calendar month and in all five years past have not failed in our commitment. This, my first sailing, was a visit of courtesy and gratitude. The English merchants of distinction and repute in Cork were lavish in their hospitality. Here are two worlds. The English of order, cleanliness, Godliness and law. The other, a kind of savagery moving towards extinction. Famine visits their indolence at regular intervals and roads and streets teem with beggars. Ports have their droves of ragged wastrels too, fares bequeathed by compassionate landlords for passage to Bristol or London. Even prison in our good country, I'm told, with food and shelter, the absence of responsibility, is adequate for these wretches.*

*At ports, whenever possible of course, we assist them. It is a cost of twenty-four pence below to Wapping and London, eighteen pence on deck, and we spare them a little, leave with them some few pence for arrival. We feel the Good Lord has bestowed us a double blessing. They will not arrive destitute on English shores and, to ourselves, even with danger of fever, they are a saving of costly ballast when homeward bound.*

*But in recompense for generosity one does not anticipate murder and madness.*

*I can scarcely summon the steel to contemplate it and in setting down its occurrence a very few words must suffice. In winter, death on deck is not uncommon and if, in east wind, some are frozen to the deck, they must be chipped off as best we can, wrapped and weighted and put over the side. Prayers are recited by the Master of course and every dignity observed.*

*At Cork, a man Sulvan brought his dying wife aboard. At Dungeness on the Thames approach she was lifeless, frozen to the boards at Greenwich. There is a fear ashore of these people, their filth, their fever, and we sunk her remains at night in the deep mud by the Jetty.*

*He was a towering madman even in beggary, this Sulvan. With an axe he smashed our bosun Maxwell's chest like a shell. And the Master, Jonathan Dowty, was split from head to windpipe. But our hangman, McMorrow, one of themselves, will have him. They put a small price on each other. He will hang for seven tides to cover him and the rats to feed . . .'*

Paul Vincent Herlihy turned the page and read from the 'ballast' list, one hundred and forty souls. He paused at '. . . *Sulvan . . . Herlihy . . . Delacey . . . Kilmartin . . . Harney . . .'*

He closed the coarse leather folio, placed it carefully beside his desk.

Fear, whatever pale shade, in the eyes of a Man of God is a beacon: mere persons, animate small things, it seems, were made to halt and squeak and scamper, not warranting a second glance: fortitude resides in the blessed.

The Reverend James Kilmartin was afraid.

He stood alone in this spacious ecclesiastical study of oak panelling, a screened empty fire grate, marble massive surround and overmantel; above it, a black crucifix and a white dying Christ.

3

The curtains were drawn on embrasured windows, except for one: this single magnificent spyhole on the world, of leaded diamond panes, was chased and cusped. Its light fell on the back of what could be called a throne – Tudor perhaps, square, heavy, clumsy – and filtered out in the ambience to embrace the robed Kilmartin.

A young man, not tall or strong, but a restlessness about him, a threat of hardness even; and he was in fear, looking at this empty chair.

Empty, it seemed, however ominous. There was a footstool but no feet rested on it.

The Chair spoke; it said "For twelve years . . ."

"Ten years, my Lord Bishop," Father Jim Kilmartin said.

"Ten." The Chair awaited silence. "Ten, ten, ten," it said slowly. "Ten years a tool, an errand boy, and whatever other unchaste roles it entailed, to this demented ageing whore . . ."

"Lucy Dory-Catchpole," Father Jim said. "She was a very virtuous person, I'm told. She was dying."

"We all die," the Chair said.

"Yes, my Lord."

"Her estate entire, immense wealth, bequeathed to an errand boy."

"He is the sole beneficiary."

"An errand boy, Father Kilmartin. An ageing anointed debauchee . . . an erstwhile curate of our dioceses."

"He approaches fifty now, my lord."

"He is damned, Father Kilmartin."

"Of course."

"These lands, her possessions, to a renegade servant of God."

"Yes."

"The Reverend Paul Vincent Herlihy."

Father Jim summoned courage. He wore a cassock to the ground, its fabric buttons and sash deepening in the scattered light.

"As I mentioned before, my lord . . ."

"Yes?"

"The estate was bequeathed to *Paul Vincent* Herlihy."

"Yes?"

4

"Not to *Father* Herlihy."

The Chair said, "He is the Reverend *Father* Paul Vincent Herlihy to his dying breath. Forbidden of course, long since, to practise his sacred duties, sent away, banished. A 'silenced priest'. But, ordained, he is a priest for ever – for ever! – and his possessions are the possessions of our Mother Church."

Stillness for a while again.

"You fill me with unease sometimes, Father Kilmartin. I wonder if you have the steel, the temper . . . yes, even moments when pity is absent . . . for the burdens that rank might bring you. You look about you a lot. I wonder sometimes."

Had Paul Vincent Herlihy looked about at his desolation too, Father Jim pondered in this moment when pity was not absent; the room was warm and airless.

"Herlihy is a strange man," he said.

"*Father* Herlihy."

"Yes," Father Jim amended. "Father Herlihy is a strange man."

"A heretical boor, Father," the Chair was arbiter, "who told his flock that the time to worship God had not yet come. We had to find Him first."

"In ourselves," Father Jim remembered: it was more than twelve years past.

"A gigolo, missing for days on end, for weeks once, I remember, his church locked and barred." The Chair was silent in its anger. "Looking for God, perhaps! Do you think he found Him?"

"I'm told he used to fast, sit in hospital warrens for the aged, that kind of thing. For the demented too. Sit through days and nights."

"Until they too shut their gates against him," the Chair said.

Father Jim was silent.

"Did you hear?"

"Yes."

"Hospitals are circumspect, discreet. Equipment was inter-fered with. You were aware, Father?"

"There had been rumours."

5

"You knew?"

"He erred of course," Father Jim said. "But there had been a great deal of suffering. A terminal agony."

The Chair – however small its hidden occupant – made a great sound. "Only God terminates! Do you hear?"

"He erred grievously, my lord."

"He *murdered*!"

"Yes."

"Sent souls to judgment before God had called them!"

"Yes."

"And how many more?"

Father Jim remained silent: only silence and even striving for humility, could rescue him from the perilous displeasure he had aroused. The lustre of high places palled; he thought of quiet measured years of honest shepherding, without possessions, a little weariness at the end of the day, perhaps the self-indulgence of an overspilling plate, a glass of wine.

But now the incubus of this Dory-Catchpole estate and its inheritor, Paul Vincent Herlihy, shaded every hour.

He could remember the expulsion, the departure, of the Reverend P. V. Herlihy, the awesome interdict, *urbi et orbi*. It had filled him with the dread of damnation. More frightening was the serenity of Herlihy, empty-handed, walking from the parochial house, unchanged, a man seemingly with direction, purpose. But what?

More than a decade now and he had surfaced again, a free-holder of golden riverside land, dwellings, immense wealth, a mile, perhaps two, from the rising wonderland of pleasure domes and man-made lakes that was creeping towards him to proliferate his riches.

There was a walled churchyard and its glebe: an impregnable church, a People's Hall: they had been derelict but cherished and tended down the years. The Rectory, set apart, was Herlihy's domicile where he had assuaged the dying years of his benefactor, Lucy Dory-Catchpole.

And there were six acres of ground to boot. It had been a village. Dory's Jetty.

The Chair said, "You have made no progress then?"

"Oh yes, my Lord Bishop. The church and People's Hall.

As you know, we have rented them, consecrated them. A kind of auxiliary parish. A foot in the door, so to speak. We are on his land."

"The Church's land."

"The Church's land, my lord. We are in residence there. Makeshift, of course, but adequate."

"We are tenants."

"There is a person, Harney, too, a factotum, my clerk, you could call him. A vigil is kept. It is a desolate place. Perhaps a great parish of the future."

"In residence?" The Chair waited.

"Two years, my lord."

"Progress?"

Absence of pity, Father Jim thought; anger stirred.

"Progress?"

He said, "There will be no bequests from Herlihy. No deals. No progress."

"Cost?"

"A waste, a ransom, a folly! I'll have a statement sent you! Cost? A hundred thousand . . . more!"

"You are becoming angry, Father."

"Yes."

"Good."

"We are skirmishing with this man . . ."

"Priest."

"We need to fight battles."

"Then fight them."

"Battles cost a great deal of money."

"Then spend it."

"I have begun to spend it!"

"Ah."

Father Jim was a little breathless. He rested, waited for a slowing pulse.

"Yes?" the Chair said.

"We need something of a hatchet-man, my lord. Unconscionable."

"Violent?"

"Greedy."

"Yes."

7

Father Jim looked at his watch. "A man," he said, "called McMorrow."

An endless empty silence; only traffic sounds beyond the heavy glazing.

Eventually, "McMorrow." The Chair spoke with authority, dignity, a clipped assurance of tradition: four hundred years of ineradicable Catholicism. Catholicism of high rank and possessions that had confronted Monarchs and Masonry. English Catholicism; a precious élite. "McMorrow. Irish, is he?"

"Yes."

"Slippery?"

"Well, clever. Greedy too."

"Do you feel Irish, Father Kilmartin?"

"I was born in London, my lord."

"I am aware."

"My parents, of course . . ."

"Yes."

He thought of them with a little sadness: that they should be dismissed in a syllable. The patriarch publican, Kilmartin, man not of one pub but three, abstemious, pinching, perhaps dishonest too; and his regal schoolmarm wife.

He said, "They were immigrants?"

"Of course."

"Dead now," Father Jim reminded. "Their money, properties, everything, the Church's, my lord."

"They are remembered in our prayers."

"Yes," Father Jim said.

The schoolmarm, admirable woman, had merged with indigenous masses, to espy them, rise above them, polished, confident; had had bestowed on her the mayoral trappings of their borough, had bequeathed him the practised accentless delivery that had lived in wireless sets of her youth.

"You crossed to Irish bastions for erudition, of course."

"To boarding school, yes."

'Bastions' had been spoken without emphasis. Another 'word', and somehow in its very tonelessness was condescension. Anger stirred again; he let it waste.

"This man, McMorrow, my lord . . ."

"Details are your affair, Father."

Calmness had returned: he could hear the rustle of shrubs when the wind gusted. The gloom of this hallowed apartment had lessened. Framed parchments were on the wall: records of distinction, elevation, knowledge of holiness and divinity. Ancestral pictures too: accoutred men-at-arms, laymen of elegant quality, their dainty spouses and broods forefronting a world of pasture, woodland, distant hills: great dead canvases beneath a patina of age. Beside them, the Victorian photographist of cowls and flares, head-clamps, props, buttresses for tiring buttocks, caught only the reality of these demigods, could add no sweep of grandeur: high-collared, frock-coated overlords, but faces from a faceless crowd; leather-bound tomes, stubby hands upon them, proud moustached men, seated, enthroned, and their grateful handmaids made fast behind them.

A clock chimed the quarter somewhere in a room or a corridor, and its sound hung there, lingered in this palace of sanctimony.

"Father Herlihy. He still attends to the aged, my lord. A single worker's dwelling on his land, the Church's land, is a hospice. A cabin, that's all. Old ones come there to die."

"There's a doctor?"

"Everything."

"A nurse?"

"A Miss Delacey. Catherine Delacey . . ."

"Who shares his rectory?"

"Yes."

"And his bed?"

"I have no idea, my lord. But there will be other dwellings. For death. Dwellings for dying. A village. He plans a village."

There were moments of silence.

"They will be 'helped' to die?"

Confusion descended upon Father Jim.

"Father?"

"Yes."

"You agree?"

"Yes, my lord."

9

"We are aware of his intentions, Father Kilmartin. The Church's chain of power reaches everywhere. We too have our knight errants, men of honour."

"Nothing has been built, my lord."

"*I* have seen to that."

Again the awful moments of silence; Father Jim stirred, prepared to leave.

"Are you afraid, Father?" A nuance of humour.

"It is a strange place, my lord."

"A strange place, a strange priest."

"Forbidding."

"Ghosts, Father?" Almost laughter now. "Gaelic goblins, banshees, little people?"

There weren't words to describe unease: the certainty sometimes of being at once alone and accompanied, a rising fear that had to be confronted, constrained. But Father Jim was ambitious. He was silent.

"A lonely place," he said, eventually.

"You are doing very well."

Magnanimity from the Chair!

"Plans need creatures great and small. Hatchet-men too. You have not gone unnoticed in higher places, Father Kilmartin."

The episcopal hand with its ring had been proffered and Father Jim knelt and touched it with his lips. At the door, he stood and bowed.

The Chair said, "We have an ageing Monsignor in our dioceses, Father. He stands down in six months or less. Your name has been mentioned. You might have things shipshape by then?"

"Yes, my Lord."

Down in the hallway again, he rang for a taxi. In a dressing-room he divested himself of cassock and sash, like a weekend footballer packed them in a holdall: this medieval garb of deference to His Lordship, a changeless liturgy, a reassurance of timeless obedience! He opened a leather suitcase, carefully began the business of dressing for the outside world.

Time had wasted: an hour, more, endured in that twilight courtroom.

10

James Kilmartin, Monsignor, he thought for a moment; it had an aura.

And now, Dermot McMorrow, at a stroke clothed with a fresh importance. Details are your affair, Father . . . Monsignor . . . Monsignor James Kilmartin.

The priming, the aiming of McMorrow would be a discreet progression, Father Jim decided, played moment to moment, watched from high places: a delicate hand on the line would be expected from the short-listed James Kilmartin.

And escape from that possessed, whispering, accursed plot by the river.

In Park Lane, the hotel, resplendent and with not a little prestige, but with only remnants of its feudal dignity, stood tall. The pale gold of October sunshine caught the windows here and there, laid a bright yellow piping along its penthouse peak. The fall was settling on park and trees too: the grass paler, the leaves losing their grip.

McMorrow's studio apartment was in the high upper storeys: smart lounge, a bedroom, the other amenities en suite. He rented it sometimes, month to month: boardroom, pied-à-terre, bolthole, bordello, belvedere even.

As you liked it, as he required it.

He stood, telephone in hand, gazing down, groomed, carefully packaged – an aura of reserve, a hint of style, even wealth – so that hardly a glint of trickery showed. The commissionaire down there, befrocked, stovepipe hat, even polished skin, stood watch on a broad arc of steps to the wrought iron screens and doors that shut out the clangour of pavement and roadway, the endless shooting rapids of traffic.

Behind was the warmth and distant hush of the foyer he guarded. His boots shone on the pale Portland stone.

McMorrow looked at his watch and the choirboy image slipped for a moment, spleen flickered. He put down the phone. They were late. He paused a moment to recapitulate the scheme, its timing, to recall the names.

Dowty and Maxwell.

They were late; Dowty and Maxwell were late.

In the lounge, two deep enveloping couches faced each

11

other across a coffee table: a plane of crazy marquetry of coloured woods, glass-topped, chromium-fixed. Over-the-top bloody rubbish, outré crap, he thought: a quartet of Bayswater miniatures, a set of hunting prints. There was a multi-purpose table for writing or dining or whatever; a couple of delicate chairs, ornamental, hardly functional. A bit of greenery too, sprouting from a transparent orb of water, the pale hydrophonic roots like bleached hair of the drowned. But the inornate warmth of carpet and curtains almost compensated.

McMorrow had sprung from a polite Dublin world of Ps and Qs, three-figure door numbers, thrift accounts.

He was well made: that choirboy innocence and fair silken hair, a forgotten religion. If he needed to be noticed, only then you noticed him and his restrained good taste: he was thirty-nine.

The telephone bleeped and the floor-steward said, "They are here. Two gentlemen to see you, Mr McMorrow."

"Two gentlemen?"

"Well . . . yes."

"Bring them."

Taddeo, floor-steward, majordomo, valet, factotum, spoke the Queen's Cockney in the tones and ancient rhythms of some Calabrian village. With dignity he presented the visitors on the threshold and was gone.

"You're late," McMorrow said. "Shut the door."

"Parking," the smaller one explained. "Half an hour. It took half an hour, I'd say. I'm Dowty."

"Shut the door."

Maxwell slammed it with his foot. "Don't play the hard nut, pussycat," he said to McMorrow. "You have a job. We're here! Take a look!" He was a Scot.

They were both young hunters, hounds, hardly thirty, shining in fitness, in handsome black leather jackets, tailored slacks, Dowty smiling, Maxwell vacant, dangerous. 'Spit and polish' traced them like a visual aid. Not long, McMorrow knew, since the flak-jacket days and combat tricks.

"Did your Ulster bit, did you?" McMorrow inspected them.

Dowty said, "Micks, Ayrabs, Argies, Guv'nor." He was a pleasant young man. "Mix it, cool it, you name it, that's us."

McMorrow nodded, waited.

Dowty smiled. "Soften 'em up? Pop the question, never a sound, sweep the floor?"

"Yes," McMorrow said.

Maxwell said, "You're wasting our time now, Mister."

McMorrow ignored it, remembered his face: you shaped, conditioned your savages to appal, frighten, terrify, or to maim and kill, uphold society's precious fabric, he thought. Armies left a stamp and a stigma. He examined and balanced their self-esteem.

"Don't give me yap," eventually he told Maxwell very quietly. "I know the rules. I pay the piper. Understand?"

"Sorry, Guv'nor," Dowty said – a flatness without provenance – and smiled apology. He said to Maxwell, "Button up, button up, you know, shut fucking down! Get it?"

Rank established itself in an instant.

"I have work," McMorrow said. "Work and pay." He beckoned.

On the table he had spread an aerial picture of the river and its waterfronts, from Tower Bridge to Dagenham and beyond. Except for an amorphous pile that might be a hotel or something in the making, and specks of demolition like random warts, empty wharves awaiting life or death, a few pubs, modern made ancient, or dwellings even, a half dozen Georgians refurbished by men for supermen, and geometric shapes of empty basins – except for these, it was a levelled scarified world of empty stores, warehouses, rot, stubs of masonry, strings of narrow footway running to dead ends or frayed edges. A dockland warren of early century and before. Only greyness now on this aerial picture where the wharf gates had been and, down the decades, gangs had clustered – 'out on the stones', they called it – watching for the gaffer's nod, the right to sweat: anxious moments day by day, a beginning of anger; give us this day our daily bread.

It was a silent world now.

McMorrow ran his finger along the north shoreline:

Stepney, Ratcliffe, Narrow Street, Limehouse Jetty, crept on further, further, a long way out. "About here," he said: he tapped on a tiny blur of microdots. "A furlong and twenty yards of waterfront, see?"

He gave them a little respite, watched them.

It was almost a wasteland. McMorrow had walked it, plotted it with care in the small hours; close enough, never too close; unseen, he thought. Almost a wasteland but for a walled churchyard and its buildings laid back from the river, on rising ground: a green oasis of glebeland with its church, its rectory, a People's Hall, trees, gravel tracks, shrubberies, old burial plots with dignified markers.

Outside the walls, the wasteland began. There had been river people once, some with psalms and hymn-verses who went in dread of God. Emptiness now, only a decay of stubs, once cabins or two-up-two-downs; now, with walls askew, seemingly frozen in a moment of implosion. One cabin alone stood erect in the weed hassocked desolation. And there were kerbed narrow footways surviving, gone astray, strangely giving the semblance of streets.

McMorrow, from his seclusion, had slowly traced its boundaries, measured it with a practised eye. Seventy by seventy was an assessor's acre: three and a half by two. Jesus! he had thought, six, seven acres of riverside ground. Two years perhaps and it would be in the golden towpath of dockland!

And all of it – glebeland, wasteland, down to riverside granite and skeletal wharfage – the kingdom of Paul Vincent Herlihy!

Beyond it, at its very fringes, a silhouette against black river and sky, a tall gabled tenement stood its ground. No glimmer of light showed.

McMorrow had moved only yards, careful, soundless, when the wind, out of a still morning, struck him. He had stumbled and fallen on rough ground. And stillness had returned! For a second, no more, the wind had lived and died. McMorrow remembered it like a scream of voices and had felt fear.

He had hurried away, back into the distant hinterland, to

the reassurance of street-lights and the warmth of his car.
He remembered the wind, the weight of darkness back
there: it might be that life had shrunk away from uneasy
ground.

McMorrow had spent a day in the hinterland too, where
he had gathered scraps. A lone wino, for a pound coin, had
said, "Do yourself a favour, matie, jump in your motor and
piss off." McMorrow had watched him limp away towards
a corner shop, bottles and beer cans . . .

"A furlong and twenty yards. What else?" Dowty was
saying.

"Once upon a time," McMorrow said, "small shacks,
people even, a village. You go there," McMorrow's finger
stabbed at the River again; he explained it, recited with care.
"Limehouse, Silvertown, Beckton Swamp," he said. "The
river on your right. Keep it there. Long, long roads," he told
Dowty. "Sometimes nothing, dead ends, twisters, nothing.
Hug the river, watch for the church, the church is the marker,
a Lutheran church, you'll find it."

"That's the job, is it?" Maxwell said. "Looking for the
lost bluetits of Wapping?" He was grinning at McMorrow.

"Where you *do* the job," McMorrow told him.

Dowty nodded.

With a thumb nail McMorrow scribed the outline for them.
"Behind the church, a deadhouse. 'Mortuary Chapel', the
padre would have called it." He waited for them, gave it
the importance it needed. "Here, tacked on, you see, the
deadhouse." He tapped on it.

A little lightness. "Padre's spare room. Overnight guests.
Once upon a time."

"Candles for company," Dowty said.

McMorrow allowed a distant response. "You'll find it a
lumber dump now, I'm told," he said. "Everything from
statues to scrubbers. Bibles too, bottles, beer crates."

He paused.

"And a Canon."

"A shooter?" Maxwell said. "There's a shooter, is there?"

"A cleric," McMorrow told Dowty. "A dodgy cleric. All
the tricks." He dabbed a little portrait for them. "Black

cassock to the heels. Sometimes a cloak, black as a bat too. A walking-stick . . ."

Maxwell was amused again. "Lame, is he, this hopalong padre? For Christ's sake!"

"Not that I've noticed," McMorrow said: for a moment he studied the great bony crag of Maxwell's head. "The stick," he said, gazing at the centre of Maxwell's forehead. "He could fell an ox with it."

There was silence; and beyond the windows, a soundless world and the distant fringes of Kensington.

Dowty said eventually, "Dog collar, has he?"

"Oh yes, a dog collar. Biretta too."

"A hat!" Dowty told Maxwell. "A hat! Biretta is a hat, not a shooter."

"Jesus!" Maxwell said.

"Not young, not old," McMorrow described the Canon to Dowty. "But stubborn. Hard, I suppose, you could say. I want him to sign something, that's all." From a briefcase he took a large heavy manilla envelope, reinforced, edged with tape.

And then, more slowly, an amount of money, in twenties.

A narrow 'window', tape-framed at its edges, had been cut near the base of the sealed envelope, and blank white parchment showed beneath.

"He signs there," McMorrow said.

"Just signs?"

"He signs 'Paul Vincent Herlihy'. Nothing before it, nothing behind it. Write it down." McMorrow gave him a plain postcard.

Dowty wrote it. "Paul Vincent . . ."

"Herlihy." McMorrow spelt it and examined it. "That's it. What's inside," he said to Maxwell: he held up the envelope, "wouldn't interest you. Understand?"

Dowty nodded for him.

McMorrow picked up the money. "No marks, busted fingers, ribs, teeth. Just a signature. Quick, tidy, expert. Expert, that's the important bit. Morons come cheap."

He counted out two bundles, twenty-five twenties in each. A little redness of respect washed across Maxwell's face.

16

"Down-payment," McMorrow said. "When you bring the envelope, the other half."

There was silence, a kind of churchlike silence.

"Yes," Dowty said. Maxwell, no smile now, was looking at the crisp unsullied notes, their silver threads woven like party scarves.

"The deadhouse," McMorrow said. "He sits there, two till three. Other times, maybe. A lot of times, I'm told. But always two till three."

"A little game?" Maxwell said.

"Meditation, I suppose," McMorrow told Dowty. "Sometimes he reads."

"In a deadhouse!" Maxwell said. "A deadhouse! A fruit-cake, is he? Rats running loose in his head!"

Enclosed within himself, McMorrow felt a sudden warmth of satisfaction: Maxwell's scrambled reasoning had slowed, calmed, settled in perfect suspension.

A bloody fruitcake!

He looked at his watch. "A lot of wheels, bottlenecks, holes in the road, from here past Stepney and Wapping, and you're looking back at Barking Creek and the marshes at Beckton. Looking back from Paul Vincent Herlihy's deadhouse," he said. "You'll have to push, won't you? You were late, see?"

"Sorry about that," Maxwell said: Dowty had prodded the response, set him in motion.

From the door Dowty raised the envelope in salute. "It'll be like you said, Guv'nor. Just like you said."

It was ten minutes after one o'clock. "I'll expect you about five," McMorrow said and ushered them away.

He went to the bathroom, tidied, arranged himself. There was a wall-mirror: from head to toe he studied the faultless image before him. The best was admirable, unobtrusive: shirts, suitings, hand-made shoes. He stood closer, looked at supple skin: no trace of age. Thirty-nine, he thought . . .

. . . Once, on the eve of his twenty-first, he remembered, a long time past now, he had bought a cheap suit and worn it to the bank on that Saturday morning: a little provincial market smudge where he had clerked and given deference to shopkeeper élite, patrician, professional, the emerging pleb: the foothills and peaks of hierarchy. The threadbare hubris of it all!

There he had been overwhelmed by the immensity of his own poverty, threadbare clerk in hobnailed plutocracy: evening wear for socialite 'balls' of wintertime so out of reach; hotel bar; golf club lounge; a clapped-out 'banger' beyond wildest raving dreams. Summertime 'hops', dress informal, he could afford, saw himself watched – an amusement perhaps – assessed for 'style' or lack of it. No off-the-rail clobber for these scions of butcher, baker, aloof undertaker, lickerish quacks, legal men allsorts. He could remember their blob Munch faces. Christ!

"Sportswear for Saturday mornings, McMorrow," the manager had said. "Sports day, you know. Saturday is sports day. Suits for weekdays, sportswear for Saturday. Slacks and jacket. Where are they?"

"The cleaners."

"Sir."

"Sir."

"Get them and change. Now."

He didn't have the money.

"Half a month to run and no money? I can't see you amounting to very much, boy. Not very much. Take your work in the ledger room or somewhere. Keep out of sight."

A long time ago, it seemed. The shrunken little sports-coated griffon now dead and in dust, he hoped: Presbyterian alum-dipped face, glaring down long tunnels of God and men gone sour.

McMorrow had come a long journey. Sportswear for Saturdays!

The bank had 'sent him down', 'with regret' accepted his retirement. He was a thief, packed off, 'transferred', not a ripple on the pond. Almost fifteen years now. Banks, like churches, keep lids on maggot cans. McMorrow had learnt to play tricks with accounts, ingenious tricks, legerdemain with systems and code-books outworn, needing rectitude for survival: a few thousand spent as he 'palmed' it, to open doors, earn nods from men of trade and profession, lift the bibs and rattle little daughters who so lately had whispered, giggled.

He looked back to it, even from this lofty perch, with a strange nostalgia: days that were precious, time running out and McMorrow dummying, jinking, with a baffled fiscal defence reeling all about.

Three years he had glittered; then returned to 'Lisieux', three-digital semi, impeccable brewery clerk father, overweening mother floating on the attainments of her menfolk.

Their awful shame! "You could be in gaol! In gaol, oh God!" They had died: two years and they had been laid to rest, or to wander in mumbling abasement through eternity. He had felt hardly sorrow but pity: they had been born for servitude and earned it.

But not McMorrow.

He had their careful savings now. Pence! But a house was 'property', an asset. You never sold, you borrowed: he had learned shrewd lessons from small-town hucksters. The 'new times' had come: banks, the usurers, were greedy as McMorrow. He had borrowed, bought, again, again, in the first spirals of the money-game. He had wealth, a great deal of wealth.

Not enough.

But this was the 'straight', there was the winning-post; he dialled Taddeo, the floor-steward. "There'll be another gentleman, Taddeo. Important."

"Yes, sir."

"Bring him first. Then malt. Malt whisky, Perrier, ice, you know . . ."

"Yes, sir."

He went to his window and looked down at Park Lane, the tangled dreadlocks of traffic dragged from Tyburn into the maelstrom of Hyde Park Corner.

The upstream poured back unrelentingly from Victoria and Brompton Road and Knightsbridge. Beyond were the

19

acres of parkland, the Serpentine space of water, distant Kensington Palace, a racing sky, the trees frantic in October wind, and great tumbles of leaves.

The park: three hundred acres or more, McMorrow estimated. Three hundred . . . three hundred. At what price? . . .

Taddeo was rapping gently on the door and Father James Kilmartin had arrived, quietly, expensively dressed: business suit, tailored shirt, careful tie, soft leather shoes; his hair in disarray had a sweep of 'now', the moment. He was unbuttoning an overcoat, light as air, a blueness almost lost in the dark mohair texture.

"Mr Kilmartin to see you," Taddeo announced. The door clicked gently as he went.

Father Jim said, "Good to see you, Dermot." A preacher's rumbling voice. He waited, was at ease.

McMorrow nodded. "I made a few sorties here and there," he said eventually. "Took a little time. To reconnoitre, to listen. A few nods and winks. But interesting. I think we might do it."

Father Jim, hardly a tall figure, a weight-watcher perhaps, was pleasantly compact in his clothes: McMorrow's age, rising forty. From different flocks, they were birds of a feather. But his smile had youth, was a flash, a glint of assessment. McMorrow pointed at the couch and watched him let himself drop into it, exhale the stifling discomfiture of the morning.

"I have a copy of probate," McMorrow said; he took it from his pocket and glanced at it.

"Unshakeable," Father Jim said. "The Will is unshakeable."

McMorrow agreed, began to read aloud, mumbled, tailed away. "Yes," he said eventually. "Simplicity, you see. You can't crack simplicity. Christ, a few lines, no more!"

Father Jim made a small reflex blessing gesture to dispel blasphemous pollution. Taddeo knocked and brought ten-year-old malt whisky, squat crystal tumblers, Perrier, ice.

"Lunch in half an hour, sir," he said to McMorrow.

"Here," McMorrow reminded him, pointed to the table. "Lunch will be here."

"Sir."

When he had gone, Father Jim poured neat malt, a careful

20

measure, and would 'chase' it with this precious untainted water; but McMorrow mixed his drink, dropped ice in it, barely sipped it.

The bottled purity of water from across the sea, Father Jim was thinking for a moment; and he thought of his daily Mass and its offertory, the mingling of water and wine, recycled water, man's recycled waste, precious blood. He found it unpleasant.

"The Will is unshakeable," he said, like a toneless oblation as he raised his glass and sipped.

"Amen," McMorrow responded. "The Dory-Catchpole Estate."

"Dorys," Father Jim said. "Ships' chandlers since mad George and the Regency. She married Catchpole, gave him to Kitchener's army . . . 1915 . . ."

"Yes, yes, I know." McMorrow's impatience was showing. "I was saying, 'simplicity', remember?"

He began to read aloud.

"I've read the Will," Father Jim said.

But McMorrow began again. " 'This the last and only Will and Testament of Henrietta Lucy Dory-Catchpole. I bequeath all my lands, buildings and their contents, wharfages and all adjoining edifices, as well as all other possessions in cash or kind, to Paul Vincent Herlihy, resident at the Church of St George and its Presbytery, where he was my faithful companion during the last painful years of my life, and to dispose of all goods, properties and monies as he chooses.' "

Father Jim said, "She has bequeathed to 'Paul Vincent Herlihy'. Paul Vincent Herlihy, a private person. If she had designated 'the *Reverend Father* Paul Vincent Herlihy' . . . well . . ."

"He's a sacked priest," McMorrow said. "A sacked carpenter is a carpenter."

"The Church doesn't 'sack'," Father Jim said gently. "It 'silences'. He's a silenced priest. Forbidden to minister, or perform the sacred duties, all that. In the Church's canon he is a priest for ever, of course. His possessions are the Church's possessions."

"Yes!" McMorrow said, irritable, rushing over trodden

21

ground. "Yes, yes, legatee, private person, Paul Vincent Herlihy who would build a village for the aged at Dory's Jetty. We've done all that."

"The Bishop," Father Jim said, "has occasioned delays, inexplicable delays, you realise? To build, there are requisite permissions, legalities, procedures . . ."

McMorrow smiled at this naïveté.

"You understand these things, of course?" he asked.

"Yes."

"We're talking about millions."

"Unfortunately," Father Jim said.

"He wears the Church's uniform, doesn't he?"

"Means nothing. In the Will, out of it, he is Paul Vincent Herlihy, the law would say. Not the Church's law, you understand. The other one."

"To dispose of as he chooses." McMorrow looked at his drink, left it untouched. "Jim," he said eventually, "Paul Vincent Herlihy – they call him the 'Canon', as you are aware – silenced priest, whatever he is, squatting with some crippled old bird for ten happy years by the river, legatee extraordinary, is *mad*." He stood motionless, watched Father Jim carefully drink a little malt. "Mad. A mad priest. Bloody fruitcake . . . rats running loose in his head."

"Yes. *She* called him the 'Canon'." Father Jim simulated doubt, uneasiness, was exuberant. "An astute man, Dermot. Rents us his church from week to week, the People's Hall for our functions." He studied McMorrow. "Seven days' notice on either side, you see? No fixity. Astute."

"How much?"

"A thousand."

"Fair."

"Includes the People's Hall."

Again, a little impatient blasphemy from McMorrow.

Father Jim hurriedly waved and purified the air. He said in what appeared distress, "I have another couple of months, Dermot. The Bishop has allowed me that. Money, of course . . ."

McMorrow held up a flat palm for silence. "To lose this bloody lunatic?"

"To acquire the land, the estate, all of it."

McMorrow would have freshened Father Jim's drink but the bottle was pushed aside. "Assure the Bishop, when you see him," McMorrow said, "that you have a tight grip on the situation."

"I did," Father Jim said; and with a show of solicitude, he warned, "Dangerously sane, Dermot. Celibate too. Nothing carnal there. Charming, courteous. Once, the Bishop, in humility, discarding rank, quietly you understand, travelled to him, down to that barren place . . ."

"Infiltrating," McMorrow said.

"The Bishop is a very patient man, a man of power. Two sterile years, remember?"

"I'm pleased," McMorrow said.

Father Jim was shaking his head in recall of outrageousness and wonder. "The Bishop! He told the Bishop . . ." Father Jim appeared to falter.

"To piss off?" McMorrow said.

Father Jim nodded. "Verbatim."

"The words of a *madman*."

"He was *smiling*." Father Jim embellished it.

"Raving mad."

McMorrow put away his reconnaissance scroll and Taddeo came with trolley and linen and lunch: the ragout was an expense of dissolving meats in wine and mushrooms; vegetables pushing out tips of colour everywhere in a sea of goodness. McMorrow nibbled a little.

Father Jim ate without respite for fifteen minutes: fortuitous moments of self-indulgence were not proscribed in his regimen; there was total silence.

And when he had considered the empty casserole with fortitude, smilingly relinquished knife and fork, McMorrow said, "Yes, I did a little scouting about at the fringes of our Canon's kingdom. A quarter-mile belt of wilderness, did you know? Desolation. Beyond that, breakers' yards, scrap mountains, the badlands, high-rises in acres of dirt."

McMorrow's rancour might be abating, the choirboy emerging.

"Some brightness surely?" Father Jim prompted.

23

"There was a pub. An Irish pub."

"Not unusual," Father Jim said.

"And a good madam of the house, piped and iced like a packaged patisserie, sang for me of 'the lark in the morning rising off his nest' and 'Greenland is an awful place' and the 'Shores of Americkay'." McMorrow remembered her in a veil of tobacco smoke. "And she wished she was in 'Carrickfergus too'. A big woman, words, words, words. Yvonne, they called her."

"You find them everywhere."

"Christ, Yvonne!" McMorrow said

Profanity brought silence.

"You enquired about Herlihy, did you?" Father Jim said, regretting the sensual ecstasy of food. He closed his eyes at the mention of God's name.

"'The poor man', she said." McMorrow quoted her, mimicked perhaps. "'With damnation awaiting him. Why did she leave him the millions, the dying old Dory gammer? Ninety-two years on her perch, but maybe she liked to see the walking-stick again. Ha! It wasn't for nothing! He must have moments of great shame. *Mad*, anyone'll tell you,' she said, 'walking down empty streets, waving his hand. Takes an hour staring at the river. Other things too, only whispered about, God forgive me . . .'"

"Curious," Father Jim said.

"Mad," McMorrow reminded him. "Mad, you see? A whole strange crew lost down there. The Canon is mad."

"A.P.U.M."

A person of unsound mind, Father Jim was thinking. Promising. But he wore a mask of scepticism.

"It would take time to establish, to prove. Most difficult. The Church, you appreciate, avoids unseemliness at all costs."

"But the land? You want the land?"

"Oh yes, the land. The wealth."

"A rich community." McMorrow felt the need to prod him.

He looked beyond Father Jim at the room's greenery, the orb of water, frail etiolated roots, envisaged it. "Holy knights, sainted men of business, men of substance, a kind of riverside Vatican guard clustering about their church. And of course a parochial residence . . ." McMorrow paused. "To give stature to its ministers."

Father Jim saw it. He drank a little whisky, looked at McMorrow's almost untouched food.

"And the checkmate?" McMorrow said.

Father Jim waited.

"Paul Vincent Herlihy – that is: Paul Vincent Herlihy, private person – has committed to paper his sorrow, his act of contrition, for past misdeeds, and his fears for his sanity. Periods of confusion, delusion, while segments of an hour, a day, are stolen from him. A passing illness, perhaps, but, that for its duration, his affairs and business should be administered solely by his trusted friend, Father James Kilmartin D.D. And, in the event of his death, his estate, entire, should pass to Mother Church." McMorrow raised a finger to restrain Father Jim. "All this while his mind is clear and undisturbed."

"Dermot," Father Jim began.

McMorrow said, "Today I get his signature. You get witnesses tomorrow."

McMorrow now took his watered drink from the table; the ice cubes had long since dissolved. He drank it back.

Father Jim stared, dawdled a few moments: conflict, shock, uncertainty should be displayed, he felt; and a striving for a forlorn brightness.

"You have an ease with words, Dermot. They come easy."

"They ought to," McMorrow said. "I wrote the damn thing. And Paul Vincent Herlihy will sign it this afternoon."

"Impossible." Father Jim poured whisky, again a careful measure, and drank it. He might be a little breathless.

"Witnesses tomorrow and the case is closed," McMorrow told him. "Paul Vincent Herlihy, once a priest, always a priest, makes amends to his Mother Church. A happy ending."

25

"He'll savage you, the Bishop, myself, everyone." Father Jim was on his feet.

"Good. We'll have him confined. The Church has its secret places for the less robust in spirit."

McMorrow poured whiskies and they sat in silence for a long time. Father Jim said eventually, "You realise I know nothing of this matter. I sent for you, of course, and you came at once. The estate is important. But you're a free agent, Dermot. Your tricks are your own." He gazed at McMorrow.

McMorrow said, "You did your sums, did you?"

"Everything is computed."

"Elsewhere? Everything?"

"Scrip, ground, brick, mortar. What we could find."

"Yes?" McMorrow said.

"Ten million."

"Good. A burgeoning market."

"Ten per cent, you asked. The Bishop's word is his bond. I speak for him."

McMorrow raised his glass a modest inch or two.

"A shame to spoil malt with ice and water," Father Jim said: he must appear a little flustered, unfamiliar in whirlwinds and choppy seas.

"It will all be very discreet," McMorrow said, smiling at last. "Very discreet."

They drank. McMorrow walked to the lift with him. From his lobby Taddeo arrived with suitcase and holdall.

McMorrow said, "A taxi, Taddeo. See to everything."

He watched the smart boyish figure, the raised hand, the sliding door, the numbers measuring his descent.

. . . At boarding school they had hung together, McMorrow and James Kilmartin. Kilmartin emerging from far-off London, a boozer across the water, dubbed by jokers and drolls 'BBC', his alien speech, so perfect its tonations, an affront. They were a little in awe of him. McMorrow had liked that, was attracted to it. He could recall the winter grip of dormitories, cold creeps, frost-riven feet, breath vapours, the spartan gleam of refectory tables.

The last day of their last term they had drunk pints at the Railway Bar. Kilmartin had entrained for God, McMorrow for commerce and battles . . .

He reached the apartment again. Taddeo arrived, was tidying, restoring order.

"Good, good," he told him, treated him generously, went back to look out at the wild October day. It was after three o'clock: Dowty and Maxwell should be about their business now.


There had been Dutch blood and a wariness even of Protestantism from somewhere in the distant past of the Dorys; they had been shellbacks, watermen, lightermen, barge masters, dogs of sea and river since the last tumbling houses on London Bridge and traitors' heads on the spikes of its tollgates.

The Dorys, born close to the mudbanks and river jetties, had laboured, drudged when it was necessary, but prospered too, slowly, without flair, for a century and decades until a more shrewd ancestor had remained ashore to provision the crawling, queuing chaos of craft stacked from London Tower to Wapping and Greenwich and far beyond. The Dory stores and jetties had spread to house cordage and canvas, the whole sweep of rigging, even to the measuring and tailoring of the Masters themselves.

It wasn't the arrival of steel and steam that had lessened them or their industry, but diminishing male seed and its final extinction, until the lone child, Henrietta Lucy, had inherited all: the riverfront battlements, the Dory hamlet of workmen's cabins, cobbled streets, granite setts, green patches, tall trees even, and the garnered precious wealth of generations. And the church.

In the centuries of splinter and splice, post-Reformation wrangles, the Dorys had been dour unshakeables; but this founding ship's chandler, urbane, grateful for his possessions, and to a generous God, had raised a Lutheran church for family and workforce and whoever might be welcomed or proselytised: Lutheran perhaps because some ancient atavistic gene of Catholicism had found warmth in the retained awesome mystery of consubstantiation; and the presence too of statuary and images, the stoups and baptismal font, incense, rich vestments and linen.

Lucy, last of the Dorys, and her wealth, had married Horatio Samuel Taylor Catchpole, the church's last incumbent, charming, loving, sterile, poetasting pastor.

She had sent him to France in 1915 and had seen him no more: three medals, like half-crowns, had arrived, and she had framed a small stereotyped letter from the Sovereign thanking her for her husband's body and blood.

She had closed the church and lived seventy years in the Rectory, most of them happily, with Horatio's poems and a vast unfinished tapestry, a kind of Dory Bayeux. The last ten years had been trying, aware of loneliness and the first faint palsy, inexorable, that would diminish her from year to year . . .

. . . But a man, Herlihy, had come, a man in black: a dull afternoon in the early trembling days and Paul Vincent Herlihy was at her door. She had never seen him before. He had addressed her as 'Lucy' which was a second name, a family preference; and, looking over her shoulder, had called out a greeting to the empty foyer.

"Who?" she had asked, looking at the emptiness behind her.

Herlihy could see a man-at-arms, a man of God, tall in his uniform.

"Horatio's been dead for seventy years," she had said.

"It was the first day of July."

She had never known exactly.

"The Somme," Herlihy said. "A morning of sunshine."

"You can tell about it?"

"Nothing."

Paul Vincent Herlihy was confused for a moment. He stood on solid stone, palpable, could feel the door surface, the breeze from the river on his face; and he might have materialised in some spirited wasteland.

28

She had followed his gaze along the panels of the unten-
anted foyer.

"Alone?"

"There's nothing now. Bright for a moment. But now
there's nothing."

"They never found him," she said. She considered Herlihy
for a long time, looking beyond him to the pavement, at a
handcart, sparsely loaded with junk, a little iron scrap, odds
and wastements.

"You called me 'Lucy'. Why?"

"Did I?"

"You're not a trickster, are you?"

"No."

He didn't seem like one.

Distantly his name was scripted on the sideboards of the
pushcart.

"Paul Vincent Herlihy," he read it for her, a little amused.
"Wandering, a mendicant."

"You were sent perhaps."

"Sent?"

"Horatio."

"Ah."

She saw a tall remarkable man, weathered, lean, strangely
dressed in black that was shiny but unspotted; even the shoes
were black and the high rollneck sweater; a handsome man,
greying a little.

"I'm a totter," he had explained. "That's a kind of scrap
collector, you know."

"Yes, I know."

And she had looked at the black garb again, and the hands,
soiled of course, but so perfectly moulded: long powerful
fingers.

"I was a priest once," he said. "Until a little while ago."

"You shunned God, did you?"

"Oh no, nothing like that. Always looking for Him, in
fact. Day in, day out."

"You were unfrocked?"

"Silenced."

"Unfrocked because you looked for Him?"

29

"The Church 'silences'."

"A strange word."

"Indeed, yes."

Herlihy was in thought then, back-tracking years of weekend pews, a midden of bodies, the absence of souls. No great numinous ecstasy had ever for a moment enveloped him.

"I was angry, you see."

"For the Almighty?"

"Whoever He is. His house full of bodies, not a soul in sight. Waste of pews and masonry. I locked them out, chained the doors." Herlihy was seeing it all, distantly, in the ghostliest of smiles. "Post offices would suffice," he said. "A salvation stamp, please, Mr Patel. A great saving of time."

"Horatio would have held you in esteem," she said. "He was filled with doubt, distracted at times."

"Churches are places of great certainty."

She thought how extraordinarily light and handsome was his face in laughter.

"Come inside, take some tea, rest a little," she said "Your pushcart will be safe out there. It's my village. Where the village was. The war, you see . . ."

"Yes," Herlihy said . . .

"Stay a while," she had asked eventually: here was his room, his study. There were dead streets and buildings all about; he should come and go.

"Home," she had said.

"A strange word."

"Like 'silence'."

"A strange place. You're ill, aren't you?" Herlihy had asked.

"Yes." She held out the faintly trembling hands. "It could be a long time, you see. A long time." . . .


A long time.

Over the space of a decade he had watched the creep of this shaking palsy in her cramped body, listened to her little trotting tottering footsteps; and because he felt warmth and protection in them, and his image gave her some strange comfort, he wore only the traditional clothes of Catholicism that she had purchased, had tailored for him: black suits, stocks and collars, cassocks, fine lined cloaks, birettas.

The Rectory's upper storey, part of it at least, was his apartment: bedroom, library, a study looking out and down at churchyard grass, the trees, dignified toppling headstones, a few table-vaults, not a cypress plume in sight . . .

. . . "Sulvan's," she had said that first afternoon tea. "Our neighbour, that's all that's left."

Herlihy had looked at the formidable pile hugging the river: a house of mismatches, afterthought gables, windows, large, small, asymmetrical. From Lucy Dory-Catchpole's drawing room he gazed at it distantly across the churchyard and the almost levelled village. A long single-storey appendage sprouted from its bulk.

"A club, I think," she said. "People come there."

"Sulvan?"

"He comes and goes."

"He calls to see you?"

"Never."

"An old man?" Herlihy asked.

"Strong. He doesn't change, you see." She thought about it. "Seventy-five years, more, I can remember. Always the same. He doesn't change."

"A son, a grandson?"

"Nothing changes."

"He comes and goes."

"Yes, he comes and goes," she said.

Herlihy was looking about the great spacious beauty of the room, at the walled glebe beyond with its church and People's Hall and this indestructible rectory; and then at the razed naked ground of the village. Why had he come, he wondered, to a strange illusory place, pushing his totter's cart into acres of desolate ground, scavenged even of growth?

Only a cabin stood in the wilderness of it all; and, not distant from Sulvan's, hidden in its shadow, a house, small, roofed, maintained. She had followed his gaze.

31

"Matthew John Sinclair," she had said. "He doesn't like churchyards. I made him a home down there, give him more than he could ever earn. My doctor, you see? A 'scoundrel', of course." She smiled. "Lazy, slothful, gambles too, I'm afraid. But I'm fond of him. And he *understands*. Drinks only rarely. When he wins, you see. Rarely. But he passes there every day." She pointed towards the main gate and its wicket, and Herlihy's pushcart. "Stops to look for my face in the window, comes when I telephone . . .

"At the end, the very end, when I'm tired, I'll telephone him too. He understands."

"Yes," Herlihy said. He understood.

At that moment then, she had telephoned: and when there was a reply, she said, "Don't worry about my medicines in future, Matthew. The Canon will be passing. Canon Herlihy. He'll drop in on you."

It was a gentle arrangement with death.

She sat again. "You can manage these pills and bottles and things for me? I forget them sometimes. You'll remind me."

Herlihy pondered only a moment or two: the merest shadow of import rarely escaped him. He wondered only how soon, and raised his teacup to acquiesce.

"'Canon'," he had said. "You have elevated me to 'Canon'." He was amused.

"Dear boy, if you could have abided it, you might have climbed to terrifying heights."

"I wonder why I came?" he said eventually.

"You were needed, I think."

She would live as long as there were moments of happiness, she had told him; and had lasted all those years, trembling, stumbling from domestic island to island, but with pain more difficult to assuage. And he had fed the spooned food she could still manage, held her nodding automaton head. Once, his eyes close to hers, he had seen a young girl's face, beautiful, untroubled, something to be caressed and kissed; and then the spoon was rattling on her gums again . . .

32

It had been an October day like this. The Canon now in the chaos of the Mortuary Chapel, in a vestment cubicle, in darkness, hidden away, he knelt on his prie-dieu and listened to the wind . . .

An October day, two years past, when he had gone to her bedroom to lift and dress her, and she had said, "I'm going away this morning, Paul. Telephone Matthew Sinclair."

The Canon had said, "Miss Lucy is leaving us this morning, Matthew."

"I see," Sinclair had said: a little sad, the Canon knew. "Half an hour, old friend. Half an hour to arrange things. No worries."

"Certificates," the Canon reminded.

"Certs! No such thing, your holiness. Take a punter's word."

Doctors went in awe of death too: Sinclair's humour was brittle as sugar-glass.

"Death and cremation certificates."

"Certs, removals, disposals, practical eschatology, old friend. Within the hour at your doorstep."

"Yes," the Canon said. He looked at the earpiece, could hear the distant crackle of Sinclair's phlegmy tubes . . .

The wind, on that day too, he remembered, had been battling with the trees and shrubs and getting in wherever it found a loose ageing window frame.

She had called it her 'parting glass'; and he had held the foxed papery hands until she had slipped away. Sinclair had stood, looking out at the ageless churchyard . . .

Two years, the Canon thought. Hardly a moment in the mind. After the fitful decade she was sleeping at last in the churchyard, beloved spouse of 'Horatio Samuel Taylor Catchpole 1916. He died for King and Country'.

He listened to the wind now and could hear the scutch of leaves on stone and gravel. She had bequeathed him everything: the rectory, the locked and bolted church, the People's Hall, the streets, the ground, the wharves, the jetties; and an empty last standing cabin in a detritus sea of masonry and weed and coarse scrub. She had left him the Dory-Catchpole village, her wealth in cash and kind.

Only Sulvan's impregnable rookery stood at her boundary. A bastion.

"Look after Matthew, won't you?" she had asked when, holding her erect, they had awaited Sinclair's arrival . . .


Paul Vincent Herlihy, the Canon, sat in his mortuary cubicle and remembered.

She had asked him once, "My dear Paul, what led to this ministry of yours?"

"I seemed to arrive," he had said . . .

. . . Herlihy had entered the disciplined novitiate priest-world on tiptoe, in naïve expectance of 'search'. 'Disputation', indefatigable search, however distant the mark, each daily failure proclaimed aloud, he had thought, might inspire. But, alone, he seemed to look out at absurdity, conforming to ritual, to rote, diurnal attrition, old as their creation of an inexplicable God.

"Is each body a worthy temple of the soul, inviolable?" had been preached at them in zealotry; and, betimes, a 'sinner', in despair at human foulness, might scourge himself or another, draw blood to humiliate the flesh, sit naked in winter bathwater, almost whimpering at the rising power of lust. Even the body's emissions in sleep, the frightening ecstatic succubus of a moment, left young warriors in shame, terror. But profligacy might blossom too for a moment: naked ones caught in flagrante, made to vanish before even first light crept over the tranquillity of morning offerings of a day's prayer, work and suffering to a compassionate Overlord.

"Herlihy?" Secretively he had been asked by a haunted disciple, uneasy in face and body, timid, the eyes spectral, "Do you have *thoughts*, Herlihy?"

The morning sounds outside of cartwheels and milk tankards.

34

"Thoughts of flesh?"

"Your voice down, Herlihy! Oh God!"

"Yes."

"Immodest thoughts, Herlihy?" A whisper.

"Of course, of course."

"Do we banish them savagely, pray aloud, strike one's self *there* until pain does the killing?"

"Dangerous," Herlihy said.

This votary, gripping him in affliction, dementia. "Do *you*? Do *you*?"

"More gently, I'm afraid."

Wonder, astonishment. "You indulge them? You pause?"

"For a little while perhaps. Strangely pleasant, thoughts of love."

"And then? . . ."

"I sing a comic song. The milkman sings it too. Listen."

But the words were lost in the clatter of tankards and iron-shod wheels.

The young man had hurried away in tears: he had been drowned that next high summer, his clothes found on the beach, a set of beads, a breviary, a note that wasn't mentioned: no prayers had been said, nor any moving panegyric enumerating his unassailable virtues for the inspiration of all. A quiet discreet family burial somewhere. Shame.

Herlihy had no doubts in which direction to point himself: you laboured from the inside. He moved through years to ordination with a competence to blunt whatever squinting scepticism was aimed at less than fulsome euphoria or compliance. Moments before the conferring of priesthood, lying prone on the sanctuary floor, an almost-man-of-God, close by Herlihy, had wavered and fled.

It wasn't from their God they fled but from His irrevocable awful punishments.

In a few weeks he would be posted: "Father Paul Vincent Herlihy, in this blessed year, nineteen hundred and sixty, you have been chosen to give your life to God in His mission fields of England. A twofold mission, Father Herlihy. To shield your immigrant brothers, their imperishable souls, from vice and eternal suffering. *And*, Father Herlihy, win back too, by your fervour and devotion, the wandering native English who were once our brothers in Christ."

"Yes," he had said.

"You were orphaned, Father Herlihy?"

"A foundling."

"Ah."

"Fostered when I could work."

"Foster parents? You visit them?"

"One dead. The other . . ."

"I see. Visit the orphanage, Father. It's called St Joseph's now."

"Still an orphanage?"

"Oh yes. The Sisters would be proud of you." . . .

. . . God's mission fields of England: it had been a makeshift East London church, a mid-Victorian building of forgotten purpose: a back-street repository, a mill, a forage store perhaps? Now its ground floor housed infant classrooms of gloom; and a wooden brittle stairway, bare boards, climbed up to the church space that could seat two hundred worshippers, or less, if ever they came.

In a year, gathering a name, a location, when he could, he had visited a half-dozen homes: shapeless neglected women, crawling children, food and body smells; absentee spouses who went from bed to work, to drink, to eat, to copulate, to sleep, to work. Herlihy brought condoms for the women and was assaulted; was visited by an ageing diocesan preceptor, an awesome visage, who had burned him with his pity. "It has been brought to our notice . . ."

"I'm very busy," he had told this venerable man.

"God will spare you a moment, Father Herlihy. He put His creatures here to seed the ground, to procreate. *We* are here to serve. Hearsay is flimsy, but smoke without fire? If you have transgressed, Father Herlihy, spend your life in penitence and you may escape damnation. We will pray for you. And be wary of you, watchful."

The parochial house, an adjunct of this bare ruined pile, was bleak as its black-backed lino, oleographs and net curtains could make it. The hallway was bare.

"Father Herlihy?"

"Yes."

"Except at times of Mass or evening devotion, keep church doors locked. Dishonesty is rife in your parish. Thieves."

"I have faith in thieves," he said.

"Have faith in God. The Church's possessions are sacred."

"Possessions?"

"The Church's posessions."

He had been left a dozen or more years with his parish eroding about him: the demolition of the past, the burgeoning of secular new spires. Only the lame and the halt, for whom even a bus-ride to a more salubrious house of God was a hazard, remained, came to his services. The school bled to extinction. Perhaps he was shunned.

Attacking, from within or without, this great crystallised monolith was charging at windmills, he knew; but there were other roads and passages to be travelled, to be searched.

For two years before he had locked and chained his church, he had walked a thousand miles of hospital corridors and wards, sitting with the mad, the dead, the doomed.

Strangely, on that final day of locking and chaining, a totter's discarded pushcart had been left at his door and it seemed to have drawn him inexorably on its wandering course to the river and Dory's Jetty. A gathering-place? Henrietta Lucy Dory-Catchpole. She had elevated him to 'Canon'!

Herlihy remembered only a ragged curacy in years of barren ministry, and smiled. Inner city, inner sanctum.

Not recall of the mild rigours of seminary and novitiate days stirred; but comic backstage moments of costume and make-up, rubric tome upon tome, stock-in-trade of a memory-man, to be mastered and conned: an actor and his lines. Defenders of the faith, perfect, word-perfect. Not a question remained to be asked.

Perhaps his fall from grace had begun there at that mountainside novitiate, looking back at the distant spires of Dublin. He had banished emptiness with egregious humour, pacing in silence – a robed silent crocodile of novices – merging in the cloistered dusk, beads or books in hand, rubber soles carefully laid on ancient flagstones.

"Who is God?"

"The Creator and Sovereign Lord of Heaven and Earth, infinitely great, infinitely good."

"We're sure?"

"You are in danger, Herlihy. In sin. Pray for humility. Before you lay your head to sleep in peril tonight, go to your Confessor, ask forgiveness for pride."

"Puzzlement."

"With faith there is no puzzlement."

"We're *sure*?"

"Of everything."

"But the mind?"

"The mind?"

"Can we put it to sleep?"

"Father Confessor will see you."

A table-book world, he had thought: 'two ones two', 'twelve twelves hundred and forty-four'. Thirteen thirteens? A pause, a pencil, a pocket of press-button digits. Beyond our ken.

Herlihy had confessed his 'sin'. Nine days of silence and fasting had been penance, a novena of prayer to Augustine of Hippo who had triumphed over pride and the flesh.


The Canon stood up from his prie-dieu now, pushed open the door of the cubicle that stood like a discarded booth, dropped from on high in the Mortuary Chapel corner: it had been a wardrobe, a mini-vestry, a place for albs and copes, surplices, stoles, all those costumes and accessories to welcome the dead in grief and incense.

But it accommodated now a chair, a prie-dieu, an inside bolt, for the Canon. He could sit in the darkness of a womb and come close to patterns of thought, real, insubstantial; or, in shrouded light, read long-forgotten lore from the Dory shelves; or Horatio's precious opuscule of love, leather-bound, 'To Lucy on going to the Wars'.

The Canon thought only rarely of his esoteric time-shifts: not clairvoyance nor any crystal vision but misdated moments, some jumbled upended metachronism, when it seemed he had rented his shell to others to look out at past grief or joy or nostalgia.

Sometimes from his cubicle door he saw the catafalque and tall candles, dead faces, full or wasted, bombazined women, men in obese frock coats; listened for organ dirges or sounds of grief or comfort. But it was always a silent world . . .

A single naked light-bulb glared down. He gazed about at the disorder of the mortuary annexe. A door from the churchyard had been sealed with bar, bolt and time. Who could remember now the last cadaver that had lain until dawn had paled the surrounding candles? But there was egress by a curtained archway, and a bare flagged umbilical corridor behind it, to the sanctuary rails of the church.

The Canon wore a cassock and biretta; under open buttons at the neck, a plain black stock showed and the white traditional collar. Behind him, on an old brass hook-rail, hung his cloak, a leather-bound beret, a scarf, everything black.

Untidiness irked him. The Mortuary, hardly more than an outsize room, was windowless except for a narrow strip of stained glass following the eaves. Old shelves now were crammed with nondescript debris, statuettes, even a headless Christ, forgotten toilet-rolls, paint kettles, a bowler hat cobwebbed from crown to brim.

On the ground were the bulky figures of the Christmas crib; rolls of tarpaulin that would yearly shape the stable at Bethlehem; the Infant in His manger, even animals seeming almost to smile in holiness.

And the Magi, the Wise Kings, too, were crowded near a flagpole, eternally resigned commuters awaiting a star.

A porter-firkin had a weighted lid and was the reservoir of holy water, gallons of it, for stoups and font and the public's domestic consumption. Union Jack and Papal Flag stood side by side, faded, intertwined in a great ecumenical symbolism. And there was a trestle-table that had seen three wars: a battered deal surface, the inspissations of black lead, sweet oils and whiting, smears and sulphate, paint drips, sweat, saliva, graphing a tacky map of domestic toil.

The cleaners' bags sat on it, umbrellas, macks, a saucer of stubbed-out fag ends. Upturned beer crates were seats.

But the great obtrusion was a mountainous stack of spirit cases. Functions at the People's Hall had a licence for the retail of alcohol; and to the lumber of this defiled mortuary annexe and its holy firkin of water were added these various fluids of life, from vodka and fiery scotch to obscure vermouth that might be herbal water or ethyl 'dynamite'.

The Bishop's incumbent, Father Jim, with episcopal blessing and imprimatur, was an anointed entrepreneur. And Harney, his minder, with smile and liquorice-paper fag, was a strange vigilante for God.

It intrigued the Canon to be under surveillance, amused him too, to pre-empt the pastoral bridgeheads and every movement towards encirclement: and, in return, *he* watched *them*. Father James Kilmartin's future eminence was at stake, he knew; and there had been fresh news along the manor of a wandering handsome man, youthful, expensive too, but with the awful glint of Celtic greed in his eyes.

All intelligences eddied at Sulvan's pool, dependable as emerging Reuter, and the Canon was a respected member.

"Bang Bang," Sulvan had said on the telephone: 'Bang Bang' equalled 'Canon' among friends. "Prowlers. We have prowlers." News transmitted, a flash without fuss, Sulvan was gone . . .

They were conspiring again, the Canon thought. A thousand a week in rent of church and People's Hall was a mere fortuitous trifle in the Canon's contingencies. Doc Sinclair's and Catherine Delacey's emoluments, in fact. But church and Hall were functional again, decay held in check. And there were no barriers.

At Sunday Mass and church holy days, Father Jim's congregation gathered with a veiled eagerness of face, an absence of devotion, seeking to glimpse this awful silenced man of God, cohabitant once of a pagan witchwife at the edge of her grave. She had paid him well. But there was a Maker's account outstanding! And now, it was whispered, there were others!

Father Jim felt no duty to disabuse them. The Hall flourished with the proximity of sinful wonderment. Mothers with offspring came to Saturday-morning catechism, and to peer. Dancing of waltz and foxtrot and ancient rhythms had a rebirth, a weekend bar prospered.

The Canon watched their comings and goings from the shadowed privacy of his study and sometimes searched the vacancy of their faces from a squint in the mortuary corridor. It was best that they came and went: fences and isolation would have bred a more evil shiver, the certainty of naked devilry, athletic caperings among the gravestones, upturned crosses, a host of mockery and sacrilege . . .

The Canon listened to the wind sweeping off the river: it came through the church, seeming to boom on a great tympanum, rattled doors for entrée and slid beneath them. The wind, the storm-flecked river, were a great roaring applause for winter.

It was early afternoon, scarcely two-thirty, but memories had been crowding him and he would stride out along the empty river tracks, make his haphazard circuit, feel lashed and cleansed at the end of his trek.

He hung his cassock and biretta on the brass hooks, put his collar and stock on the prie-dieu, wrapped himself against the weather: a rollneck coarse as tweed, the cloak and upturned collar, a beret peaked low on his forehead. From the ground, almost hidden by prie-dieu and chair, he took his stick: japanned, exquisitely polished, a rod of lignum vitae. It was iron-ferruled, the head delicately carved for grip like matted hair.

Some Dory worthy of the past had brought it ashore and a deep brass ring had been engraved, '*Ich kann nicht anders*'.

The Canon shouldered it like a guardsman and was gone.

From the lee of the People's Hall, Harney, agile Father Jim's factotum, watched the Canon's emergence, one moment the cloak wind-twisted about him, the next filled and broad as the wings of a bat, as if he might fly.

The Canon was in the middle distance; he had come from the church. A sudden eddy caught him and swung him

41

towards the People's Hall. Harney's peering face vanished to cover, but a yellowed handkerchief dabbing wind-watered eyes was snatched away; he pressed back against the stone-work.

"Christ!" he said, looking at the sweeping plagues of leaves, gravestones, grass. Had he been sussed? That rambling batman had the eyes of a hawk. He peered again, watched the Canon out of sight.

A dark horse that, Harney was thinking. And that stick like an iron bar.

He ran with his jacket held across an orb of belly, and through charges of wind to the church, his buttocks pulled sphincter-tight against the cold. One moment he was tossed in the storm of wind and leaves and dust; and then, mercifully, he had found refuge. The outside world was muted and distant; but in God's empty house what was loose rattled in the sudden flurries. Then almost stillness. Harney coughed: a kind of dry bark, and sound seemed to cannon and thunder in the void. He felt he had offended the kingpost roof, the carved hardwood seats, windows of leaded panes, mullioned; and in the cusps and tracery little trefoil lights of stained glass that he sometimes sat and watched.

Father Jim had covered the Lutheran statuary with heavy purple cowls, had sent them 'for an early bath', brought on life-size images of Gabriel spearing the serpent; Oliver Plunkett, sainted now, a face hardly known to most, who had been hanged and hacked at Tyburn; Anthony of Padua; and Patrick, patron evangelist, six foot three with crozier and outstretched hand banishing from Ireland the snakes clustered about his feet.

SS Patrick and Anthony, on lofty plinths and pedestals, stood inside the sanctuary rails before votive candelabra, sentinels of the high altar and its tabernacle; and from a pendant crown of ironwork hung the never extinguished light of God's presence. Holy Anthony of poverty and gentleness was beloved of Father Jim: the enforced roles of hustler and pitchman sat uneasily on him but he bore them with fortitude, a daily avowal of humility and obedience.

The images were of cheap Italian plasterwork and the

hand-painting had the hotchpotch of long-ago Woolworth lead soldiery. St Patrick's mouth had an odd twisted grin and his eyes were dots; he might have been inviting the snakes to return, Harney thought.

Father Jim had also placed in position two confessionals: eight-by-four chipboard and light oak stain. Diabolical, was Harney's verdict: like thunderbox johns in a fairground. At any rate, there was need only for one, but Father Jim had thought that the symmetrical emplacement of one at each side would enhance the dignity he had rented.

These additional furnishings were portable, of course. The Canon had seen to that. Oh, no flies on that bucko, Harney thought again. He moved along the church, past the sanctuary rails and through the corridor to the Mortuary. He stood in the confusion and listened: rattles, door-slammings, moments of silence.

The sight of spirit cases comforted him. He took tobacco and liquorice paper from his box and as he rolled his cigarette his wristwatch tilted into view. Two-thirty and a shade; an empty cubicle, the Canon gone early. Down by Sulvan's, Harney supposed, to that Crippen-Sinclair, to hot up the pace for whatever dying old duck was in 'sick-bay'. Dodgy work at the crossroads, you could be sure. A man might be safer on the trot. Oh, they didn't fool Harney!

He moved to the spirit cases, raised a half-bottle of scotch. He lit his black cigarette first, then took a good round mouthful of whisky: the comfort of tobacco and alcohol was God-given. Suddenly he listened: footsteps in the church.

"Bollocks!" he said.

But he didn't hurry; he drank twice from the whisky bottle, replaced it, and, cigarette in mouth, was stocktaking when Father Jim arrived.

"Ah, Harney!" Father Jim said. "Have you seen him?"

"The Canon?"

There was an impatient gleam aimed at Harney. "The Canon. Of course, the Canon."

Harney held out empty palms. "Ten minutes ago." Harney nodded towards the noise, the wind, the world outside. "Took off like a bat!"

"Took off? Gone? Where?"

"Christ knows," Harney said. "He likes the wind, maybe. This place is haunted."

"Don't swear, like a good fellow."

A mordant shrug from Harney. "Absent-minded, I suppose. Forgets to tell me where he's going!" He fixed his glare on Father Jim. "He tells *you*, does he?"

Father Jim offered peace and waited. "The noose is tightening, Harney. He's *mad*, the Bishop thinks. We'll need proof, of course, ample proof, reasonable."

"'The noose is tightening', did he say?" Harney was amused. "A clever man, that fellow. I can see why he's a bishop."

"Watch the Canon, Harney. Every move, understand?" Father Jim paused, made a gesture of apology and helplessness. "I'm being pushed, Harney! From high places, other interests too, I feel. Who? Ghosts, shadows? Strange, the whole business. I couldn't manage without you." He flicked Harney's shoulder in gratitude. "Your experience is invaluable. Bar manager, ship's bosun, psychiatric nurse. I had no idea, Harney."

Father Jim, seeming hardly thirty, with some protean gift of mood and image, seconded from a less demanding diocese to be tested in the Canon's village, was nimble as a Thomist. Gone was the medieval robe and sash, the business suit, its appurtenances. On his rented parochial ground, he was the mod young man: trainers, jeans, sweatshirt, bomber-jacket, black cloth cap with a green centre-stud on its crown; compact, gleaming teeth for a smile. He was the harassed Father Jim now.

Harney was mollified. "We'll nail him down," he said. "We'll nail him."

"He never stops, Harney. Always in motion."

"Down the old back-doubles again, I suppose?"

Father Jim said, "Those unspeakable empty back-streets he keeps wandering about! Standing there, looking up to the sky, amused, as if people gaped at him in a wilderness. Then down that alleyway, narrow as a crack, to the river. Smiling, waving to big ships long gone, that couldn't see

44

him for rubble." Father Jim was pained. "What do you think, Harney?"

Harney had a stock-book in hand and he put it away, drew on his black cigarette, paced about: an air of professionalism. He wore cords, a Harris tweed jacket, a cravat. He said, "He's clever, of course. They all are. Oh yes, clever." He gazed at Father Jim's feet, the black-and-white trainers, and then slowly lifted his gaze to Father Jim's face. "Was he ever, shall we say, confined to barracks for a spell? You know, a couple of months in the country to let the old brain cool down?"

"I have no idea, Harney."

"Mmm," Harney pondered. "Some of them, when they've heard the clang of the door, had the key turned on them like a trap, can't get rid of the sound, you see. They want to be out all the time. Walk, walk, walk, like there's a happy land somewhere . . ."

"Yes, yes!" Father Jim's apprehension gathered, almost a weariness settled on him for a moment. "There was another accident at the school on Saturday. The catechism class, you know? Yes, another 'accident'!" Father Jim was toneless in his scepticism. "Francis Xavier Murphy 'fell' over the Canon's walking-stick and crashed against the statue of St Brigid, so recently donated to the People's Hall. Head on!"

Harney smoked and considered it. "A nice statue too. It'll be missed by one and all."

For a moment Father Jim eyed him with manifest displeasure. "Half a dozen stitches in Murphy's not very vulnerable scalp, Harney! And his mother?" Father Jim might have had an awesome vision. "Not to be trifled with ever, a member of the Altar Society, a singular female who can reach the sanctuary lamp, Harney, without the aid of a stepladder. You know her?"

"A very savage woman, I'm told."

"Swears the Canon invited Francis Xavier to *jump* over his stick. And when he's in mid-air . . ."

Harney snapped finger and thumb like a nutcracker. "Gives him the old flip, does he? Up and under."

Father Jim seemed to feel the pain. "Something like that."

"Well," Harney said with finality, "the man's unsafe, that's

45

established. GBH. Three counts in a year would make him a doorman in Soho. Guy Fawkes' Night in the car park, like a wounded Samurai, he swings round, puts two West Indian yobboes in the bonfire.''

Father Jim momentarily closed his eyes in thanksgiving. "Scorched only, by the grace of God." He crossed himself and Harney nodded devoutly. "They were urinating on the fire, I believe.''

"Oh yes," Harney said. "And exposing themselves a shade enthusiastically, we all agree. But the man's unsafe. They must take that stick away from him."

"*We* must take it, Harney."

Harney smiled. "He said to me the following day: he was tapping me on the shoulder with the stick, 'Shock therapy, Harney, is the message of the Scriptures.' 'Oh no doubt about it, Canon,' I said. 'Not a doubt in the world.' ''

The wind attacked again, hammered strange percussions with doors and windows; the curtains in the archway bellied. Outside, a dustbin might have been upended and driven away in a frantic jangle.

"A fair blow that. No let-up," Harney said at the abatement; and then to fill a moment's silence, "A wind to make kites out of sheet anchors."

"Yes.''

Father Jim's attention was pulled hither and thither, scattered. "There's wisdom in not preaching to the unstable. Understandable," he said suddenly. And then he listened to the wind and came in step with Harney again. "Force eight and rising. Think of the coast. A respite tomorrow, they say, and worse to come." He made a little blessing gesture to protect himself, goods and chattels and staff. "And he's out there, Harney. That distracted man is out there, at large." He looked anxiously to Harney for a moment or two. "In your psychiatric experience, Harney . . . ten years, was it?''

"Give or take, Father Jim," Harney said effacingly. "Oh, I've seen dozens like him. Eventually they go too far, you see. Suddenly there's a powwow in the consultants' office. 'Diminished social responsibility, delinquent tendencies'. All the big stuff trotted out. Verdict? Top-security confinement.

And that's it! Bang slams the door, click goes the lock, and for the first week they're like hyenas in a net. A scream or a laugh, Christ couldn't tell. Nurses driving home the jabs, you understand, and 'security' lying low in the shadows.''

"We must be discreet, Harney. Maintain a foothold. Remember that. Remember it . . .''

The People's Hall, from its beginnings and more venerable days, was equipped with a committee room, handsome, panelled, where vestry members had convened to manage the mundane necessities of even God's business. Now, its committee room had a central corridor – portable screens, really – and openings to Father Jim's and Harney's bedsits, adequately furnished by the Canon, of course.

"We must maintain a foothold," Father Jim reiterated. "And trust in God . . . our daily prayers . . .'' And 'Monsignor' James Kilmartin, he thought.

"And John James Harney, psychiatric 'charge', para-med first class and trouble-shooter behind twenty-foot madhouse walls!" Harney didn't raise his voice but there was menace in every word.

"Yes, yes!" Father Jim retreated, escaping the blunder. "Deep-sea bosun too, east or west . . .''

"And now," Harney said, "everything from beer-slinger to bell-ringer, arsehole allsorts in this bloody Van Diemen's Land. The air is full of noise in this place . . .''

"Harney! Harney! . . . please!"

Harney found a lower key but the menace simmered. "We'll wind up in clink, in clink, I tell you! What goes on down there? Tell me, eh?" He pointed towards the wind beyond the windowless walls. "That shack down there, blinds and locked doors, some dying old stick ready for the 'off'. Ambulance-trips in, smoked glass and the undertaker's van for the outward bound.''

Harney paused only for breath.

"And the staff!" he said. "Canon Bang Bang, of course. And the mad tart he keeps in the Rectory, floating around like a madonna on wheels. I'll bet she lifts her bib for him.''

"Harney!"

"Holds their dying hands, I'd say, the misfortunate skinbags

47

with a lifetime's loot signed over. That's the entrance fee, I'd say."

Father Jim remained silent, paced about, through the open doors of the cubicle viewed the Canon's stock and cassock and biretta. Harney was upset. Not surprising. Watching and being watched. But these declamations of nefarious practice, skulduggery, even death, would have to cease.

"There are no payments of any kind," Father Jim said. "And Miss Delacey? Qualified and registered, Harney. Highly qualified. Are you listening? They all pass through my net, you must remember that. And, from what we can see, dedicated to these moribund wretches and the Canon. Is that clear?" Father Jim fixed him with a cold eye, awaited the interruption that didn't come. "She lives in the Rectory? Yes. Evidence of lechery? None."

Harney didn't face Father Jim; he looked towards the whisky cases and thought how the explosive warmth of a mouthful would distance him from this little pious itch.

Silence, acquiescence would be the thing, but he found himself thinking aloud, too loud. "A whole rectory for Bang Bang and that legs-crossed Delacey mare. A couple of partitioned horseboxes for cash-on-the-nail lodgers. For us! Two hundred blues a week. A thousand flags!"

"A thousand for church and Hall. Not exorbitant, Harney." Father Jim softened a little. "You mustn't upset yourself, old friend. I know you mean well."

I mean bollicks, Harney thought. He said aloud, "And that quack, Sinclair, is a juju mixer, a cast-iron nobbler."

"Qualified, Harney," Father Jim said again. "The world opened its doors for him. But twenty years squandered, wandering in strifes, upheavals, destructions. Godless work. Talent spent. This Dory person paid him a great deal of money to sit on her doorstep." Father Jim thought of the strange ways of God, the divine vagaries. "What we would call nowadays, Harney, a 'dropout', I suppose."

"Look," Harney said. "People ring him now when their cats have the clap. Ten pounds a knock and he has it laid on some three-legged mutt at Hackney before he leaves the manor. A cocktail shaker, I tell you. Watch him."

48

"*We* watch him, Harney."

"He watches us."

"The Canon, Harney. I'm going now, out into this raging day. Listen to it. I'll keep him in my sights. God is on my side."

He has a habit of disappearing, Harney had an urge to say, but he restrained it. The prospect was joyous of aloneness and his whisky.

Father Jim said from the archway, "You could stock the bar, Harney, a heavy stock for our Saturday gala. A double-header, I didn't tell you, did I? 'Maverick Flynn and the Riverboat Men', of course. But an incredible guest appearance! Incredible, Harney. 'Nunz v Narcos'! Providential, is all I can say. Passing through, Harney. Incredible!"

"Who?" Harney said.

Father Jim might have been contemplating degrees of heroism. He said, "Five fearless young handmaids of the Lord from our homeland, Harney, leaving the peace and holiness of their cloisters, to perform, to push from gig to gig, as they say, town to town, a weary task, to raise funds against the great evil of our times."

"To perform?"

"Oh, excellently, Harney," Father Jim said. "'Heavy Metal', they call it. Heavy Metal."

Jaysus, Harney thought, the whole world is gone mad. He steadied himself.

"The cleaners?" he suddenly thought.

"I've instructed them. The Hall will be spotless." Father Jim smiled faith and encouragement. "Keep going, Harney. The end, you could say, is in sight. The Bishop's administrator . . ." Father Jim's voice dropped to a soft murmur ". . . is making arrangements in a suitably equipped nursing home. Somewhere up north, remote, isolated, you know. We should have word in a day or two." He smiled with an unexpected warmth. "Almost two years we've weathered the storm, Harney, and your efforts have been noted in the highest places." Father Jim listened to a fresh onslaught of wind. "Dear Defender of us all, he's out there in that wind and turmoil, waving at the river. Guide me to him."

Harney said, "Watch that Delacey piece. A jiggy mare. As they say in the Cosa Nostra, she puts the finger on, Bang Bang is the hitman."

Father Jim, about to leave, was struck as if by sudden ictus. He tried to unravel Harney's oblique inside wire.

"The casualties, Father Jim. Francis Xavier Murphy and the short-taken West Indians, the bully boys, the hard men." Harney was amused, teeth bared in a dangerous grin. "They rub Virgo Delacey the wrong way, if you'll pardon the expression, and before you know it, the Canon is riding in like John Wayne with a walking-stick."

"Oh God!"

"The kind of knight-in-shining-armour-maiden-in-distress syndrome. Not uncommon, Father Jim, in the psychiatric field."

"The Canon and Miss Delacey!" Father Jim prodded a hand out for silence. "No more!" he said. "It's a profanity on holy ground." He rubbed his hands slowly, then more briskly, a rhythm, an act of discipline? He stood erect. It might be some strange nostrum for dented sang-froid.

"We have other works to do and must not be diverted, Harney. Saturday, a great gathering out there for our Show Band of the Year, 'Maverick Flynn and the Riverboat Men'."

"And of course Narks on the Nuns."

"*Against*, Harney! 'Nunz v Narcos'. Narcotics, you see." He was gone.

Harney listened to his footsteps diminishing through the church, the rush of wind, the slam of the doors as he left. He moved to the whisky case, drank, and began to roll another black cigarette.

The Canon, wheeling about in the wind, had seen Harney's half-moon face peering from the buttressed gable of the People's Hall, had seen his handkerchief carried off in a swarm of leaves. There was great vigilance and plotting of movement these days.

The Canon pushed on towards the Rectory. Daylight had

been stolen, he thought, the clocks put back: not yet three o'clock and the flight of grey cloud from the wind, the tight ceiling, had the first traces of evening.

He visualised Harney's dodging scamper to the Mortuary and whisky cases. And could little Father Jim be far behind? Harney gauged with precision for his wants: measured portions of whisky and peace so that when repleted darkness fell, he would have found remission, escape. There was good in everything.

The churchyard shrubs and trees were tossed, bent, dragged in the sudden squalls from the water: they gave the wind its howl and shiver. The Canon left the gravel paths and crossed the grass of the burial ground, lay against the wind, shouldered and jostled with it; the grass fell flat for a moment and bristled again. Only the stones and vaults were unyielding.

He saw the harsh granite monolith, straight from the blast quarry, that he himself had brought to the churchyard: an undressed glinting rock, spiked and sheared surfaces; mica, like flame when sun shone, a single level face where he had mounted a bronze tablet:

HENRIETTA LUCY DORY-CATCHPOLE 1986

She Died in Peace.

HORATIO SAMUEL TAYLOR CATCHPOLE 1916

He Died For King & Country.

He had grassed the open scar of earth too, with churchyard turves above her ashes: honest grass that had seemed to him at once a dutiful cladding of warmth for her memory.

He was suddenly at the rectory steps, hardly worn over so many decades, and the door was opened for him.

Catherine Delacey smiled. "Walking early today."

"Ghosts," the Canon said.

She took his hand, shut out the wind. He was honed as a travelling man: watered humorous eyes, skin weathered tight.

"We have a 'departure' this early evening," she said, looking out.

"Ada?"

"Yes."

"I thought she might want to leave very soon."

"Soon."

"Early darkness too."

"Yes."

"I'll go to her in a little while," he said.

She took his cloak and beret and stick: and watched him hold the drawing-room doors apart for a moment before he nodded and went inside.

It had been Lucy's drawing room all those years but he and Catherine Delacey shared it now: a beautiful corner space, windows towering almost from the floor: two pointing east with the flow of the river; three looking across rolling ground, shrubs, trees, to the gateway and the encircling sweep of corniced ragstone wall.

Age-buffed pine gave warmth to the floor. There were rugs and window-seats, cushioned divans facing each other across a marbled mantel surround, an open grate with brass-railed fender, gleaming fire-irons; tables, a lovers' chair, an escritoire: everything seeming to have been dropped fortuitously and where it looked most beautiful. The heaped coal fire had a kind of pulsing glow: he could feel its radiance.

He crossed to the last of the southerly windows, stood close to it where he could look obliquely to the churchyard . . .

*A young girl in flimsy summer finery stood there and her tall loving Horatio holding out a hand: they stood in some enclave of imperishable summer beyond the blemish of storm or coming winter; they were smiling. He often saw them there . . .*

And then at the gateway, almost hidden from him by shrubs, he saw a flicker of movement. There emerged, for a moment only, leather jackets, black, a pair of them: daring young braves, light-footed as cats. Villainous faces, the Canon thought. In seconds, hugging the wall, they had reached and entered the church. Hardly to pray; and if to meet someone, not God.

The Canon pondered it. The Bishop's men, carabinieri? A patrol, a sortie? The prelude, in that case, to battle.

Catherine Delacey had entered with wine and glasses. His back was to her. She looked at the greying hair, the tall wiry frame in black from rollneck to matt black shoes, oiled, heavy as fieldwear.

Without turning, the Canon said, "We have prowlers, I think."

"Prowlers?"

"Yes."

"Harney and the Reverend Jimmy prowl," Catherine Delacey said. "Savages behind rocks."

The Canon smiled.

"Parishioners prowl, everyone prowls." Then suddenly she wondered aloud, "Musicians, could it be? The advance guard. 'Roadies', he calls them. 'Roadies' set up 'gigs', did you know?"

"Fascinating," the Canon said.

"Saturday night, 'Maverick Flynn and the Riverboat Men'. And Flying Nuns, or something. With warheads, I should imagine."

But the Canon, at the window, was engrossed in surveillance. "On their toes, these roadies. Smart as Indians. One with a bag."

"Ghouls, perhaps." Catherine Delacey put port and glasses on the fireside table.

"And hard," the Canon said thoughtfully; he turned towards her. "Hard, very hard. Harbingers of a kind, I would say."

"Where?" Catherine Delacey was apprehensive now. For him.

"In the church," the Canon said. "Collectors, men of vertu? In search of Father Jim's confessionals, perhaps?"

He considered for a moment the practised stealth, the curious drive of some exigency. "Assassins, nothing else," he said and came across to sit facing Catherine Delacey. "Take care," he said.

She poured the wine. The room, the reassurance of its massive walls, shut out the fading hours of daylight. Catherine Delacey smiled again and the Canon wondered at her beauty.

But Catherine Delacey had only an attractive plainness: delicate plaited hair, healthy skin and teeth; a healthy body too that could suddenly be charged and in action.

"You look fine," the Canon said.

She leant over to touch his hand for a moment. Like the Canon, though almost a decade his junior, the years had softened provenance and faction . . .

. . . They had met at a gory street calamity, a strange fortuitous moment for them both, suddenly corralled in a gathering cluster, looking down on a body of shattered bones, the horror of limbs awry; a jagged crater high on its forehead and scalp, crazed bone pressed on tissue, grey ooze and blood. A young face already distorting. Above them, the motor-cycle, horn-locked with steel railings, reared upwards like a doomed animal. Catherine Delacey had bent down to the awful mess.

A rebuke had come from somewhere. "Don't move him, silly bloody bitch"; and Catherine Delacey had said, "Piss off, there's a good fellow. Get an ambulance, will you?"

She had felt about at wrist and neck for a pulse and stood up with bloodied hands. The Canon had offered his handkerchief. She saw grey-streaked hair, weathered skin, the cloak, the rollneck, the beret: a strange vision perhaps but no longer remarkable in an eccentric world, she thought; a tall figure holding a magnificent polished ferruled stick.

The Canon, silently, had been praying a moment or two, thinking of the arrival of pain, and escape from it.

"Alive?" he had asked.

"Yes."

"Ambulances take a long time in traffic."

"I hope so," Catherine Delacey had said.

It had been early December, cold, cloudless, the sun etching the kerbs, the cheap façades of Asian sweatshops, the ancient brickwork above them. Traffic, multi-horse-powered, moved at the rate of spavined Victorian hacks to the convergence of Whitechapel.

In a little while the ambulance was sending ahead its heehaw at the speed of sound and arrived only when the crowd had tired and all but dispersed. The Canon awaited his cloak that was placed for warmth on the body. Catherine Delacey waited. Salvage men dragged the Japanese mechanical bull from the railings.

Red blankets, expressionless uniformed men were there. The Canon took his cloak, only a little bloodied.

"Nineteen shopping days to Christmas," Catherine Delacey said.

"I was walking through the old streets," the Canon told her.

"Somewhere special?"

"Walking."

He was looking at the calm grey eyes, tied-back hair – her changeless fashion – a tweed coat, belted, high-buttoned, elegant, unfashionable in denim days.

A regal indifference, he thought. The morning shone.

"I'll walk with you," she said.

"Delighted."

"I'm Catherine Delacey," she told him. "You're Paul Vincent Herlihy. It's embroidered on your bloodied cloak."

The Canon saw a beautiful face.

"A very old lady with trembling hands embroidered it for me," he said. "She died this autumn past."

The ambulance, the salvage men, were pulling away. The traffic would soon crawl over a fading smudge.

"Aldgate isn't far," the Canon said. "A drink if you like."

"Blood doesn't worry me," Catherine Delacey said.

"Will he survive?"

She pondered it. "A whole team at battle soon," she said. "To keep him pumping. Whatever gangling brainchild emerges."

"People of compassion?"

"A challenge too."

"Hanging days," the Canon said. "Counsels flung down the gauntlet for each other, a ceremonial joust. The accused could watch."

"Something like that."

55

They had coffee at Aldgate, drank a little wine.

"Is port addictive?" the Canon asked.

"I hope so," Catherine Delacey had said.

The fringes of the City, the unsleeping square mile, reached fingertip to Aldgate and Whitechapel once, now they creep over dockland, the riverside, the quondam congeries of barefoot immigrant and whore, lues and ritual murder. The élitist City, its friendly canyons beyond sunlight, beckons: Palladian and baroque are stunted now, crouch beneath towering glass cathedrals of a commonsense God who knows about bread and on which side it is buttered. There is an untroubled peace on the façade of the City, and behind it, a crazed world of electronic dementia, horrendous colliding shrieks of tallymen and fairground barkers.

At Liverpool Street, Catherine Delacey said, "This was Bedlam Asylum once."

"Yes," the Canon said.

"It was an outing to come and look at lunatics and their chains."

They went through Bishopsgate and Shoreditch with its graceful church, into Kingsland, the gateway to miscegenous Hackney.

"This is a hospital," Catherine Delacey said. "A hospital. It was a workhouse once."

There was a great rambling complex of brickwork, stained, in decay, neglect showing on windows and woodwork.

"A workhouse soon again," the Canon said.

They climbed the steps to its hub. Great wings shot out like spokes left detached from an outer rim: a design of confinement for destitute and bereft of Empire days. It rose four storeys, towering above the last small dwellings of ilk and identity.

The hub was 'Reception' now: oil paint and dull marbled lino; a phalanx of tubular chairs was spotted with people. There was a counter and a bald peering man in dark steel-rimmed glasses. Blind, the Canon wondered.

The 'blind' man said, "Good morning, Miss Delacey."

She nodded. "A lazy bugger," she told the Canon.

"Not blind?"

56

"Lazy. Sleeps behind his windows, you see."

Corridors stretched away from this hub of infinite waiting. But they climbed a stone staircase, more than a century old, worn, black as basalt; there was a wooden latter-day handrail on iron banisters.

"A workhouse *now*," the Canon said.

To each floor, its corridors, its signposts, jumbled cartons, soiled linen, another flight of stone, forgotten trolleys, rubber sheets.

"Journey's end," Catherine Delacey said.

The Canon nodded.

She held open a door for him. "My wing, my patients. You must see them."

Close-packed beds, shared unused lockers; fumigant, germicide, faeces, urine, clung to whatever trapped aeration filled the space.

The Canon counted.

"A dozen," Catherine Delacey said.

"Dying . . . dead."

"A day, a month. No years here," she said.

She faced him. "The old embroidering lady with trembling hands? You helped her, did you?"

"Yes," the Canon said.

He thought: we need help to arrive, to stay a while, to go; he looked at the opposing lines of death, stillness, restless hands, a gaping mouth, rounded as a burrow, sucking down threads of pain.

"Yes," she said: he might have spoken aloud, left words smeared on the rancid air. "We need help to 'go'."

"You help them?" the Canon said.

"When they ask." . . .

They had gone down the stone steps into clean December frost again.

"I'm going to build a village," the Canon had said.

"A village? A whole village?"

"A street. A cluster of one-roomed firesides where they can wait, look about them at things gathered in a lifetime, go when they ask."

"Soon?"

"There's nothing now. A single shack."

"Empty?"

"Yes."

"One is before two," she had said.

Everywhere gods fighting gods, the Canon thought, the world their killing-field; battles fought too, savage, for that first spark of foetal life, to save it, create it, bequeath it this interminable game of soldiers.

Gods don't weep.

And the aged, beyond combat days, without use, must cringe in shame, exit from their own filth.

Gods don't grow old . . .


Catherine Delacey was touching his hand still; he turned back from his thoughts, saw the warm beauty of the Dory-Catchpole room about him, the close lambent crown of the fire, blue and amber flickering.

Catherine said, "You were remembering . . ."

"When we met," he said.

"Such bloody hands held out to you."

"Nineteen shopping days to Christmas, you said. Full of wisdom."

He stood and went to the window, looked out beyond the churchyard at a single refurbished shack, a place to die. A single shack. The village street, its plan, its every detail, two years in sterility, propped by his bedroom desk.

Men of power, in holy places, could discountenance, abort.

"Ada," Catherine Delacey said. "Ada is ready to leave." She could see him looking down at the lone windswept cabin.

"Yes," he said.

"Waiting for you."

She brought him his cloak and stick and beret again, wrapped him carefully against the elements; brought Matthew Sinclair's physic of peace. He put it carefully in his pocket.

From the doors of the drawing room she watched him cross the lobby and called to him, "My love to Ada."

"Yes."

He turned back to her, took her hands in his. They stood

58

in silence: there came always these strange forlorn moments with the closeness of death.

Then he was off, pulling the great panelled door behind him, battling along the gravel paths in the wind . . .

*. . . Lucy and Horatio, again in their high-summer enclave, seemed to smile from the grave and its granite marker. He raised a hand to them . . .*

On the vanishing pavement and empty ruined street at last, he looked back through the iron gateway, across the undulating ground to Catherine in the warm glow of their window.

The cloak twisted and flapped; he moved into the sweep of wind, breathless in the exhilaration of it, the roar of it in his mind. Across the scabrous ground he could see his tracks, the wasting pavements, the cabin, a patch of survival where Ada awaited him: the moment of journeying . . .

*. . . And he was aware, suddenly again, of silence shutting him in: he stood in a crystal dome of storm and buffeting, and looked out at another place of frantic movement, postcard stillness sprung to life. The cobbled alleyways returned, ground-level hovels, flaked limewash brick: a door, a twelve-paned window apiece, a single chimney, the coarse slate of the roofs, eaves low as a raised hand. In front, cabbage patches, precious as life.*

*Hidden behind was the river and visible beyond the roofs only the tips of a forest of pennants and masts. Stillness, soundlessness, but movement everywhere; hands at work, fists raised, heads thrown back in a great mime of speech and uproar; women clad from neck to heel, aproned across great bellies; the rolled sleeves; tight peaked caps or battered bow-brimmed bowlers of the men. He waved to them, but they had passed by on the track of time, a great journey beyond his reach. He watched them fade, the rags, the silent uproar, their whole world of frantic stillness. It was gone . . .*

Desolation returned: the salvaged cabin across a space of creeping detritus and weeds. The wind was everywhere again as he pushed towards it, wondered if he too was being watched from some crystal dome as he was hurried past on an infinite cyclorama.

The cabin was roofed, faced and painted now: solid doors and frames, a stout window, bright curtains. The Canon selected his key and entered.

Once it had been a place of two rooms: a kitchen for waking hours: the bedroom for all – to sleep, to listen, to peer, to copulate, to relieve the body's lumps and fluids.

Now it was a single space. Catherine Delacey had chosen tiles of warmth, colour; rugs; the reassurance of a wooden bed and its locker and shaded lamp; shelves for a lifetime's bric-à-brac, even a whatnot from where remembered faces smiled in attendance, framed in brown distant moments of time. There was a glowing gas-fire and polished wooden surround; pictures too of matinée gods and angels, long perished, imperishable.

Only in one corner did creeping mortality have its show: behind a floral screen, the chrome of trolley and hand-basin, a flush toilet bowl for disposals, Catherine Delacey's gown. What was necessary.

"The dying need living rooms to fall asleep in," the Canon had said. "Not iron beds nearest the door."

Ada was drowsing, a beak-like face that might have been pert and sparkling once. Her hair was brown, had never greyed, and was cared-for and arranged on the pillow by Catherine Delacey; her hands lay on the counterpane, the fingers made a little clutching motion and were still again. There was a bellpush. The Canon went behind the screen and prepared Matthew Sinclair's measured anodyne. He sat beside Ada, took her hand and gently awakened her.

"Miss Delacey told me," he said.

She gazed at him: a distant smile.

A blessed mercy, the Canon thought, that for some, at the time of leaving, came these hoarded moments of youth. The pains, the dread, the trauma, the decisions were behind.

Ada's was a small voice, a little hoarse in weakness. She was somewhere in memory. Her hand was a small delicate claw in the Canon's palm.

She seemed to look past him at a journey completed. "Like a day at Southend, ain't it, all this? Sun, tide at the wall, milk stout and mild, a kiss and a crush when you can, salt on your chips thick as the sand, pearlies, knees-ups. Then it rains, rains, rains. You're glad to go home."

The Canon nodded.

A little tide of strength seemed to come to her.

"My fella, him in the picture. A lad," she said. "A diamond too, when he wanted. All them Southend tricks . . . no end . . ." She was smiling into the memory of it. "Getting dusk like now an' he tries it on in the phone-box." She gazed at the Canon. "In the phone-box, know what I mean?"

"Tried to give you one?" the Canon said.

"That's it, love. I let him too. God, it was heaven."

The Canon looked across at the face laughing from the whatnot, the body that had imprisoned a 'boy' for ever.

"Oh, he went early," she said. "Dead as a doornail I found him."

The Canon brought her the picture.

"I'll see him down the road, will I?"

"At Southend maybe," the Canon said.

"Coronation is what killed him," she remembered; she tired, a great weariness, and it passed. "Coronation, that effin' coronation. Whole street like a fairground: pictures, bunting, jack-the-lads, beer buckets and he never makes it. Comes in pissed with his flag and upstairs to fix it. Falls out the window, flag and all . . ."

She slept a little while.

Then it was raining: the hammering squalls came and diminished; and came again.

When she awakened, she was in pain, overpowering. No words.

The Canon pressed the fragile fingerbones. "Miss Delacey," he said.

He raised her up and she drank carefully, slowly: it was very precious. He arranged her pillow, her hair, but she was already asleep, drifting away. She had passed through the gate, the Canon thought, to wherever it led. Southend, he hoped.

61

The rain had ceased. He would walk a little, then find Matthew Sinclair. He listened. While he had sat with Ada there had seemed a great peace. Now there was the impingement of everything. He took his stick from behind the screen, nodded farewell to the still face of Ada as he left.

The leather jackets, he remembered. In the church, like jungle cats, were they? And the handsome young man, expensive too, reconnoitring, fishing with smiles. For shadows, persons unknown?

Where now were they all? Along the distant shoreline, there was a flicker of light and then gloom again.

Harney was in the church, in the Mortuary; the cavernous slam of the door on Father Jim's exit still echoed, lingered like a spirit. God couldn't find the Canon, Harney thought; or the Canon find God. A lunatic road-show, the whole thing; the howl and screech out there, a rackety wind-machine at the end of its run.

He looked at the dust-webbed discarded candles, grease-bearded, drank again, smoked the black cigarette. He was hardly tall, but a powerful man, and his gut sagged a little. Except for the eyes, it was a forgettable round face. Harney could stand immobile, suspended, seeming to listen with a blind man's stare; or instantly he could smile, clothe his visitors with warmth. Nothing escaped him.

He lit a match now and held it beneath the webbed candles, sent a hidden spider from cover, quick as a kill. Dirt, rubble, God in a crib, plaster faces of sainted animals and men: like a blob on the box after midnight, he thought.

One more drink; the balm of it! Mouthfuls might be missed but blessed water filled the void. Always a fresh bottle, was the trick, a drink-down, a top-up, keep the record straight. Father Jimmy wandered in Limbo.

The ineffable flame and solace of alcohol was spreading now, the tang of tobacco drawn in, and the clouded fragrance about his head before draughts and flurries swiped it away.

He looked at the open door of the Canon's cubicle, the

holy trappings lying about: breviary, collar, stock; cassock and biretta on hooks.

This was a place of performance, Harney thought: Camden Town cowboys, nuns on a gig, Bang Bang, the magic Canon.

Not a cleric at all, says Father Jim!

He stood in the midst of the Christmas crib and its images, still as the images themselves, for minutes.

Harney could perform for them all! Once he had dived fifty feet into a six-foot tank and broken his leg. A circus trial. "Come back when it knits," they had invited him. Enthusiasm had waned but he looked back with pride: it took 'balls' to perform.

He was pleased: he would drink to 'performance'!

This time he took his own half-bottle from an inside jacket pocket. Personal stock.

Harney, ex cathedra, had advised wholesale suppliers to Father Jim's bar that discounts should be discreet and generous. And in kind. And to Harney. Or no business.

He raised his drink. "To performers, by God!"

Importance flowed with the warmth now, a sense of command. The careful diminution of bar-room stock, the conservation of his own, was more efficacious than prayer: a barrier against the world and its pain.

He removed his coat, his cravat, laid them carefully on the whisky cases and crossed to the Canon's cubicle. A mirror? There was a discarded sheet of window glass and he propped it on the trestle-table where the light-bulb's glare caught it and gave him a dim reflection.

The dog collar and stock first: he snapped the back stud of the collar in place, tied back the strings of the stock at his waist. The moments of transfiguration had begun; he was lighter; he pulled in the protuberance of belly; a less rotund buccal face seemed to stare from the darkness of his mirror.

He raised himself up to gain an inch or two, tightened the jowl with a lifting and jutting of chin.

"My dear brethren in Christ," he said, and blew out a cloud of smoke. The black cigarette, he thought, was harmonious. He let it droop from his mouth and studied himself again. A bit on the racy side, on reflection, he thought, and ground it out.

The cassock then, with buttons to the ground, and a high neckband cut to show the collar's confronting white square and a surrounding edge of authority. It reached to the ground and trailed a little, of course, but there was a certain statuesque dignity in the drapery, Harney thought. He was pleased with it.

"Listen to the sound of the crying wind, my dear brethren," he said.

Now, the biretta. He had looked forward to that. It was a shade small, but he gently pushed it down until it gripped, gave it a tilt for dignified style. He took up a paperback for a breviary, held it open before him.

An aura of grace and joy enveloped him. He would drink to it, an honest drink. But a smoke first: he rolled his tobacco and liquorice paper and put flame to it. An honest drink. He took the half-bottle from his discarded jacket and sipped with reverence. A great peace was hovering. He let the cigarette dangle from his mouth again, held the breviary in one hand, the bottle in the other.

"'They have sown the wind and they shall reap the whirlwind,'" Harney declaimed, closed his eyes, turned as if to a congregation, intoned, "'Let us eat and drink, for tomorrow we shall die.'"

When he had raised his lids and vision had returned from beyond, he saw young men in black leather jackets, human, framed in the archway. Two young men. The invasion of his canonical privacy set off a blast furnace of rage.

He boomed, "Your business here, gentlemen?"

Maxwell said, like gravel, "Looking at a padre's piss-up, Jimmy, with a fag in his gob like a yob. What's in the book? Knickers and tit?"

Harney, behind the clerical garb, felt as if the profanity had flailed his 'anointed' body. Aphasia gripped and released; he stared at Maxwell in frozen wonder. When the 'stroke' had passed, he said, almost secretively, "Move off, arsehole, very quietly, so I don't hear you. Out of here. Out of the church. Off the premises. I don't like to blow a fuse, see?"

64

"A sin, is it?"

"Dangerous."

"Doctor's orders?"

"That's right. He said I was dangerous."

Maxwell giggled: a shock of amusement, speechless a moment, then braying out a great derision of Harney.

Dowty waited for him to recover. He said, "I do the talking. All of it, remember?"

"He's a bloody turn."

"I do the talking."

"You do the talking," Maxwell said.

Dowty smiled on Harney. "I have the pleasure, have I not, of addressing his reverence, the Canon?"

Harney was mollified at once: this was a deferential clean-cut young man; there was respect. "Yes indeed, I am the Canon, my child," he said, remembering the benign smiling images of Hollywood's men of cloth. He saw that Dowty carried a holdall: a small zipped canvas cylinder.

"The gate was open," Dowty said. "Not a bell in sight. We took the liberty."

"The Rectory has a bell, you see." The Canon would forgive this impropriety. "The parochial residence, it has a bell."

"We thought we'd find you here in the Mortuary."

"The Mortuary?"

"Yes."

He was still the avuncular Harney but behind smile and bonhomie caution crept and waited. This familiarity? The Dory-Catchpole topography might have been studied with care. *The Mortuary*.

"Salesmen, representatives, that kind of thing, are you?" Harney said. "I'm afraid the parochial needs are in the hands of the Bishop's administrator." He was sympathetic. "A great distance from here."

The wind had come on with a rolling breaker of force, it seemed, and drove rain before it. It hammered on the mortuary roof and against the surrounding narrow fringe of stained glass at the eaves.

Harney raised a hand in blessing and protection; he found

a strange dignity in this new role. Had it suddenly flowered, a blessed vocation latent all these years?

"The Lord will protect us from harm," he said.

Dowty nodded. "We only came for your signature."

Harney had to ponder that.

"Signature, you know? The old 'John Henry'." Dowty made a scribbling motion, took a brown outsize sheet of paper from his bag. Or an envelope, perhaps.

"Ah!" Harney cracked it. "A petition, my child! Harassment on offshore Britain? Chastity in Soho? Dockland for the Darkies?" He held out empty hands. "A wasted journey, I'm afraid, gentlemen. I never sign anything."

"Never?" Dowty's face was tighter, less gentle.

"I might make an exception," Harney said, "in the case of 'bring back the rope' and medical castration."

"Nothing like that," Dowty said. "Just a signature."

Harney shook his head, a dismissal, became aware of the cigarette dangling from his mouth. He stubbed it out, put away the whisky bottle, snapped the 'breviary' shut with great finality. "Well, I bid you good day, gentlemen. You'll find your way out. God be with you."

"While we're waiting for this shower to pass," Dowty moved to the trestle-table, brought the envelope with him, laid it flat for inspection. "You sign here," he said and ran a finger along the bordered 'window' and the underlying white parchment of McMorrow's document.

Maxwell said, "And the Lord will protect you from all harm."

Dowty aimed at Maxwell a finger like a gun. "No more! Right?"

A different package altogether now, this civilised one, Harney was thinking. He had seen a lot of faces like Dowty's and Maxwell's, lived with them, clattered one or two when the chips were down. Harney didn't take fright easily.

"Messenger boys. Who sent you?" he asked.

"Clients are confidential. Just sign," Dowty told him. He put a ballpoint pen and postcard on the envelope . . .

*

. . . Harney's thoughts raced back across years, down corridors infinite, 'nurses' at steel doors, a surgery desk: the glitter of everything, the square gold-rimmed lenses bringing him, Harney, the 'specimen', into focus . . .

"You're coming along nicely, John." Sweet disarming familiarity that enraged Harney. And he hadn't then learnt to conceal it, to smile. The 'screws' at his shoulders were blank as cutouts.

"Transferring you to K Block."

"Yes."

"The next move is 'out'! Back to the world again, John! Happy about that, aren't you?"

"Yes."

"Not long, I feel. Time heals the emotions, the scars." Great compassion, reassurance there. "Keep on the rails, that's the thing. Last week's little battle is forgotten, John. Nurses deSilva and Barnett are back with us again. Only a few bruises to show. Nothing on the record."

Harney silent.

"You'll like it in K. A good bunch, lively, on the move . . . you'll like it, John. Sign here."

He had never reached K. On the march to it he had sensed the smell of torpor and oblivion come close. And then he was in the steel and glitter of surgical furniture, penned down; he could feel the thread of needle in his arm and he was fading from consciousness when the penny dropped. The bastards! But he saw the waiting table, straps in readiness, the head-clamp, a rubber wedge against the sudden locking of teeth, the console trolley and its dangling electrodes. They would blow away his brain . . . Jesus!

He had sat in aloneness for weeks, spent, uninhabited. You never argue, he had learnt, you never tangle, you never sign. He had battled them for three years, then: it was time to learn, time to 'crawl'. Another four would pass. Mop the Victorian urinals, skiv in the kitchens, smile and arse-lick, move nearer the gate. He had made it. Seven years, by Christ! . . .

Dowty was drumming on the table.

Harney said, "I told you I never sign papers. Now move!"

Dowty's fingers, rigid, stiff as a blade, jabbed forward at the cassocked bulge of Harney's stomach: Harney's chin went up, air and a kind of retching groan burst like a joke-shop eructation. Dowty turned the envelope, ballpoint and postcard towards him, and waited.

Harney waited too, held the table, sucked in air, made a noise like the dying; but waited, gathered seconds.

Dowty leant forward, slid the postcard. "You sign here. Just like the postcard. No tricks."

Harney was ready. Backhanded, he uncoiled like a spring, caught Dowty's face, left him on his buttocks; blood came from his nose, reached his chin, dripped on black leather.

Then Maxwell was in, to savage him.

Dowty shouted, "No marks, you stupid bastard!"

One hand of Maxwell's had tightened into a fist about Harney's ear, the other was clamped round his genitals.

Dowty got to his feet. "No marks!" He took cotton wool from the holdall and plugged the little streams of blood. "No marks. Nice and calm. You ready?"

Maxwell tightened the screw of Harney's ear by half a turn, closed the grip on his testicles, only for a second or two, until Harney's voice quavered as if he might blubber. Maxwell relaxed, showing teeth and the ugliness of gums. "We're not going to hurt each other, laddie, are we?"

Wind-rush caught church doors and windows broadside again, shook and rattled them for moments; the rain was like pebbles.

"Who's expected?" Maxwell said.

"Anyone. Anyone can come."

With a handkerchief and spittle Dowty cleaned his face, his jacket. He stood for inspection.

Maxwell nodded.

"A quick job, I think," Dowty said; he studied Harney, the Mortuary. "This is a dirty hole."

Maxwell said, "Quick is the trick for this shitbag."

"Now!" Dowty said.

Maxwell's hands tightened and screwed; Harney roared in the storm and kettledrums of rain; Dowty threw a black cowl over his head and shoulders; Maxwell clipped cuffs on his wrists. They began to spin him like a top.

A minute, two minutes. Nausea swelled in Harney's body and mind; a band of pain crushed his head; his eyes blurred. Three minutes. The world was suddenly an explosion of colour, then dark and light and colour again. He tried to shout but sour whisky welled and trickled from his mouth. They stood back and let him fall.

"On his back," Dowty said.

Maxwell rolled him with his foot, pulled the cowl off. They stared down until sight returned and the eyes began to focus on them.

"If you want to sign, just nod," Dowty said.

Harney was motionless, jaws clamped tight.

Dowty went to the holy-water barrel, lifted the lid. "Cuffs off," he said to Maxwell.

Maxwell nodded.

"Everything off."

With a single tug, Maxwell ripped open the cassock, sent buttons flying into the crevices of debris and rubbish. They stripped Harney to the skin, frogmarched him at speed across the Mortuary, pushed him, headfirst, down in the icy blessed fluid: his fundament, like a cyclopic face, stared up at them, his scrotum floated. When the bubbling started, they dragged him out.

"Now?"

Harney's eyes seemed sightless; little retches of water came from his mouth, but he shook his head like a weak old man.

They plunged him again, waited for the bubbling, dumped him on the floor, cuffed him at wrists and ankles. Dowty fitted him with earphones, cowled him, let a little cassette tape start turning.

Harney had been drifting away into a shelter of sub-consciousness, the balm of silence, when the sound ripped through his mind: his brain was a fabric torn in shreds, the rending terrifying agony was death. He gathered strength to scream; pain was a blinding strobe light. And then it ceased. From behind it came a deep rumbling moan of low-frequency horror, reaching like fear into bowels and bladder. He was terrified. And then again, the unbearable white scream of noise blasted him!

He was finished; he tried to signal with feet and shoulders and head.

Dowty switched off. "He's ready."

They hoisted him, balanced him on a beer crate at the table, again arranged envelope, postcard, ballpoint.

"Dry his hands," Dowty told Maxwell; he opened a fresh bottle of Father Jim's whisky, pushed it to him.

Harney raised the bottle with both trembling hands and poured a quarter of it into his swollen gullet, waited for it to reach stomach and gut.

"This is what you sign." Dowty held the postcard before him, laid it on the envelope.

The fire of whisky was burning at last in Harney, the pain diminishing; the easement was blessed. But for the moment he was a stranger, touching, groping, astray in the Mortuary, discovering it and its turmoil afresh. A stranger: crates, cases, the open door of a cubicle, grotesque figures from a Christmas crib. He fought against the confusion.

Dowty was putting the ballpoint in his hand; he could hold it. He focused on the postcard.

Unpractised block letters spelt out: PAUL VINCENT HERLIHY.

"Paul Vincent Herlihy," Harney said: the sound of his own voice, restored, startled him. He was swaying: Dowty fed him a little whisky.

"That's it," Dowty said. " 'Paul Vincent Herlihy'."

"I'm John James Harney."

There was silence.

"The name is John James Harney."

Maxwell leant over his shoulder, looked down at his genitals. "I could give your nuts a nice little work-over, add a dash of brandy to that dirty mess down there, strike a match, set you off like a Christmas pud."

Dowty fitted him with the earphones again.

"Jesus!" Harney shouted. "No, no! Whatever you want . . . whatever you want! . . . whatever you want! . . ."

"Paul Vincent Herlihy. You sign it. Not print it."

70

Harney signed.

In seconds they had packed and vanished; the doors shut silently; only the rush of wind to the church and corridor reached Harney. He drank heavily again, forced himself into motion; dried, dressed as best he could, restored the Canon's vestments to the cubicle, looked at the almost buttonless cassock.

"Christ!"

It struck him: a great shattering hammer-blow! The vestments! They had come for the Canon! Paul Vincent Herlihy? The Canon?

He could only sit and gape.

He would drink and smoke. Fifteen minutes, he would drink and smoke, drink and smoke: he wasn't ready to think yet. He looked at his watch, wondered at its fifty-bob durability and the fragility of his own God-given, still trembling fingers. Rage unsettled him, almost brought nausea. He might kill someone, he thought. From a shelf he took a leather-sheathed knife, looked at its blade, drove it deep into the trestle-table. One, two, four, six times. He threaded it on to his belt, out of sight.

The bastards, the bastards, they had come for the Canon! 'Discreet', Father Jimmy Boy says, the little tricked-out bunkoman!

Hired squaddies, marshalled scum, for a holy army! Everyone would pay! Everyone!

Harney sat and rested; he was shivering. He dreaded the blessed icy run to the People's Hall and his room where he could restore an appearance of calm and dignity.

The Canon walked across the open ground and towards the river where only the blind skeletal frames of warehouses followed the shoreline of wharfage.

They had been stout buildings once, windowless, with formidable gates, and loft-cranes facing the cobbled road: fortresses against thievery. The rattling clangour of iron-hooped wheels, the Canon thought; the smell of animals; the dung scooped up, still steaming, for the minuscule patches of tillage.

He walked on the flagged naked floors now, held a rusted stanchion to anchor himself against the wind. The rain had ceased; only at moments river spray was caught and flung ashore.

The gentle passing of Ada, her chosen moment, comforted him: all those years she had remembered her Southend moments of love. Catherine Delacey would tend to her now, dress her, find a little beauty to enhance. Spirits, they always bided a while, Catherine had told him; they looked back, a little wistfully, he supposed, at the shell, the tenement left empty at last.

And then where, what journey ahead? The sky was a torrent of cloud, evening almost spent and night-time down. It was after four!

The Canon turned towards Sulvan's; it was in darkness, its scattered pile perched on the river, two storey, three storey, showing the grafts and additions of close on two centuries: brick, slate and chimneypots, ancient and modern, the small windows of long ago, the steel frames of today.

Fortified in its high-walled compound, shoulder to shoulder with the Canon's village, its stone steps went down to the river, time-worn like the flaked mooring-rings leaded in the side walls.

Sulvan's was a place of shadowy concourse, an entrepôt, not of goods, but of intelligences; a place of anonymity.

The Canon was a keyholder, one of a few. He let himself into the club's single-storey sprawl. It was in darkness: the only windows, small, multi-paned, overhanging the river, were heavily curtained. In business hours it was a place of warmth, unremarkable, shadowy, seemingly decorous as a Victorian parlour . . .

. . . "Who is Sulvan?"

"You've known him ten years."

"Yes."

Lucy Dory-Catchpole had answered him once; she was smiling, months only from death, rambling perhaps. "I was a child when the century came in," she was saying. "Sulvan then is Sulvan now. A Dory born when the flags came out for Waterloo knew Sulvan's brothel down at the water. Sulvan then, Sulvan now? Time, does it touch him? He comes and goes. Goes where?"

"A ghost."

"Ghosts have come back. He never died."

"We are on strange ground," the Canon had said . . .

In the pitch-blackness of Sulvan's club now, he found a seat, stretched, took moments of rest.

He had hoped to find Sinclair; but he would still be on the High Road world of punting and odds and percentages.

The Canon would wait.

The dead were for Sinclair: he had his arrangements with worthy morticians who would take Ada in a van of smoked-glass windows to a chapel of rest; and thence to cremation. 'Due to advanced age', would always qualify a Sinclair certificate and its truth was incontrovertible. And, of course, the Canon's discharge of debts was immediate.

A dedicated alliance.

The Canon thought momentarily now of Catherine who would bring dignity to Ada's remains: the touching of limp hands growing cold; the chill of her own fingers before a sleeping peaceful Ada was achieved. She would think of him too: there was a great embrace of tenderness in their administering of death.

Catherine would say, "Peace."

The Canon listened to the hollow slap of water against the stone edges below the windows, the spray flung against glass in the sudden treacherous whips. Yes, they had a love for each other, unproclaimed, but when there was bleakness, the loneliness of departures, it brought them hurrying to each other's thoughts.

In the darkness, he heard the approach of voices from the house, familiar male and female, with sometimes a trace of unease, or tenderness, gaps of silence, sudden discords. And higher up, in the rambling stairways, a small childish treble, scarcely audible, diminishing now as the footsteps

73

came. The wind, perhaps. The footsteps louder now; it was gone.

At the furthest end of this lounge a spotlight was flicked and a stage, rising hardly eighteen inches above floor-level, was caught in its brilliant amber pool. There was a polished upright piano, a four-legged stool of sheet-music days, microphones at its side, mounted speakers; its backdrop, a tinsel wall of purple, gold and yellow. On the piano stood an old spool tape recorder, covered, carefully tended.

A mounted billboard said: STAN-STAN-THE-PIANO-MAN.

They came onstage, Stan and Lottie. The amber light seeped only a little way into the lounge and the Canon was in deep darkness: it might have been a ragged end-of-season matinée, an empty prom out there, wet wet seats, only rain and wind and salt spray.

Stan was compact, hardly in shape, and battered, as if dipped in weariness; smart though, in check slacks, loose tweed jacket, shirt, flimsy red scarf knotted at his throat, ends hanging awry.

Stan had killed, had spent ten years locked away, and Lottie had waited.

In grief it had been committed, a great blundering revenge: that was his murder. He had stood down from Sulvan's ranks – with Sulvan's blessing – to carry out his private manslaughter.

He said, almost in anger, "I've lost it, doll, lost it, haven't the spunk for it, for Christ's sake! You know it, I know it, Big Sulvan knows it. I'm the piano-player."

"*I* don't know it," Lottie said.

She was dark and smart, shoulder-high to Stan: the silky hair, the dark Latin eyes, a romantic legacy perhaps coming with Spanish aid to Irish rebels and virginity. "Look at you," she said. "You fought the bloody wars. How many years? And he gives you the piano! Stan-Stan-the-Pianoman!"

"A whole army fights wars, love. I was a soldier."

"The best."

"Christ!" Stan laughed.

She kissed him and he put his arms about her. The Canon

watched them in their happiness and felt warmth and gladness for them.

"I'm forty-six, Lottie gal," he said. "There's a new army out and about, young soldiers, new wars. I'm forty-six."

"The best. I know it, you know it."

"Look," he said. "You wasted all them years for the big gates to open, a long long time, for Stan-Stan-the-Pianoman. You're thirty-two."

"Thirty-four."

He sat at the piano, rattled it. "Not Casablanca, is it?"

"We love each other."

The old house was full of sound, even the low moan of wind as it piped at the end of a blow. There had been timber but the first bricks and mortar had been laid when Waterloo was past and the riverbank teemed with disbanded rankers, destitute, dissolute: labour for a song. A time to make wealth.

Then, even then, the starving Sulvan had set his brothel there. And who was Sulvan now?

The sweet singing sound crept downstairs to the Canon again. "Do you hear it?" he had once asked Stan and Lottie. "A dozen bricked-up flues in them walls," Stan had said. "Draughts and winds and shifting timbers." . . .

No trace of Sulvan yet, the Canon thought: he came and went, his stays and absences uncharted. A day, a week, a month. Sulvan without kith or kin. Without death, without escape? Sometimes the Canon looked at him and saw ageless eyes, hands that might have dug the ancient river muck, saved pence per week to build a whorehouse . . .

Onstage, Lottie was saying, "Sulvan. He never heard the clang of an iron door!"

Stan pondered it. "People say."

"Not a mark, like he'll live for ever." Lottie studied the grey thinning hair, Stan's hammered face. ". . . like he'll live for ever."

"Maybe," Stan said.

"How many Sulvans, Stan? How many years?"

"You don't ask," Stan said. "No one asks."

"When he talks, we listen!"

"Right."

She reached for his shoulders. "You were a class man, love. They took you once, the law, the fuzz, the filth. Once, that's all. Gave you ten. A lifetime, I thought."

Lottie remembered they had never sung, 'Twenty-one, the key of the door, never been twenty-one before'. She remembered it with a little moment of regret.

She kissed him. "All set, fixing up my party, Stan, remember? And you run that bastard down. Ten, they give you. That's when I thought it. Jesus, a lifetime, I thought!"

Stan remembered.

Lottie said in a little while, "You were going to ask, pop the question, had the ring, hadn't you?" She waited.

"They took the ring," Stan told her. "Said I nicked it."

"Did you?"

"Yeah. It was special. For you."

She laughed. "We don't need rings. Ask me now."

Stan gazed at her, the warm skin, all the shining admiration for Stan-Stan-the-Pianoman.

"I'm the piano-player," he said. "The piano-player! Three years out and a piano-player for ever, that's all. Sulvan pays the piper, keep it in mind. Pays what I'm worth, maybe more. You're his barmaid. We live."

"Manager! I'm his manager!"

"Seven days a week you manage, love. Pays your whack, don't he?" Stan smiled. "We could afford a night on the town come Christmas, maybe. Look in the windows at Selfridges."

Lottie felt anger, resentment; impatience with her Stan-Stan-the-Pianoman. "I was fifteen when he took me on, room and board, three nicker a week and watch my step."

"But you never got shafted."

"Sees me once in my skin and he says, 'Dress, dress, cover it up', like I was a mess."

Stan smiled and the old handsome face was beneath the scars.

"You're straight, love, see? Safe lip, safe till, safe books. This is a wash-house. Everything needs washing, bar towels and bankrolls, the time of day. We're the 'props'." Stan pointed to up above. "More than you'd ever spend, locked up there in that lookout. A laundromat, love! And whispers

come too. Whispers can save a man 'time'. A big place this."
Stan shrugged. "We're the 'props'."

Lottie brought a fist down on the rickety keyboard. "I only waited for *you*, Pianoman! Nineteen years he has me! We should have *our* place, *our* 'wheels', the spot on the coast, place in the sun. Everything!"

He stood, hands held up in surrender, for calm.

She said in a whisper, hard as a rock, "While we can, my love."

"Big dreams, gal! For Christ's sake!"

"A door up there and enough behind it to float us for home."

"Or down past Thames Haven with the tide. I'm not much on doors and safes with Sulvan on my back."

"Sulvan dead."

"He don't even bleed."

"Say he's on his balcony," Lottie said quietly. "I bring him his cash." She suddenly jabbed at Stan, sent him staggering. "Can he walk on the water too?"

"Christ!" Stan said. Recovered, it stopped him in his tracks. "You're out of your mind!" He was shocked at her innocence. "Mad!" He took her shoulders; he pointed towards the pitch-black where the Canon was lost. "If Sulvan's out there in the dark, clocking you and me and the wind, customers won't see us no more. Or ask, even."

Lottie said, "Sulvan comes and he goes. A week, a month. Nobody asks."

Stan said, "That's how it is."

"Then one night he's back. Like he hopped out for five minutes and here he comes again."

"And nobody asks."

Lottie walked the perimeter of Stan's rostrum and back as if following some chalk line to redemption.

"A balcony up there," she said. "Over the river, love. Curtains across it. You go in his pad all you see is his shoes. Weekends, when he's home, he's there. Not even a bottle. Looks at the river for hours, like he's fixed. Drop his tills on the deck, shout my 'goodnight, guv' and I might get a grunt."

77

The Canon watched Stan's tough scabrous mask; it had felt pain in ten years. Lottie touched it now with her fingers.

Stan peered at the empty lounge; he might be searching the darkness. He said, "And you bring him his cash, is that it?"

"The door's open."

Stan shook his head. He looked back at a decade of stairways and rods of iron, the catwalks, safety nets for flyers. "I should piss off from you," he said. "I can see dog-food again, hear the flop of it, smell the vomit of slopping out on my hands all day. Three hundred and twenty-two steps round the ring of the yard and the sky to look up at. Doors clanging again. Get yourself a yobbo. A harebrain might try it. I'm finished."

Lottie said, "A jab on the curtains and he's gone, staggering like you, only fifty feet down. And, late Friday, the small hours of Saturday, the tide's on the run. See, Stan, no one gets out when the tide's on the run. He's off with the crap for Tilbury and Canvey. Where will he be in a week? Nobody asks. Or a month? Nobody asks, Stan. That's how it is."

"Look," Stan said. "We'd screw it. OK?"

"You've done your stint, Stan-Stan-the-Pianoman," she said. "Minded the shop, didn't you? It's up there now, we want a piece, that's all. That safe, like a wardrobe, black with gold lines to make it all nice." She stood gilded in the spotlight. "You've done your bit. This bit is mine."

"Yours?"

"That's right."

It left him groping, spitless with anger; he fought with it. The darkness down in the club would be a friendly oblivion if he could reach it.

"You do the push, do you?" he said.

"And you do the safe," she said. "Sit down, Stan."

But he stood tall by the mike like a frozen first-timer, pale, gone dry.

"Sulvan?" he said again, to be sure.

"I'm going to kill him."

"Oh Christ!"

"For us. Will I be different then?"

"Different?"

"Not soft to touch any more. To screw."

"We won't change," Stan said. "But no one knocks Sulvan."

She came hurrying to him, embraced him, searched in his face for hardness. "Listen to it," she said. "Out there. The river and the wind. A night to have a place of our own, my love." . . .

Sulvan, the Canon thought. Who would remember the beginnings of Sulvan or the end?

Lottie was beckoning her Stan. "We'll dance," she said, held out her arms. "Then sit, have us a drink, be safe together."

Stan smiled; he put the spools turning; there was a grinding snap of age in the old recorder tabs. His voice, boosted out on the speakers, filled the black emptiness of the lounge. "Ladies and gentlemen, this is Stan-Stan, the thirsty man, and it's time for his jug, OK? I know you'll miss me, all you dollies. Ain't I lovely, eh? So I won't take everything, I'll leave you with me music."

Bar noise was good for Stan's music, live or taped. It filtered it through a woolly wrap, dulled the sharps, blotted the flats, distanced it.

It was an old tune, slow as Stan could make it: the leaves all brown were tumbling down . . .

"Remember?"

"In September . . ."

"In the rain . . ."

They danced, swaying a little, hardly moving.

"October," Lottie said.

"Near November."

"Love you, Stan."

Stan said, "Will you marry me?"

They were embracing again: an old silent B clip, the Canon thought, that might have excited tears long ago; and music coming up from the man in the pit.

A ring on the doorbell now, two longs and a short, distantly from along the corridors.

"Balls!" Lottie said. "Sinclair, bloody flying horse doctor."

She moved off reluctantly, then with a bounce was out of sight. The bell sounded again and Lottie's indelicate response echoed back to the music.

Stan, unease returning, flicked off the recorder.

Love and murder, the Canon thought; Ada set free. Murdered? Was it love to watch final pain, or kill it? He wondered at the certainties and absolutes that lived in high places, the comfort of gods that had yet to be espied; the knowledge of them: compassionate eyes, beards and flowing hair, flaming swords, screams of hellfire. How long could He listen to the screams of hellfire?

To every man his God, the Canon thought; we still had to find Him.

He gathered his cloak about him carefully, took his stick, waited for the gentle stir and confusion that Sinclair's arrival would bring, and slipped from the darkness of the club to the darkness of the wind again. Darkness, the Canon thought, but not yet night-time; he could see the trees pushed, battered, and a whole maelstrom of leaves caught in the churchyard. The warmth from the rectory windows was the fireglow coming through the shadows of the room to make three motionless banners in the wind.

Black jackets, the Canon was thinking again: when he had emerged from Ada's, had he seen vanishing tail-lights? A moment, a half-remembered moment? So many things. Ada gone on her journey at last. Catherine . . .

He followed the rambling walls of Sulvan's house, in and out, from shelters to tunnels of wind, till he reached its private door. He let himself into the hallway of tough polished lino; a stairway ascended to the upper regions and levels, but he walked ahead through storerooms and bar space with its counter, table, chairs, stools: almost a dispense-bar only, except that it could offer, in moments of business exigency, a snuggery far from the crowd. Beyond was the curtained passageway to the lounge.

The Canon entered. Stan was at his piano, an uncertain warmth on his face that showed the streaks and curves of scar tissue; and Lottie, at Matthew Sinclair's request, had brought drinks.

Sinclair drank only halves of bitter, the cheaper the better, a habitual economy. Money was for gambling. But he was generous or frugal with the vagaries of fortune. He checked betting-slips now, pondered, made thoughtful assessments and, as was his custom with most mortals, talked to Lottie from a kind of tiny brain-implanted Ansafone.

"Didn't disturb you, Lottie, I hope."

"Not me, never you, Dr Sinclair."

"Rang twice, you see."

"You did?"

"Thought you wouldn't hear it in this 'blow'."

"Good thing you did. Heard only one."

"Not impatience, you understand."

"Oh no!"

Sinclair saw the Canon's arrival, put away his paperwork, and raised a hand in salutation.

"I walked the minefields unscathed today, old friend. I'll send up a bottle of Taylor's for Catherine. Have a drink."

"A little whisky," the Canon said. "Old Ada has passed away."

Everyone allowed moments of silence and solemnity.

Sinclair took his cue. "A good age, a good age. Peacefully?"

"Fell asleep," the Canon said.

"The way to go, in my book," Lottie philosophised, filled in a little time. Denizens of Sulvan's – a respectful discretion – didn't intrude on the dying. "Took my old man six months hard to get himself out of Homerton General in a box. What was left of him. I'll bring your drink."

"Big?" Sinclair asked.

"Small," the Canon said.

It was continuing to be a good day, Sinclair considered. Catherine Delacey would be with Ada and he would join her to view the remains. Death certificates were an 'extra over'. The Canon was generous. Removal, chapel of rest, cremation: Sinclair's exclusive furnishers talked death and discount in a single breath. Then the next 'voyager' on Catherine Delacey's list to be collected and installed. The immediate future had stability.

Lottie came with whisky.

Sinclair said, "I'll make a call or two, join you later for a drink perhaps."

The Canon nodded farewell, watched him go. Sinclair was small, fleshless: a scurrying trot always, as if he were in flight. "A third-generation quack," he had told the Canon. Turned sixty now, he had grown up in dignified days of medical practice, his father's house, a residence, a sacrosanct place that could offer a drawing room to wait in, a capped and aproned maidservant to usher the sick into the reassurance of the great man's study: rolltop desk, pictures, framed scrolls of qualification and avowal; and, memorable, the great coal fire of dancing flames in wintertime.

Sinclair couldn't make the jump to kerbside derelict shops where people wandered in to sit moping, backs to the wall, reading inversed 'SURGERY', right to left, on a painted window. "I'm a bloody snob," he would say. "Glad of it too!" Keeping the 'dead' alive these shameless days was a spurious mercy; helping them move on when they had tired of it was dignified.

The Canon admired the reserve, the pedigree, the impeccable clothes for all times, all seasons. His small isolated house, a Lucy Dory-Catchpole usufruct, hidden against the sprawl of Sulvan's, had an elegant comfort and Matthew Sinclair's own contributions were racing prints and shelves of bloodstock and turf history, form books, astrological tomes and a wall chart. He was a Libran, and his delicate laboratory scales gleamed in conjunction. A faddy eater, hardly a drinking man, gambling seemed to satiate all other needs, even passion for man or woman. An admirable citizen who gave the world no heartache, the Canon thought . . .

Lottie was saying, "A good age, the doctor says. Poor old duck."

"Eighty-nine," the Canon said.

"Your drink all right?"

"Oh yes." The Canon drank, nodded to Stan too.

Stan's upheld glass was his high esteem.

"Not from these parts, was she?" Lottie said: a mile on a country road was a 'step'; but, in London, it was a voyage to a distant land.

"Hoxton," the Canon said. "She had a barrow on the Kingsland Waste for fifty years, I'm told. A long time."

"Her 'old man' gone too?"

"Died young," the Canon said, remembering the flag and the open window. "A loyal subject of the Crown."

There was restlessness about Lottie. "I'll put something on for Stan and me," she said. "Something for wild raging nights. Something special, I think."

Stan nodded.

"Will I tell him?" Lottie asked.

"Course you will."

"It's going to be Stan and me," she told the Canon. "Stan Traynor and Lottie Lee!"

The Canon bought them drinks and they touched glasses. Lottie was suddenly tearful, beautiful. She could kill, the Canon reminded himself. She went off, swaying her lovely body, and Stan watched her.

They would, the Canon hoped, have some moment like Southend to remember. Everyone should have a moment to look back at . . .

Stan went down his repertoire of chords and arpeggios and the Canon pondered if, on arrival, he had said "I killed Ada a little while ago"; and if Lottie had smiled and whispered that she would kill for love too?

The strange melody from upstairs came again, faded, oscillated in pulses of wind.

Stan said suddenly, with a shrewdness that didn't surprise the Canon, "Why do you do it?" There was no malice: a moment of curiosity.

"They ask me. Dignity is very important, don't you think?"

Stan was thoughtful, in silence for a long time; they drank, listened to the outside.

"A kindness?"

"Something like that."

"My old man was a thief," Stan said. "The best, you know, respected. Even the fuzz. Had enough at thirty-five, all he wanted. Took a 'fruit and veg' in Plaistow, house overhead. See him in the pub of a Sunday, dressed up." Stan was remembering it all. "And the shop! Lights everywhere. Respected man."

"You were proud," the Canon said.

"Every inch."

"Dead now?"

Stan's head was up, eyes peering back at the memory of it. "Someone's collecting *houses* then, you know? Collecting, snapping 'em up, big deal," he said to the Canon, slow, pondering it. "Christ, two here, three there, like grapefruits and Granny Smith's. Big scalpers out there somewhere, on the make, my old chief says. He has it right. Clearing the waste, burning the scruff. Not him though, never a move! They send him 'messengers', of course, very big 'messengers', and he sends 'em back." He looked at the Canon. "He's a rock!"

The Canon nodded.

"Then early of a morning, coming for Christmas, setting out his stall, colours and lights, a bit here, a bit there, standing back like a painter to look at it . . . that's when they fixed him."

"Killed?" the Canon said.

"A fifty-tonner, flat out for Tilbury, goes through the lot. A hill of stones and bits of furniture hanging down."

The Canon sipped the pale warming whisky.

"Everything gone."

"Your mother?" the Canon asked.

"Her too. I knew who done it," Stan said. "I run him over. Got ten, did ten, every day of it." It was water under the bridge. "Never knew who sent him though."

The Canon looked at a face of battle-marks, the fingers of his left hand gnarled at the joints; index and thumb strangely twisted where they had been broken.

Stan held the hand up, studied it himself. "I used to play a fair old joanna once upon a time." . . .

"It was hard in there?" the Canon asked eventually.

He looked at the Canon's rod of lignum vitae. "I took

stick," Stan told him. "Not the screws, oh no, not them. Screws has jack-the-lads to do the business."

Black leather jackets, distant men of holy cloth.

The tinsel behind Stan and the piano moved and rustled a little. "You made a stand," the Canon said.

"They busted me."

"Yes."

"A way of busting everyone, you know?"

The Canon waited.

"Stripped me down, six big ones, on to the table, greased me up, buggered me till blood runs."

"Yes," the Canon said.

Stan's hands were restless, trembling a little. "Busted me. How do I know when I'm bust? I know it, that's all."

"I understand," the Canon said.

Stan thought about it. "Yeah," he said. "I think you do."

"Times don't change." The Canon stood and prepared to leave. "Take care," he said to Stan. "Take care."

Stan nodded.

"Sulvan?" the Canon asked. "He'll be here?"

"Any time," Stan said. "Soon . . ."

The Canon left. When he had passed the stores, the corridors, and opened the door on the wildness of the evening, he could hear the faint chords of Stan-Stan-the-Pianoman.

He hurried away into the total darkness, knowing every scar and hollow of the razed ground. The Erith shore, across the river, was a string of light and, beyond it, how many warps and wefts of street-lights, lonely roads, the great encircling suburban ramparts? Trains, drains, beneath his feet, an underground race, a timeless world.

There seemed to be a great urgency.

He found the lee of the church and, for moments, respite from the full push and spin of the wind. Beyond the hidden vaults and shrubs and mounds, light came dimly from the People's Hall; Harney was in his room too; his window shone. The cleaners would be scutching and polishing and

Harney, he supposed, stocking his bar for the weekend soirée of God, the faithful and Father Jim.

The Canon entered the church; it was an escape. There was sudden peace. Outside, the world battled against stout walls. He stood in the nave and looked at the tiny red glow of the sanctuary lamp: God's presence. It hung above the wooden rails of linen and communion time, a bulb, a minuscule filament.

Behind him was the tower and louvred belfry with broaches and spire lights. There had been bells once but now a cassette player only, and Father Jim's cluster of Japanese speakers on the bell-loft floor. Father Jim had chosen his tapes – 'peals', he thought, more prestigious – for all times: workaday prayer, marriage, death. The flick of a switch put bell-ringers to shame. There were even carilloned hymns for appropriate saints' days.

The Canon thought of Matthew Sinclair who had a dislike of them, could associate bells only with disasters in the City: and from thence, a train of thought to stewards' enquiries and favourites pulling the outside trap at Hackney. The Canon smiled.

Once – he remembered the days – a sanctuary lamp had been a floating lighted wick in colza oil; and a bell had been a bell. God was moving house like the rest.

He looked at tokens of beauty and homage the Dorys and their peers had found to give praise: the arcade, the carved lectern and pulpit, the delicate slender lights of the clerestory, wall tablets, an ancient hatchment, stoups.

Father Jim's appendages, temporary, portable, of course, were an offence. Still, the heaters helped, and the grand dames of the Altar Society. And his cleaners, Doll and Flo, with mop, broom and duster, had slowed the clock of dilapidation: they were the seed of some Dublin exodus to the Mersey and thence to London. From riverbank, to riverbank, to riverbank.

The Canon walked beneath the vaulted arcade and entered the almost concealed corridor to the Mortuary.

Coming in from storm or, in dog-day, from polluted air of city and riverside decay too, one was assailed always by the lingering whisky and tobacco of Harney. But now the Canon was instantly aware of a fresh disorder scattered across the familiar disarray of this bedraggled place of the dead: the uncovered cask, splashed and standing in a pool of its own precious fluid; the table, wet too, always unclean but now wounded with a half-dozen deep elliptical stabs.

The Canon counted, tapped them with his stick. Strange, he thought, and looked towards his cubicle. Collar, stock, biretta, all out of place. On the floor, by its open door, he saw a button. His cassock. He went to inspect it: a dogged battle, he thought. Other buttons too. Battles, battles.

Hard stealthy men in leather jackets, he thought, didn't journey hither and thither only for the ripping off of buttons . . .

The whisky, water of life, lingered comfortably in the deadhouse, but Harney had gone. The light had been left burning. The Canon patiently searched and gathered his buttons, lodged them in the pocket of the cassock. He put out the light at the wall switch, walked sure-footedly to his cubicle and sat in darkness behind its closed and bolted door, still in cloak and beret, walking-stick held like an offering in both hands . . .

. . . It was at the interment of Lucy Dory-Catchpole's ashes that he had looked out beyond the churchyard walls at the bare forbidding acres and envisioned his hospice: the gateway to his walled estate: a road of access, pathways restored, flowers and shrubs and grass tended: a village of whatever shreds of peace could be garnered and clustered about church and Rectory, a place of rest for those in transit. A village of a single winding street, he thought, with grey slate and chimneys, lanterns in the embrasures of doorways, windows looking out unimpeded at the age and vagaries of the river. The river would be time itself . . .

He heard the voice of Doll, her adenoidal chainsaw, coming through the church and corridor, and the responses of Flo, a recent recruit of Father Jim's to meet the growing demands of cleaning in the church and People's Hall. She was shrill as a tin whistle. The wind had followed them in and a sudden rataplan of rain hammered the roof.

"Listen to that!" Doll said. "Like the Plagues of Egypt. Forty days of cats and dogs." She switched on the naked bulb, plugged in an electric kettle.

They put their buckets and mops and brooms among the redundant performers of the Christmas crib and its livestock.

"That cow don't look like it'll make it to Christmas," Flo said. "And them Wise Kings!"

"The Magi," Doll said.

"Might be outside Sambo's Minicabs with beer cans and fags. If there was jobs going somewhere, I'd be off like a shot."

"Give it a chance, love," Doll counselled. "Harney's a pisspot, we know, don't we? And you *listen* to Father Jim, nod, nod, nod, that's all. Can you hear me, eh?"

Doll and Flo wouldn't see forty any more but they were spry as kittens. Doll wore her old man's cardigan over a battered party dress, high boots, her hair tucked in a kind of baseball cap against the dust: she still looked slick and gamey. Flo might have been caught backstage between changes: check slacks, stiletto heels, a fisherman's rollneck, earrings like decades of the rosary and diamante glasses; her blond hair looked good but was a little tired beneath a tulle scarf and the earphones of her Walkman.

"Switched off," Flo said. "I can hear you." But she hung the earphones about her neck. "What about that other one? That batman?"

"Quiet, love!" Doll warned. "The Canon, the Canon!" she whispered. "Call him the 'Canon'." She pointed to the cubicle. "Might be in there, see?" Like a gun dog she stalked close to the cubicle and listened, edged closer, put her ear against the door.

The Canon, motionless, even through the pervasive pong of Harney, got the reek of some market-stall splash of eau de rose or worse.

"Anything?"

"Not a sound," Doll said, moving away. "Just as well. He'd have a seizure with the stink of whisky." She became aware of the disorder, the pool, the splashed floor, the seemingly strange deliquescence of bone-dry dust and rubbish.

Flo looked at it too. "That Harney bull, ain't it? Must have pissed all round the room tra-la." Flo held her nose. "The pong, don't you get it?"

"That's me eau de rose, love," Doll said. "Harney's ain't that special."

The Canon listened to their choked wild amusement, moments of silence, fresh descents into helplessness.

"Give it another week, love," Doll said, looking about. "And it'll be like home, cobwebs, cobblers and all. If that Harney gives you the touch-up, put the broom-handle in him. Slow him down for a month. Full of steam and whisky is Father Jim's minder. A smile painted on his gob when it suits him. Here!" Doll came close with a grimace of confidence. "Not a bad number, has he? Caretaker, church clerk, buyer-in-chief, head barman, money, money, money! A tenner every time he switches on them bells for a death or a wedding."

"A tenner!"

"Twenty maybe if there's a widow and seven kids or a best man hopped-up to his eyeballs."

Flo was indignant: from her bag she took dainty mugs and rapped them on the table; spoon, milk carton, two rock cakes on a paper plate. She punctured a tea bag and shared it, shake by shake.

Doll brought the steaming kettle.

Flo said, "A tenner! Well, that's a bloody liberty, ain't it?" She rapped with the spoon this time. "There's people out there of a Sunday morning, on their knees, thinks he's up above, stripped to the waist, ropes on all sides, knocking out 'Ave Maria' or 'Hail Queen of Heaven' for a half an hour nonstop."

"Takes a half-bottle of whisky to fix his cassette, love! Real bells? Roped hand and foot, I'd fix him. And one round his johnnie, if he has one. God forgive us!"

They were off on a flight of helplessness again and the Canon thought suddenly of Ada and her halcyon days of sap and Southend, and the pier endless as youth. Flo's laughter

89

speared out like an all-clear, tapered away to silence. She said, "What about batman, then?"

" 'The Canon', they call him, love!"

"Vacant room on top, you said? Off his trolley, is he?"

"Not 'mad', I didn't! Not like that. Just simple, love. All that money, all that land. Him and that mare at the Rectory playing doctors and nurses." She whispered, "Going to make rooms like at Butlins for a lot of dying old crows, down there." Doll wondered at the hopelessness of it. "Let 'em pop off, I say. Where they are don't count."

Flo suddenly remembered. " 'Losing his marbles' is what you said."

" 'Losing his marbles' is what Father Jim said."

Flo had poured boiling water in the mugs; the tea was brewing; they lit cigarettes. Rods of smoke, like snorts of a Chinese dragon, came from Flo's delicate nostrils.

" 'Keep an eye on him', Father Jim tells me," Doll explained. "But I don't see nothing." She nodded at the cubicle. "Sits in there for hours sometimes, saying whatever he says, poor old bugger. Yesterday, he's in the churchyard, touching the trees, the gravestones . . ."

"What about touching the duchess? Up in the Rectory."

"Up where?"

"Need all his marbles for that! And something in his porridge!" Flo was in rigor for a moment, then waving about. They were swept off in a tide of merriment. "Mind the bleedin' table, sod it!" . . .

"Silly old farts," the Canon said charitably in the darkness.

"You hear something?" Flo said.

"Naw."

Silence crept back, they smoked, sipped steaming tea. Doors were banging again and the thump of wind was like sea-swell.

Doll said, "That rain's unnatural. And the wind. Listen!" She took whisky from Harney's stock and spiked the tea.

"More," Flo said. "This place is the creeps." A moment of silence fell again. "Now you can't hear a bloody thing. Not a sound."

"Used to be a deadhouse," Doll said.

"A what?"

"A deadhouse, this place. No windows, see. Only the coloured bit up there. A gaslight over the door and, where we're sitting now, the candles."

"The candles?"

"Yeah." Doll nodded. "Six brass candlesticks tall as your head. Three each side so the soft light falls on the corpse."

Flo pondered it, floated her hand above the plane of the table, almost in conjuration. "The corpse would be about there?"

"Oh, right in front of us."

"Bollicks." Flo took her mug from the table and held its warmth against her bosom lost in the fisherman's rollneck. "Don't feel like them rock cakes now."

"They do look a bit waxy." . . .

Without warning Father Jim had arrived; he was so suddenly framed in the archway that he might have materialised.

Doll and Flo were motionless.

"Ladies, ladies, you mustn't stir! I intrude. Tea-time is free time and weekend hours are demanding. Rest your old bones."

Flo, over diamante frames, vetted him from trainers to the green stud of his cap. "Not so bloody old!"

Father Jim could only ha-ha his gaffe. "A manner of speaking, ladies," he made amends. "I was in search of the Canon." He glanced towards the cubicle. "Not in his cell, is he?"

"His cell!" Flo twittered in a strange jarring treble. "You ain't going to throw him in the slammer, are you, Father Jim?"

The bolt was too close for comfort; disturbing. "You see, ladies," he interrupted their amusement, "in monasteries, monks have cells where they pray and meditate. A cell is their home. They sleep there, live there, die there."

Doll was understanding about it all. "Well, if they like that kind of thing, I suppose."

"Yes," Father Jim said patiently. "The Canon hasn't been here then?" He became aware of the fresh disorder, the great aspersion of holy water that had fallen on the desert floor; the mutilated table. "Or Harney?" he asked. "Have you seen Harney?"

"No," Flo said, nasal as she could drag it, as if a fleeting memory of Harney was a night-long incubus.

"Maybe he's composing in the bell-loft," Doll said. "Something catchy for Christmas."

Father Jim arranged a smile for this banter: he was thinking that he would be considering changes in the cleaning staff in the near future. He had a growing parish now, a bar, a disco at weekends, revenue. He could suffer fools for a time . . .

"Have a cup of tea, Father Jim?" Flo said without zeal or fervour.

"Thank you, no." His face was gentle, amiable as ever, and careful; just a trace of anxiety allowed to obtrude. "I hope he hasn't wandered off. The Canon, you know. In this weather." Father Jim, in the comparative nakedness of trainers, slacks, cap and bomber-jacket, shrugged at the inconceivable folly that surrounded him. "Hardly a young man, is he? And a little 'troubled', you know. We must take care of him. All of us."

"Yes."

Doll remembered she had an aunt did a streak in Spitalfields once. "Stopped the market dead. And she was fifty-two."

"God has a purpose in everything." Father Jim paused for restoration of rank and decorum. He briefed them. "If you see the Canon you could mention that I was looking for him. And if he's had a drenching, tell him to change at once, poor man. Have you got it?"

They nodded.

"Now to our tasks." Father Jim's teeth shone in the glare of the naked light. "This weekend, a vast concourse of the faithful in our hall. Churchmen of standing, administrators to our bishop, even a councillor or two, some very important people to be impressed with our development. Things must be perfect, ladies. These bar alterations, you understand . . . workmen, slovenliness, last-minute rushes at everything! You have my sympathy, such thorns do not escape me." Closed eyes, compressed lips, were his Ecce Homo, visualising Augean labours ahead. "Rubbish, litter, floors, counters, tables, toilets, ashtrays, shelves, chairs . . ." A sad histrionic pause for breath. "You are my front-line troops, my experts. I'm not very skilled in these matters, I'm afraid."

Doll said, "You'd be smart as a whip at it in no time."

He stood in the archway, clipboard in hand. "Flattery, ladies, ha-ha! Now I have a dozen things to attend to and tomorrow, a wagonload of beer from the brewery. Special delivery. Most Christian co-operation from the brewery. The arrival of our musicians too. It will have been a long day for you good ladies but . . ." A conspiratorial partisan Father Jim now ". . . we'll perhaps manage a little extra in the pay envelope. A little extra."

He bestowed his customary mini-blessing and was gone. Doll and Flo sipped whisky-tea and smoked and listened to the turbulence of the other world.

Doll said eventually, "That fellow should be up in Hampstead Heath doing the three-card trick." . . .

The Canon, in his cubicle, smiled, yawned, allowed himself to make a low attenuating sound.

The ladies froze like window dummies. Flo whispered, "What was that?"

"Under the table, was it?"

They were both on their feet, Flo holding her skirt like clingfilm; Doll, crouched, elbows at her groin.

"Bleedin' deadhouse!" Flo said. "Shithouse! I'm off!"

They grabbed the cleaning gear and stampeded through the archway.

Harney, at that moment arriving, was upended, left on his buttocks.

"Bloody mad-arsed mares!" he roared in their wake. "Ease up, ease up!" He was dried and dressed, but all his pain returned.

From the distance he heard, "Up yours too, you pisspot!"

He recovered, examined the table, smelt the whisky in the teacups, went to his stockpile and found the freshly opened bottle.

He stood, holding the bottle raised aloft in both hands, so that the glaring light shone through its discrepancy.

The Canon, suddenly, stick on shoulder, was striding past. "Celebrating the Black Mass, Harney?"

"Ah, Canon!"

There was a fabric-ripping split of thunder; the lightning, instantaneous, for a moment lit the stained glass and left silence.

"Your prayers have been heard," the Canon said.

"Stocktaking, Canon," Harney was mouthing. "Stocktaking."

"Stocktaking, taking stock, a labour of love perhaps." The steel ferrule of his stick tapped away into the corridor.

"Canon!" Harney shouted.

The Canon returned and from the archway gazed at him: Harney, if not afraid, seemed raw and skinned of confidence.

"Paul Vincent Herlihy, Canon?"

"Yes," the Canon said.

"Your name?"

"Precisely."

"I signed it on something."

"Something?"

"Something. Can't remember. All fogged up." Harney's fingers, unguided, traced the table's knife-wounds.

"You *had* to sign it?"

"I had to."

"A little while ago, Harney?"

"Yes, Canon."

"Men with leather jackets?"

Harney's eyes were damp, glistening with rage.

"You must remain calm, Harney."

"And, Canon?"

The Canon waited.

"I was trying on your gear at the time. Collar, cassock, hat, the lot."

"Have a drink like a good fellow," the Canon said. "And a smoke. You'll feel better. We won't talk about it. To anyone."

Harney looked towards the archway in gratitude, but the Canon had vanished.

Harney had been demeaned: the sound of his blanched fists hammering on the table, the awful weeping groan of abasement followed the Canon down the empty church. He stood for moments by the graceful baptismal font and pondered it. On a lectern, Father James Kilmartin had arranged an attendance book for his cleaners . . . Florence Rorke . . . Dolores Durkin . . . Doll and Flo. He would remember the names, Florence Rorke and Dolores Durkin. And Stan and Lottie. Stan Traynor and Lottie Lee.

In the distance, Harney groaned again. Harney lessened was a dangerous inmate.

That was good perhaps, the Canon thought: let him micturate on his territory, be savage in defence. The predators would return.

The Canon tightened his cloak about him and stepped into the night . . .

*. . . Leaves, torn trees, the churchyard, its environs, dissolved into silence again. He was pacing a narrow cobbled street, familiar with every door and window, with a face here and there, but unseen, strangely untouched in the jostling pushing crowd. The stillness. He raised a hand to them, a reflex, in the long narrow alley of barefoot rags, the beershops with lamplight touching lamplight across the span. He waved unseen.*

*A cart, against a gateway, rested on its shafts; and a drunk, nosed and sniffed at by dogs, slept beneath it. Children clustered, watched, came like flies to a midden for what was discarded; spent whores in loose hanging bodices showed themselves from windows, or stood in doorways, drawing up trailing skirts from the ground, along stockinged legs and thighs, until flesh gleamed.*

*A black or a bronzed face was here and there, a great concourse of blood: Norse, Lascar, Dutch, quadroon, octoroon, a silent babble of languages. A crucible. And the hardy sharp glitter* of native *Thamesmen*. Irish too were creeping in at the dregs of the hierarchy to scavenge, to heave the dirt and coal and river muck; the women for brothels all the way to Ratcliffe and Wapping: they had fled from hunger, and hunger had never left their faces.

The Canon passed a street stall and knew a bearded Jewish face beside it. He raised his hand again but the sad careful eyes looked at him, through him, towards the huge glaring street lantern, mounted high on the brickwork. A crepuscular world within a world, he seemed to walk unimpeded in both. He stood in the smoke of gin-houses with tosspots and brasses, the ailing, the work-wasted. There Stan Traynor held his corner, big, unscarred, his special dish for sale: Lottie, his stock-in-trade, flimsy skirts, gleaming unbuttoned white skin, nipples high. Pimps, breast-feeding doxies, scum.

And proprietress Miss Catherine Delacey on her rostrum, calm as in a nunnery, drawn-back hair, plain, formidable, her door-men alert for blood and knuckles, awaiting her nod. A house of repute.

Out and through the choking streets again as if he had known them for a lifetime, somehow insulated from the merest touch of flesh or fabric. There was the faint greyness of river fog hanging against window-panes and distantly spaced street-lamps throwing back the palest luminosity on this turbulent silent stream. He went through the narrow alleys where the ground was wet and window-light fell across litter and the spread of rotting body-waste; he was untouched by it. He emerged by the river: a forest of masts and spars, stacked riggers at the jetties; barges, lighters, watermen; or long strings of moving craft out on the midstream, hazardous as a crowded carriageway. Mast and cabin lights bled into the vapour, diffused: a strange aquarelle world of beauty resting on the filth all about it.

The Canon's cloak hung limply about him in the stillness. The riverbank had the same pushing streams of humanity and he moved along through it, effortlessly, as if he were the ghost in this soundless insubstantial world. He was moving with purpose somehow and then the vast ironwork frame of the land-dredger came in view: he knew every prodigious joist of it, monstrous rivets, ladders, bollards; mud, wet or dry, an appalling grey *impasto everywhere. Barges, down to the gunwales, brought glutinous muck and filth alongside, the snout of the dredger's long boom of moving buckets dipped in the troughs, raised up the load that was slid or flumed ashore: a flimsy diurnal stratum of new ground.*

*But beyond the reach of boom and buckets the residue sat, drying, compacting. Work for scum: thighboots, high-crowned hats, jerkins of mud-soaked frieze, square deep-panned navvy shovels to 'stage' the filth from belly to deck, and thence ashore. The Canon looked at the men knee-deep in brown or ochreous 'jelly' and for an instant seemed to see himself, shovel in hand, in fading final nausea. A moment.*

*The river's excreta of mud carried its human ordure from land and ships, carried the dead too, animal and human. A moment of memory in this silent place. Behind the dredger, the precious dirt spread layer upon layer, inspissating, wasting away its stench in slow cracking settlement.*

*Men from green fields, the Canon was thinking, hungry men, and suddenly the wind whipped against him again, and it was an empty river, empty streets, desolate . . .*

He looked at the lights glittering from the far shore to infinity, stone jetties and riverbanks now, and they too, usefulness outlived, mouldering in desuetude.

He looked along the stretch of flagstone and granite setts, the stanchions and stripped roofs that reached close to Sulvan's boundary wall. He had been en route to Sulvan's when he had 'strayed', confused his worlds.

Harney, he thought, fit in an instant of madness to blubber and rage: he had been shamed. The men in leather, in harmonious black, had turned a few screws from time to time. Harney in cassock and stock and biretta! The Canon held his stick by the ferrule-end and felt its weight. He was at Sulvan's door; he let himself in. A pilot burned in the lounge now, made a twilight world: a single flood beamed on the stage. Stan was there.

And Sulvan.

Sulvan's welcome was the merest flicker of warmth. The Canon smiled.

Sulvan, the ghost.

A man, a ghost, of good taste, the Canon always thought, from faultless clothes to square, welted shoes. Tall, hard, a great shoulderspan, forty or less; or fifty! Who could tell? Dark hair, a faint greyness that might be brushed across polished stripes of burn tissue. Only the face was at odds, a hungry sculpted piece of bone; eyes that could smile perhaps, or watch or hate.

The Canon joined him under the bright light.

Sulvan said, "I missed you on the move out there."

"I wander about," the Canon said.

"From time to time."

"Yes."

"The wind isn't everywhere."

"A bereavement a short while ago," the Canon said.

"A strange night."

Sulvan glanced at him for a moment, let silence fall, noticed the stick held like a bludgeon.

The treble wandering music, above, had rain for an eerie percussion now. Sulvan listened; the Canon.

Lottie watched Stan.

Stan sat on his piano-stool, encapsulated still in those moments of Lottie's fire and steel but looking now at Sulvan. The faithful soldier inside Stan was hammering to escape treachery.

He said to Sulvan, "No, it don't ring a bell, Guv."

"In leather jackets?" Sulvan said.

Stan shook his head.

"Prowlers." Sulvan nodded to the Canon. "We like to know when we have prowlers."

"And why," the Canon said.

"And why."

"It don't ring a bell," Stan said again.

"Of a sudden, a lot of prowlers," Sulvan said, thoughtful, as if he might be listening to the wind and the distant hymnody from above. "Prowlers, soldiers of the Queen not long ago. Square-bashers once, bastards for ever, that's how it goes. Leaves a mark in the eyes. Like blood."

"There's the expensive one too," the Canon said.

"Smart," Sulvan said. "Dressed for the town. A nice place too on the Park."

"Good," the Canon said.

It would be opening-time at Sulvan's soon; warmth was building up towards comfort in the lounge and when the soft amber of lights would suffuse it, and tables were peopled, it would have the staunchness of a secret chapel. Weekdays were days of business: bills of exchange, doors opened and shut, marks of respect, balancing of power; and Stan's slow music, unobtrusive, almost melodic, loud enough only for privacy.

But Thursday had the rumble of weekend, smart gear, dandy dolls. Stan-Stan-the-Pianoman. Play it again, Stan!

Sulvan looked at the Canon, the shouldered knobkerrie, the calmness: a man-at-arms. They went out through the corridors and climbed the stairs: solid timbers, plain as a gangway.

Their feet sounded on the bare treads: no covering. Sulvan said, "When people move about, noise is a watchdog."

"Yes," the Canon said.

It was a house without pattern, each landing unmatched, unalike; wainscotting rose with the stairway and, above it, oil-painted walls, stark as a death-cell.

They climbed to the topmost landing. It had a single window looking down on the roofs of lower storeys and the long spur of the club.

The walls, the Canon thought; he looked at the deep embrasure of the window: three feet, perhaps more. Like the Dory structures, it had the secret strength of a fortress.

In twelve years it was the Canon's first visit to this sentinel tower of Sulvan's.

Sulvan said, "Twelve years you've been around, Bang Bang. You came with a pushcart."

"I wonder why?" the Canon asked.

"You needed to."

"Sent?"

"Everyone is sent."

"You haven't changed," the Canon said. "Not a line."

The door of Sulvan's room was pine, stout, unremarkable, brass furnishings, a mortice lock. And, in the wall beside it, a slim chute where, in his absences, Lottie parcelled and posted the surplusages of trade.

"For Lottie," he said, as if asked. "She pays the tallymen, leaves the rest."

Sulvan opened the door.

Beneath the chute was the bare floor. "Parcels just lie there?" the Canon said.

"On the deck."

"A lot of parcels?"

"Sometimes."

"A lot of money."

Sulvan crossed to the safe, taller than himself: a single key, a single lever. Trays of banded notes almost filled it.

"Who stands guard?"

"Fear," Sulvan said.

He switched on the lights: ships' lanterns of long ago had been fixed to the walls: a single lantern hung motionless from the low-raftered ceiling. It should sway a little, the Canon thought, with the motion of this 'ship'. It was a Master's quarters. The wooden cladding of the walls sloped with the curve of a bulkhead; there was a desk and a padded chair bolted to the flooring; and a table of charts and instruments.

This was a spacious room: the original would have been small.

And at variance too were heavy drawn curtains, hanging almost to the floor. Sulvan parted them: glass doors and an iron balcony. The wind pushed against them, swept the glass clear of rain streaks and flurries. Beyond was the river with the push of flow and driven tide raising it high.

Sulvan brought tall winged chairs and they sat looking out from the warmth.

"You stand out there sometimes?" the Canon said.

Sulvan nodded.

"For peace?"

"There used to be a gallows out there once," Sulvan said. "Far out. Marshlands, a spike of jetty and a gallows. Gone now."

"Who remembers?"

"Remembers?"

"Knows?"

"Written down somewhere, I suppose. Alleys, whores, thieves. A man with a book told me once this was a brothel." Sulvan might have smiled.

The Canon said, "Books at Dory's say it too. Books that remember Trafalgar and French wars; streets out there, a whole babble of Europe. Irish scum too, coming year by year."

"When you have nothing, you're scum," Sulvan said. He brought the Canon whisky and water, took his seat again, and left him to drink alone.

"Possessions," he said.

"When you *have* something?" the Canon asked.

"Be careful every day." He looked at the knurled head of the Canon's stick. "Every day."

They sat in silence. Across two thousand feet of river, windswept, was another desolate shoreline, the ground climbing away for miles until its carpet of lonely lights fell over the distant skyline.

"There's a song," the Canon said:

> " 'In the year of Our Lord 1806,
> We set sail from the fair port of Cork,
> We were bound far away with a cargo of bricks,
> For the great City Hall of New York.' "

"Bricks and scum," Sulvan said.

"It took gold sovereigns for escape to the New World," the Canon said. "Expensive for scum. But *pence*, on the deck out of Cork into Wapping and London Bridge."

Sulvan looked at his hands. "On deck?" he said.

"Eighteen pence on the deck out of Cork into Wapping. And when the seas came and the east wind too, they froze to it."

"Like fish with open mouths and eyes," Sulvan said.

"Dory can tell stories in a ledger." A good man in his way, he thought. The Canon looked at Sulvan's unfinished face, closed eyes as if he were resting. "Took them at eighteen pence in a pinch. Asylum for eighteen pence. Ballast."

"From the grave to a madhouse."

"Chipped the dead off the deck and buried them," the Canon said and watched him.

"Chipped?"

"For eighteen pence a shovel and a pick would be delicacy, I suppose," the Canon said.

Sulvan was looking out across the river now. "Dory," he said. "The scum should have killed him. But his breed is dead."

The Canon sat in silence. "A madman slaughtered his Master and bosun. Slaughtered like animals."

"Executed," Sulvan said; he stood and drew the curtains again, took the Canon's glass. "Whisky and water, Bang Bang. It was a long time ago, was it?" He moved out of sight.

"1806." . . .


. . . *Diminishing lights were bringing a stillness. The Canon looked: there were oil lanterns now. The room was smaller but the desk, the padded chair, the table, the charts were there. And there was the empty motion of being afloat. For a moment the central lantern, in its stirrup, hung awry and righted itself and tilted again. A seaman, Maxwell, in reefer and high boots, was there; and the Master, Jonathan Dowty, in black Dory fustian, at his desk, a white scarf wound and tied at his neck.*

*The Canon stood and watched the soundless terrible slaughter beside him; voiceless, he shouted into the silence.*

*The door had been smashed with a single blow; something amorphous, clothing and canvas roped about it, feet clad in rags, swung an axe. It shattered the bosun's chest, slithered him away, gurgling blood and yellow food and sputum. The Canon saw the face, a mask of dirt and rime, a shapeless scab. Sulvan. He would remember the eyes: a smudged decal face, perhaps; but the eyes had survived.*

*The axe swung again, cleft the shining head at the desk from scalp to gullet so that it parted and hung like offal; the braided fustian arms were spread on the desk and severed at the wrists.*

*The room was a battlefield. The Canon watched the dragging away, naked, battered, scored, of whatever it was. For a moment he saw again the animal face, on the gangplanks now, turned back to the last moments where the filleted frozen body had been wrapped and sunk in the mud: hessian wrap-around cerements: frozen head, torso and legs first, a single piece; then dismembered outstretched arms. Good axemen, steady as dentists, careful of decking, clearing the scum. Sulvan's woman. The rolled hessian pile sucked down in the grey muck . . .*

"Whisky and water?" Sulvan was saying in the bright fortress of his room again.

The Canon nodded, saw in a momentary glance the savage awful blood-letting. "Long life," he said.

Sulvan sat at his desk.

"There was a gallows out there?" the Canon asked.

"They say."

"A long time ago?"

"They say."

"A lot of bones down beneath us here," the Canon said.

Had this great emptiness been raised for a headstone? The brothel, a first wooden cross; now this shapeless pile of remembrance.

"Why do *you* kill?" Sulvan asked him.

"I kill pain," the Canon said.

"A kindness?"

"Yes."

"Love?"

The Canon took his cloak and stick and prepared to leave. For a moment he saw the frozen female on the deck, the open mouth, the fish eyes: and then the cleft skull and the bloody vomit of the seaman.

"Kill for love. You could forgive that?" he asked.

Sulvan didn't reply; eyes closed, he sat at his desk; he might have been a tenantless shell.

The Canon said again, "You could forgive that, could you?"

"You came to tell me something," Sulvan said. "Downstairs, I looked at you and you had something to tell."

"Can you die?"

Sulvan waited.

"Tomorrow night," the Canon said. "The small hours, the tide's on the run." The Canon threw back the curtains. "And rain or storm you stand out and watch where the gallows used to be."

"Watch the river," Sulvan said. "In rain or storm. Tomorrow night in stillness. The wind has other ports of call."

"You stand and draw the curtains behind you."

"And watch the river."

"Lottie will come for you. A push, send you out with the tide."

Sulvan said, "She loves the Pianoman."

"She'll kill."

"For love, Bang Bang."

"Yes."

Sulvan nodded.

From the door, the Canon said, "Harney, the curate's minder, at the church. He was punished today. The men in leather jackets."

Sulvan said, "He wore your clothes. They'll come again. A lot of eyes out there, Bang Bang."

The curtains were open. Sulvan stood there, watching the river, the tide, the vanished gallows.

Even the Canon's soft footsteps tapped and creaked on the bare boards: noise was a watchdog. He descended and went carefully out into the darkness. Sulvan was right. The wind came only in weakening squalls now.


The Canon went along the pieces of little broken streets and between shreds of pavement, winding through wharves, away from Sulvan's and the prone silhouette of the club.

The wind had lessened, hadn't yet died, came in vicious charges and was gone again. The river was a great floor of darkness, reaching across other shores and jetties. Sulvan, in his 'ship', would be watching it.

Indestructible Sulvan, the Canon pondered, murderous, staring back at the frozen rattle of corpses? He pulled his cloak about him: the cold was not the bitterness of the night, it was the chill of death itself.

As he rounded the church he looked upriver at the distant electronic corona of the hallowed square mile, Londinium Fiscal City, itself a tenuous printed circuit, and wondered what ghosts it might leave behind . . .

There was a glimmer of light against the strip of stained glass at the Mortuary. Harney would have licked his wounds by now. The slap of water still came from the riverfront and the Canon strode away across the churchyard slopes. He would bring solace to Harney, offer him a little importance, restore him. What freak wind had blown Harney to this mortuary creek? What wind had gathered them all?

In the church, he moved through the dark arcade, by Father Jim's confessional, close to the mortuary passage-way. He listened. Father Jim's voice was there and Harney, in alcohol, confident again.

Nuances of drunkenness, its perfume, profanity, erosion of stock, were prices acceptable to Father Jim for some glimmer of light in this awful tunnel.

But Father Jim had lost his minder.

In the wounded mind of Harney, the leather jackets were Father Jim's animals: abasement, nakedness, shame, physical pain, however misplaced, were offences to be punished.

Harney would be clever, unchanged, about his daily business. But a moment would come! Harney would punish!

Father Jim was saying, "In fact, Harney, I also have Miss Delacey in mind. She has fixed ideas about music, I gather. Fixed ideas. Very rigid standards. I'm told she winced at the mention of Maverick Flynn; and our pioneering holy Sisters. 'Winced' was the word, Harney."

Harney was considering it. "Well, I suppose she's more the Clair de Lune, Magic Flute, Air on a G String school of thought. Takes all kinds."

Father Jim had dropped a tone or two in search of exigency. "I was thinking if she informed the Canon, as you say, put the finger on them. Maverick Flynn and the Riverboat Men." Father Jim was suddenly stricken. "The Nuns! Oh my God!"

Harney's kind dismissive laugh bled off the tension. "I don't think he'd strike in the open, somehow. He's more the urban guerrilla man, wouldn't you say? In, out, gone in the smoke."

After moments of silence Father Jim said, "He must be located, kept under surveillance at all times! Understood?"

Harney took unkindly to these changes of tone. "Willco," he said.

Father Jim allowed himself a few moments of camaraderie. "Your experience in these matters is a godsend, Harney. When I engaged you as church clerk and future bar-steward, I had no idea you had devoted so much of your life to the mentally afflicted. Wonderful. And a seaman too! A man of the world, not easily ruffled."

It seemed that Harney would keep the spill of the afternoon's shame from ever blotting Father Jim's portrait of a heroic world-weary figure.

The Canon understood, listened.

Harney was cocksure. "Ten years bosun on the deep-sea runs, Father Jim." He paused and declaimed in a soft nostalgic cadence, " 'The happiest hour a sailor sees, Is when he's down at an inland town, With his Nancy on his knees, yo-ho!' "

Father Jim applauded but there was a period of silence following the jolt of this sudden performance.

"Harney," Father Jim said eventually, "would you consider the Canon has deteriorated in recent months?"

Harney took a very professional stance. "A difficult prognosis, that." He might have paced about for a little while. "If you know what to look for, of course, you'll find the telltale signs. Certain spastic movements of the fingers, a smile in the eye, even the ability to vanish, as we know, at the drop of a hat. It all adds up." Harney exhaled. "No, much as I regret it, in my opinion, certainly no improvement."

"Thank you, Harney." There was the snap of Father Jim's clipboard. "You'll finish your stock soon, I hope. Tomorrow is another day." He was preparing to leave. "These cleaning ladies, Harney," he said. "Catholic, of course, recommended by the convent, the Mother Superior herself. But nowadays a lot of valuable stock lying about?"

The silence, the Canon knew, would be the exchanging of knowing glances and Father Jim's anxiety.

"Save in your presence, I'm never too happy about these foreign Catholics," Harney said. "You see that latest addition out there, dusting down the Stations of the Cross in diamante glasses, stiletto heels, and more bangles and beads than a head-hunter. What comes to mind is lack of reverence."

"Watch her, Harney. Watch them both. I'm going now. I'll survey the battleground and strategy again. And again! Goodnight, Harney. Vigilance!"

The Canon stepped into the seclusion of Father Jim's confessional and listened to his rapid pace through the church, the slam of the doors as he left. There was silence.

Harney was orating, "Study the strategy again and again, Father Jimmy Boy, till you're blue in the arse. Measure twice, cut once. A golden rule on land and sea. Or in the bloody nuthouse!"

The Canon went quietly back to the church door to re-enact his entrance, less discreetly now with a snap of ancient mortice and warning taps of his stick on the paved floor.

He would have expressed hope that wounds were in healing process and offered commiseration; but Harney forestalled him.

He stood stiff as a post. "Canon!"

"My good fellow!"

"I ask a favour."

"Granted, granted." The Canon took an empty crate and seated himself at the head of the trestle-table. "Indignities are best laid to rest, aren't they? This afternoon? Forgotten, never happened." It was dismissed.

"Have a drink, Canon."

"A drop of your whisky, perhaps." Harney was already pouring from his private stock, a mark of respect; and the Canon was discreet.

"Another weekend of music," the Canon said. "Busy times for you, open-ended days."

Harney stared his resignation. "Maverick Flynn and the Riverboat Men," he said. "A bulldozer driver, two town-hall clerks and a dustman. A great sound, they call it."

"Riverboat Men? From far afield, are they, Harney?"

"Well, it's a fair spin to Camden Town, I suppose."

"Indeed."

They drank.

"A strange title, don't you think?" the Canon said. "But it has a ring to it. 'Maverick'? That's something to do with cactus and prairies and that kind of thing, isn't it?"

"In point of fact," Harney explained with authority, "it's a kind of stray undernourished animal without an owner. And Riverboat Men? More than likely were tricksters, thimble-riggers and con men."

"But they play music, don't they?"

Harney had a kind of paternal gentleness. "They pick these names, Canon, to catch the eye, upset the ear. That's all."

"Ah."

"I mean, 'Rosary Reynolds and the Five Sorrowful Decades' wouldn't bring you out in a thunderstorm."

"I suppose not."

"And, of course, we have the Narcotic Nuns as well."

"Yes."

Harney poured genteel measures of scotch. His squat frame was bulging a little but there was a smartness about him; he wore brogues, brown twill slacks, shirt, cravat; and a conventional blazer, dark blue, with some meaningless jungle of crest on its pocket. They drank. The wind was an occasional flurry now and they could hear the rattle of leaves.

The Canon said, "Would it distress you to tell me about it?"

"But to no one else," Harney said eventually; he sat at the table, rubbing the knife-wounds with his hand, caressing them. "They stripped me down to my knackers, Canon. Stuck me, arse up, in the barrel." Harney apologised. "I thought I was dead. Then earphones and noise belting through my skull. You never heard noise like this, Canon."

"My poor fellow."

"And then," Harney said in sorrow; he glanced towards his crotch, "and then, it would have been a bottle of brandy on the 'meat and two veg', and a match to it, set it off like a Christmas pud, burn it to a cinder. I signed your name."

"No harm done," the Canon said. "My *signature* is a different matter, you see."

Harney brightened. He was a strong man, the Canon thought; clever too. When he sat, the Canon could see the bulge of a sheath knife at his belt. A spark to set him off, the Canon thought; who could tell?

He said suddenly, "Would you say I'm mad, Harney?"

"Mad, Canon?"

"Yes, mad. A shortage of marbles, that kind of thing."

Harney gave it full consideration, not a hint of impulsiveness. "Oh no! Definitely not!"

"Good."

"Mind you, a funny thing the old brain-box," Harney said. "I remember once, storm-tossed between the Canaries and Freetown, the West Africa run, you know, and the cook has a mental explosion!" For a moment Harney seemed to see it all. "He's sound as yourself sitting there and then without a flicker of warning he's over the side. Gone! Like he's jumping a bus to make the first race at Hackney."

The Canon sighed, drank a little: deadhouses, madhouses, chapels of rest. Once, with his totting cart, he had stood before the gates and manorial walls of Colney Hatch, on a summer's day; behind him, the traffic hurrying between Friern Barnet and Southgate; across the lawns and beautiful awful flowerbeds, the great sprawling pile of brick and barred windows to protect its mass of flawed inexplicable software, buzzing whirring tearing mechanisms beyond the remoteness of control, cross-wired and rejected when God was nodding. The Canon had looked at his empty barrow and moved on . . .

He said, "Understanding of the human mind is God's

cross, Harney." And then suddenly, "Would you say Father Kilmartin has all his marbles? Father Jim?"

Harney's laughter was a rabid throaty bark. "He could spare a couple of handfuls for you and me and take on the High Priests in the Temple."

"Mmm, interesting," the Canon was saying, waiting for the laughter to diminish. "I think he's mad, you know. Quite dangerous. You mustn't mention this, of course, Harney. It might accelerate the progress. Fresh forces might be unleashed, delinquent, violent even."

The Canon sat motionless, rapt, as if listening. Harney's voice had deserted him. He looked at the depth of calm in the Canon's eyes, the kindness, the tight weathered skin of his face. Harney listened too.

The Canon said, "Do you sometimes get a feeling of turbulence here, Harney? And sometimes, peace? Great everlasting peace?"

"All the time, all the time!" Harney trembled in a great frisson of excitement. "Turbulence and peace!"

"The wind is dying."

"Getting its breath, having a breather. I know winds," Harney said. "She'll be still tomorrow, and then she'll blow! And rains too! I dreamt of the scrubbers on surfboards last night and they screeching like owls. A force twelve, maybe."

"Scrubbers?"

"The cleaning ladies."

"Ah," the Canon said. "Would you say *they* are mad, Harney?"

"As mad as fiddler's bitches, Canon."

"Dangerous?"

"Well, between ourselves, I wouldn't turn my back too often."

"Yes, yes, I must remember that. You have a very sound knowledge of these matters, I find." The Canon refused a little whisky. "Sanity and madness and the Beaufort scale." He nodded appreciation of Harney. "Force twelve wind. A great deal of wind."

Harney smiled.

The Canon said, "You went to sea as a young man, they

say. Adventure, the call of the wild, girls in every port, Harney?"

Harney's esteem for the Canon, for himself, glowed in the suffusion of whisky. Could they lock away this excellent man? Father Jim, the forward scout, and his black army over the hill; the leather jackets, Harney suddenly thought, and the terrifying kiss of holy water over naked skin, from head to scrotum. Blood and rage raced to his head in dizziness. Girls in every port, he could hear the Canon saying . . .

"Ha, ha, the landlubber's dream, I'm afraid, Canon." The laughter was sharp as glass. "Now you take the West Africa stint. Out of Liverpool to Port Harcourt. A dirty spit off the equator, if you'll pardon . . ."

"Of course."

"The women, it can't be denied, are a bit over-suntanned, you know what I mean? Beauty in the eye of the beholder, of course."

They had been the lickerish days, Harney thought. He was still breathless with anger. But for moments he remembered dancing naked with the screeching Obalende tarts, his erection trapped between black and white bellies, great pendulous mammaries glistening in sweat, a gramophone of the twenties scratching some Volteuffel humid waltz.

The Canon said, "You chose the celibate life, I imagine?"

Harney hid his shame. "Well, one week in six or seven, when I planted the old feet down in Liverpool Town, I used to trot out a little scouse piece that strummed the guitar and sang, 'Springtime in the Rockies'." . . .

There was silence and Harney's face hung in sadness; he remembered his fingers tightening about such a tender neck, the arms hanging limp, the lolling head.

"Delightful," the Canon said. "Marco Polo smitten by love. The future Mrs Harney, was it?"

Harney drained his glass and refilled it; the Canon listened. There was anger and sadness. "She had it off with a West Indian piano-tuner," Harney said. "Preston Foster Mackenzie. I could never understand it. He had a face like Neddy there." Harney stared in wonderment at the pious face of the Christmas crib donkey.

111

"Cheer up, there's a good fellow!" the Canon said. "What about these musician people, these riverboat chaps?"

Harney said tonelessly, "Maverick Flynn and the Riverboat Men."

"Cowboys, campfires, riders of the purple sage?"

"Something like that."

"'Springtime in the Rockies', Harney! Father Jim might get them to play it for you."

"Musicians?"

"Yes. Are they mad, do you think, Harney?"

"At four hundred a night?"

"Four hundred?"

"That's knockdown. Special rate to Father Jim for parochial survival. A great man for the bargain, Father Jim."

"I can believe it."

"Six hundred tickets flogged to date. Plus what comes in at the door. A bar like Las Vegas! If we don't stick away a couple of grand, then *I'm* mad."

"You seem quite sane to me, Harney."

"Thank you, Canon."

The Canon nodded farewell, raised his stick. "Give my good wishes to Father Jim. I see him so rarely."

Father Jim had rung the rectory doorbell: he had pulled a porcelain knobbed handle and, inside, the bell mounted on a coiled spring tinkled musically. It was his first visit, as episcopal nuncio, briefed and determined. He looked at the churchyard and surrounding walls, the ageing graves; but Lucy and Horatio Catchpole, at their tryst, were beyond his vision.

Catherine Delacey opened the door and viewed him. "Would you care to come in?" she said without any trace of welcome.

He followed her across the hallway, comfortingly lit and furnished, glittering with care. The drawing room and its beauty enveloped him. Here he might stand one day, looking out from his parochial residence, guardian of the spiritual and the temporal, host to bishops and monsignors, and the selected worthies of his domain.

"You're looking for the Canon?" she said.

"And your goodself, Miss Delacey. I'm looking for Mr Herlihy and your goodself."

"The Canon isn't here."

"Ah." Father Jim was at his most gracious. "The church would like you both to be our guests at Saturday evening's entertainment and insisted I should call in person to invite you."

A desperate flurry of wind pushed at the windows, spent itself, and there was silence.

"The weather will be kind," Father Jim assured her; he smiled. "A little quatrain of mine, embroidered and framed by parishioners, dominates our blessed box-office:

> "Hail, rain or threatening storm,
> God's welcome is forever warm,
> When others failed abysmally,
> He stilled the seas at Galilee."

"Did he?" Miss Delacey said. "And on Saturday evening He makes one of His rare public appearances at square dancing. I'm pleased for you. There were other matters, were there?"

"Well, yes."

Father Jim, with episcopal restraint, let it pass him by. He improvised, "A little additional heat for the People's Hall at weekends wouldn't be amiss."

"Adequate, I think," Miss Delacey said.

"You are skilled in heating, of course?"

"My mother, an excellent woman of North Kerry," Miss Delacey said, "used to cut her own turf, quite expertly. And drop a load or two in the curate's shed to ward off voodoo, pestilence and black magic."

Father Jim said, "Miss Delacey, let us be calm." He sent out little messages of solicitude, empathy, anxiety; he smiled in apology. "Are you quite well, Miss Delacey? I hope I haven't upset you. I'm a trifle impatient at times, so many things to do, overstretched. Little rules and discipline mean survival."

Miss Delacey was thinking of Ada: she had combed and curled her hair, framed it about her small face, trimmed her nails, creamed her hands and folded them. The wind had been high then and she had felt moments of great loneliness.

"Miss Delacey," Father Jim was saying.

"Yes."

"Mr Herlihy is in need of care and attention."

"The Canon?"

"Mr Paul V. Herlihy."

"An abandoned love-child?"

"I'd hardly put it like that. He is at a time of life when there are significant changes, biological changes . . ."

"Giddy spells, agoraphobia?"

Father Jim offered hands of patience. "These changes do not necessarily confine themselves to our physical life-support." Father Jim stood, head bowed, in motionless silence: he might be praying. Eventually he pronounced, "The Canon, as you call him, Miss Delacey, is mentally disturbed."

"Aren't we all, thank God. Sanity would be unbearable," she said.

"I intend to help him. I must pray devoutly that it is a passing disturbance." Father Jim looked pleadingly upwards. "Reach out to the Great Designer Himself. *Ad peccatorem, mens sana in corpore sano*, Amen."

"The Canon is a lunatic, is that it, Father Kilmartin?" she asked.

Father Jim found the formality of his surname somehow slighting in Miss Delacey's tonation. Anger was stirring. The banishment of them all, the toppling of their sinister geriatric bothy, the purification and restructuring of everything!

He gazed at the dignity of this room and felt he belonged; he said, "There have been accidents, you are aware, of course, people pushed in fires."

"The burning alive of human flesh is God's prerogative, Father Kilmartin."

Father Jim's face was still placid; the rage burned in his gut. The venomous bitch, blasphemous too!

"People *pushed* in fires, Miss Delacey." There was a forensic sweep about Father Jim's delivery now. "Pushed, you see.

Savage reprisals in which I hope you are in no way implicated. Are you? And then, Francis Xavier Murphy!" He paused for a prosecution's withering attack. "You know, I presume, that Francis Xavier jumped over the Canon's stick?"

Miss Delacey said, "Failed to jump over it."

"Yes." Father Jim took a letter from his pocket. "I have received a communication from his mother, that remarkable Christian woman, enclosing a medical report." He held it up momentarily as an exhibit and then, with dignity, in broken phrases befitting such indelicacy, struggled on. "There is a possibility . . . fortunately a remote possibility . . . but for all that, a possibility! . . . that Francis Xavier's . . . reproductive system could be affected."

"Please God," Miss Delacey said.

"Take care, madam!"

"The prospect," Miss Delacey said, "of his increasing and multiplying is more appalling than nuclear waste."

Father Jim gaped at this fresh outrage. "I am shocked, Miss Delacey! You force me to consider, in the very minutest detail, your suitability, not only to treat the godless dying, but to share even remote ground with our Christian community dedicated to the shaping of a brave new world."

"Shaping is your job, dear Father Kilmartin. I merely lubricate old rusty downhill cogwheels." She smiled farewell. "And now, if there is nothing further?"

"There's Paul Vincent Herlihy, Miss Delacey. A silenced cleric, deranged and delinquent! I suggest that until such time as I can spirit him discreetly away to a place of treatment, you assure me that you will avoid his company. There is the matter of complicity, you see. Even in the oiling of rusty cogwheels. I am not a fool, Miss Delacey."

"Come," she said; she shushed him across the hallway and, as she opened the door, the Canon stood there, key in hand.

"My dear," he said. "And Father Kilmartin! A pleasant visit, I hope."

He stepped inside and Catherine Delacey shut out the world and Father Jim.

She took his cloak and scarf and beret and stick: he looked handsome, she thought, wiry, almost youthful, a tall black

115

figure in slacks and rollneck. He put his weathered shoes in a doorside closet.

"Tea by the fire," he said.

She smiled.

The Canon washed hands and face, felt the comfort of warm water and soft towels. He went to the drawing room, to the fireglow; only a single table-lamp made its pool of light and the fire sent its own unpredictable spears into the shadows . . .

. . . *Lucy Dory-Catchpole was there in the twilight, and her dashing, so unwarlike second lieutenant, by the window, holding hands, gazing love to each other. For them, at least, and at that moment, they were shut away from a long-ago tiring down-at-heel world: ugliness was out there for others and beyond rectory walls. It was distanced, might creep up from the alleys and waterfront to buff the windows and fall away. They stood in safety . . .*

The Canon turned away. It came now on lighted screens to firesides: the good, the bad, the unbidden: private tabernacles, perhaps, these rented boxes, with God looking out at gaping faces . . .

*The Canon looked at Samuel Taylor Catchpole again, the Sam Browne, its authority, the broad buckled belt to carry revolver and explosives that would be ludicrous in his pale tapering hands. Lucy ran a finger along the polished leather. They were fading, gone . . .*

The Canon sat and remembered all the years. The faded tender revenants of Samuel Taylor Catchpole and his Lucy had stirred the youthfulness of ordination days . . .

. . . "It's 'St Joseph's' now."

"Still an orphanage?"

116

"Oh yes. The Sisters would be proud of you."

There had been time to spend before his hegira to the scabrous mission fields of England and battles and conquests and defeats. This was a time of returning briefly to homesteads for the many, for all, to be humbly paraded, to lay blessed hands on friends, kin, on the ailing, to be addressed with a strange new deference, distant and cautious.

Herlihy, unencumbered, had been free to wander. There had been generous invitations from fellow anointed to their family homes but he had carefully sidestepped them without offence.

In two days he had found St Joseph's, his orphanage. The trees had grown taller about it, it was hidden, but the slate roof was its changeless grey; and windows and concrete facing had aged. Somewhere, in unison, a class recited prayers, and teaching-voices were erratic as bursts of gunfire.

The steps, the hall door, its furnishings were unstained; the pathways, the great spacious parterre without blemish.

"I would like to see the Mother Superior," Herlihy had said.

A teenage uniformed inmate allowed herself only a momentary glance before she led him to a reception room.

Mother Superior was not in awe of clerics, and neophytes at that.

She was pleasant and brusque. "Ah, Father. Can I do something for you?"

Herlihy remained silent long enough to drain her superiority.

"I am a past pupil," he said. "You found me foster parents a long time ago."

"And now you are ordained!"

"A week ago."

She was kneeling before him, a pious woman, and he hoped his blessing would outflank the impenetrable barriers to God.

"Come," she said.

In her shelved record-study, in moments, putting computers to shame, she had found a volume and his record sheet.

"You were a foundling," she said. "Sister Paul Veronica Herlihy took you in charge, gave you her name."

"Veronica?"

Mother Superior smiled. "She is with God now and you must remember her."

They walked in the grounds and she prayed that the good English people would return to the fold.

Herlihy had noted in her meticulous documents his year of arrival. He saw it again on an elegant detached building, the residential home of the holy Sisters. A stone tablet said: 'This building generously bequeathed by SAMUEL KIRK-FORTESCUE'. No more.

"The year of my arrival," Herlihy said.

Mother Superior nodded. "You must see our dahlias, the pride of our gardens."

There was lunch and mineral waters and blessings and farewells . . .

Directories didn't list Kirk-Fortescues: but racing almanacs and bloodstock manuals have a wealth of starting-points. In a week he had found a fifteen-hundred-acre, walled estate, its magnificent gates at the apex of a semicircle. In sportswear he had walked four hundred yards of statued avenue when the manor house came in view: cars, peacocks, a fountain, a gardener on his knees pulling weeds. He had turned and walked back three miles to a village pub.

An hour passed.

An old man said, "You're travelling."

"I called to the estate."

"Fortescue."

"The estate."

"He'll pay in a year if you're lucky. He rides horses and women, the sire of his yard. Twenty bastards to his name. More. He goes to faraway nuns with his presents from God. A bundle in one hand, a wad in the other."

"He's a Protestant?" Herlihy said with a show of naïveté.

"A Protestant Mason."

Herlihy had laughed . . .

Catherine came with tea and switched on a mantel light that caught them in their own fireside enclave. She toasted bread on one side only, buttered it, chopped the brittle edges. She drew the curtains.

"Our storm has gone with Father Kilmartin," she said; there was only the faint sound of wind now; she was pouring tea. "Our Father Jim."

"Father Jim," the Canon said. "I can never get quite in tune with it. Today they encourage that kind of thing, I'm told. Everywhere." The Canon found it difficult to say 'home'; to him, after fleeting decades, it seemed an alien place now. "Not very reassuring."

Catherine Delacey smiled. "It pleases him, brings him happiness. 'Call me Father Jim', he tells the dancing weekend flock. 'There you go again with this "Father Kilmartin". Father Jim, Father Jim, that's better.'"

"A strange discord, an echo," the Canon said. "Papa Doc or Fearless Fred or something. Undignified at any rate."

She looked at him, considered the danger that approached, but was silent. She remembered Ada again and her peace in leaving.

Without warning, the Canon said, "My father, you know, a respected man, shaved on Sundays, changed his cap, donned the navy-blue suit and polished boots. And a tie. Oh yes, a tie. And walked two miles to Mass."

Catherine Delacey looked back at it all. "Those dusty roads and hedges," she said.

"If it rained he had a woollen coat heavy as a sheep."

"For winter rain and summer showers."

The Canon smiled. "And a prayer book, small as a matchbox to hide in the palm of his hand."

"To hide?"

"A squint at it and a squint at God in the tabernacle. Shrunken prayer books, shrunken gods squatting in cages. The clang of the little brass door, the click of the key. God in the darkness."

119

"Your mother?" Catherine said; she reached over for a moment to touch his hands.

"Once he bought her a length of serge to make herself a coat," the Canon said. "And on Saturday nights she cleaned it with the cold dregs of tea. A big dangerous barren woman who might smile once a year. They fostered me." The Canon thought about it for a little while. "To milk a cow, shovel out dung, sweep pools of grey water away from the door? I suppose so." He seemed to listen now. "I used to watch a reverend priest go by, a canon too, feel pain at the unattainable comfort of him, the glow of his face, the ring of his ferruled stick on the road."

"And you began to believe in God?" Catherine said.

The Canon said a little wistfully, "I decided to *find* Him, ask Him for a job."

"They took you on probation, at least."

"Strange people, strange people."

She said, "Finding Him. A bit difficult, isn't it? Madness, I suppose."

"Beyond understanding."

"He stands with Father Jim each week in the pulpit, they are told."

The Canon nodded. "Old friends, who can tell? Declamations of certainty, spouts of indulgence."

This might be a moment now to speak of danger and madness and confinement, she thought; but the Canon was laughing and she laughed with him. A time too precious for squandering.

Instead she said, "Ah, I must tell you!" She joined her hands in anticipation. "My father, on his tin whistle, gave praise to the Almighty in the key of C. 'And now!' he would snap for silence, 'a slow air for the Man Above.' Spinal trouble, he called it. 'Chained to my chair, God pity me!' he'd say. My mother helping him to bed at night, tiptoeing about in the morning in fear of waking him. The kitchen full of saintly relics and the names and addresses of discredited bonesetters." She paused. "I was the youngest of five," she said.

The Canon said, "Five. Determined, even in pain, to fulfil his conjugal obligations. A saint perhaps."

Catherine Delacey nodded. "The agonies of procreation tonight." She fingered an imaginary flute. "Tomorrow, 'The Rakes of Mallow'."

Suddenly she laughed: in such a plain determined face, her eyes, unguarded, had an extraordinary beauty. Her happiness was the Canon's. Calm returned, the faint wind, the fluttering movements of the fire.

Eventually she said, "You never went back to see the grey pools of water again?"

"No. There isn't much time. There never was. I see old streets on country roads," he said. "Worn doorsteps, shop windows where oil-lamps hung, and stockings and holly at Christmas. A long time ago. Yesterday."

There was silence.

"Do you think we'll find Him?" she asked.

The Canon said, "'Searching' is the thing. Only Father Jim finds Him."

"But you've chased Him down the narrow streets so long. It isn't fair."

"I saw His shadow once or twice," the Canon smiled to her. "A flicker at the end of convergence." He looked at the curtained windows, towards the bleak foreshore and his single home of the dying. "A little while ago, old Rumbold is giving up the ghost, remember? Sleeping gently her last moments of captivity. There was stillness there, so much happiness. I could have sworn He touched me."

Catherine Delacey looked at him for a little while. "Yes," she said; she gathered the delft and left.

When she returned she had composed herself, was ready to face him. "You are in danger," she said.

"Only a little."

"Didn't you know you are mad?"

"Only a little."

"Ask Father Jim, the Bishop's recorder."

"He came to tell you?" the Canon asked.

"You will be spirited away."

"I should be enraged now, you see, goaded, a raging lunatic. He's a clever little fellow," the Canon smiled.

"He wants your church?"

121

"Yes."

"And the Hall?"

"Everything."

"Everything!" Catherine Delacey took a brass chased poker from the fender.

"You see?" the Canon said. "You are in anger, my dear, out of control. Lunatics are like that. And I have a great love for you."

Catherine Delacey said, "I have loved you since my gory hands on the High Road. No one takes your village."

The Canon smiled: everywhere, love, he thought: Lottie and the Pianoman, Harney and his Nancy, God and Father Jim.

Catherine Delacey was silent.

"Love is confusing," the Canon said.

"A kind of greed."

"Greed," the Canon said and was silent for a little while. "There's a young man of greed and fashion among us. McMorrow. I should have told you," the Canon remembered. "He sends us his prowlers, men in leather." The Canon took her hand. "Men of greed. Be careful."

"They'll come again?"

The Canon considered it. "Yes."

"If they come?"

"I'll kill them."

"*We'll* kill them," Catherine Delacey said; she laid the poker carefully in its fender; she kissed him on the cheek and left.

Yes, love was confusing, the Canon thought: he sat by the fire for a little while to retrace the twists and vagaries of his day: it had brought a restlessness.

He left the comfort of warmth and reassurance, crossed the foyer and climbed the stairs to his bedroom.

1806. He read again the parchments, the passenger-ballast lists of Dory's voyage out of Cork, carefully searched and found his names.

Traynor and Lee – the Pianoman and his love; Harney, Kilmartin, Herlihy, Delacey, McMorrow; Father Jim's sweepers, Durkin and Rorke. And Sulvan, his name mutilated with quill strokes.

There was a brief note: *Two fine men lost to this Irish savagery. Ship's Master, Jonathan Dowty, and his bosun, Maxwell. God give them rest.*

The Canon wrapped himself against the weather; and from the granite edge of the river he flung the coarse leather-bound folio into the darkness.

# Friday

Yesterday's gale and scouring rain had left a limpid morning
in its wake: the vaporous blue of this early winter sky,
sunlight catching the church and People's Hall, the stones
and vaults of the churchyard putting out long shadows. The
trees shone with what colour remained and their torn leaves
were splashed on turf and pathway. The Canon gazed at
it all, and the river. To remember one moment like this,
he thought, was something for ever. He thought of Ada's
moment of love at Southend.

At Sulvan's Stan had arrived. The Pianoman was sweeper
too. He emptied glutted ashtrays in his bucket, wrappings,
packages; he swabbed and washed and dried and polished. He
felt no resentment: every step was a step walked in freedom
and on friendly ground; he had a fag to smoke, a drink to
reach for: all he could want. But Lottie loved him more than
he was worth.

The Canon came onstage and sat at Stan's piano.

"Busy," he said, looking at the waiting hillocks of
litter.

Stan brought a plastic bin and hardboard squares to grab
and lift. "Busier tonight . . ." he started out to say but reality
loomed and fear gripped for a moment. "Friday night, you
see? Busier."

"The small hours of Saturday when you're clear?"

"No rest," Stan said.

The Canon looked at his face. "You've seen a few battles,"
he said.

Stan nodded. "In the nick and out of it." He thought of
Lottie again. "But I never killed nobody. Only once," he
said. "Different. Had to. A job, that's all. My old man was
a king."

"Yes," the Canon said.

He put his fag end on the floor, ground it out. "Couldn't do it like *that*. Not 'cold', I couldn't do it."

"No."

"An eye for an eye's different."

"For love?" the Canon asked.

They heard Lottie's footsteps on the stairs and she came softly down on her special day.

Stan gazed back at the lounge taking shape and order again. He said, "Real love?"

"Not cold," the Canon said.

She arrived: Lottie, even in headscarf, baggy slacks, a cast-off jumper, had excitement and style. She came and leant across the litter-bin to kiss her Stan.

"Early," she said to the Canon.

"After a death always the tidying," he said.

Lottie had all her snap and quip, but she moved a little quickly, over-gestured: there was an edginess.

"Murder," the Canon said without warning.

It spun her like a top.

"Yesterday. Rain, wind, storm. Today there's beauty," he said.

Sulvan's footsteps sounded in the hallway; he made his entrance: raincoat, scarf, tight leather gloves. He nodded a greeting.

"A clear morning, Canon," he said.

Last night's shadow and substance were hidden away.

The Canon raised a hand.

Lottie said, "I got twelve dozen glasses to shine, spirits to do, tills to float . . ."

"Wait," Sulvan said.

Lottie was fighting to screw down her courage.

"I'm 'out'," Sulvan told her.

"Out?"

"Journeys to make."

Stan stood still at his rubbish: you didn't ask questions.

Lottie waited.

"I'll be back," he said. "In good time, Lottie."

"Yes," she said.

126

"Soon maybe. Or later."

He went out with the Canon: Sulvan, man of power; the Canon, godlike, with open cloak and greying hair.

"What do you see this morning, Bang Bang?" Sulvan asked as they looked at the river.

"A beautiful morning," the Canon said.

"Good."

"I try to remember days like this."

He thought of the churchyard, the trees, the carpet of leaves, the stones of building and remembrance caught in the brightness.

"And your village."

The Canon gazed towards the lingering wilderness. "Two years. A single cabin in the weeds."

"Possessions," Sulvan said.

"A lot of dead ends and talk and silences. Danger, maybe. Strange finesse, divine intervention."

"You could be losing a battle."

The Canon nodded.

"Let no one take your land. Green field or a jetty. Whatever it is."

The water lapped gently at Sulvan's steps, a launch waited there; the river was a sheet of pale winterish gold.

"You're going to Park Lane?" the Canon asked.

"Yes," Sulvan said.

"To bring him here?"

"Or kill him."

"Bring him here," the Canon said.

Sulvan nodded.

"There was a gallows at Park Lane too, a long time ago. At Tyburn Tree," the Canon said.

"Gallows everywhere. Possessions, you see."

"Yes," the Canon said.

Sulvan came close to him: if there was compassion in stony eyes, it was there. "You'll have a village, Bang Bang."

He watched Sulvan descend the steps; a cabin door was opened and he was gone out of sight. The launch pulled out into midstream and swung upriver for Westminster . . .

127

He turned and looked up at Sulvan's towering mausoleum, memorial, brothel. The sun shone on his balcony up there and the windows behind it.

Possessions.

The launch was small now, moving out of sight on the riverbend from Woolwich to Silvertown.

The Canon walked back through the taproom and stores to the lounge and its stage. Stan still garnered litter and brushed and polished.

"A drink?" Stan offered.

"No," the Canon said.

Stan brought him coffee.

"You're afraid," the Canon said.

"You know?"

"Yes."

"An eye for an eye. Different, you see?"

The Canon gazed at Stan's music centre, a pile of fifties forgotten junk left behind, but cared for, tended; distantly, the scrape of chairs and tables, the rattle of Lottie's mop-bucket came from the bar space beyond the curtains; and the sharp rap of Lottie's heels behind the servery.

Stan held out his twisted hands.

"You love her?"

"Yes."

"That's enough," the Canon said.

Stan was at the curtains; then his footsteps fading. The Canon sat; silence crept in over the extraneous muffled noise until it was absolute . . .

*. . . He moved through Sulvan's ancient brothel, untouched, unmolested. The salt-skinned, wary, greedy faces, with jingle to spend, could take their timed debauchments in cubicle dens and boxrooms where teenage whores were stripped and poked.*

*The Canon stood and watched the mechanics of pleasure and trade; the low wooden cots, grey blankets, the sprawl of thighs and hammering buttocks; the pipe-rooms of sweet smoke; dope, hand-rolled, pushed in long-stemmed pipes, sucked with concave jaws into lungs and blood; the eyes, the sleeping faces, the blackened globes of oil-lamps.*

*The bar-room then, of taps and copper sinks, pewter drain shelves, a swelling pool of bodies, battered hats, rags, scars: a lamplit haven of warmth away from fouled cobbles, beggars, children, animals.*

*At low-water, drunks might doss on foreshores, or in open boats, or up beyond Ratcliffe, under the London Bridge arches, on dried mud and filth.*

*Beyond the bar-room, the 'Banquet Suite', spacious in such constriction, where Masters brought their doxies to feed and wine before consummation. Everywhere bodies in movement, on corridors and stairs. And then he saw the brothel-keeper himself, Sulvan, big-chested in open jerkin, peeled scalp, tight-cropped hair, sweat rag at his neck. The Canon looked: the unfinished face, the eyes distant as spans of time . . .*

Stan was at the curtains again; he drank from a beer jug. He seemed restored, an old contentment returning.

"I'm obliged," he said.

The Canon walked down through the aisle of the club and out into the morning. He could see the river again.

Sulvan was gone. He looked for a moment towards the Rectory and then at the lone cabin where Ada was at rest.

He would go to his cubicle at the Mortuary, the Canon decided. The beautiful gilded day had some fragile quality in it, evanescence: it might vanish and leave him trapped in a sweep of cloud and river fog. A strange day.

In the near distance, in the shadow of the People's Hall, he could glimpse some unhurried activity, movements of goods and persons: ugly twinned abraded cubes, black, large as funeral caskets, stands, tripods, electronic consoles, a Frankenstein display from another world: cable, kilometres of it, it seemed, being toted from place to place.

A small cowboy, a mannikin in tilted stetson, thumbs in studded belt, spurs even, seemed to supervise it all. So small, the Canon thought. He moved on.

In the church, great shafts of sunlight raked like buttresses

129

from the windows and spilt along the floor. Harney was in the Mortuary: from the passageway, the Canon could hear his baritone, its gravelly hum, a sudden interpolation of words: Harney, almost healed again, cauterised in burning alcohol.

The Canon sent warning noises on ahead of him and arrived in the turmoil. "Melodious, my dear fellow. A plaintive strain too."

Harney's face flamed with bonhomie, a hint of emotionalism. "A beautiful day, Canon. But short-lived, I'd reckon. Not meant to last."

"All days are beautiful, Harney," the Canon said. "Wind and storm, words whipped away like smoke. A wonderful thing, to shout. The words, where are they now, I wonder?"

Excitement was growing in Harney's eyes.

"Have you ever laughed with the wind and rain hammering at your face, your skin, your brain? Ah, such beauty, Harney."

Harney was breathless; he said, "'Springtime in the Rockies', Canon."

The Canon smiled. "It sounds idyllic," he said, "but it escapes me, I'm afraid."

Harney was close to tears. He sang, "'Once again I'll say I love you, While the birds sing all the day, When it's Springtime in the Rockies, The Rockies far away'."

The Canon pondered it in silence. "You render it with great emotion, a depth of sadness. Associations, Harney? 'Old unhappy far-off things, and battles long ago'?"

"A lot of my family," Harney said, still in melancholy, "were what you could call eccentric. An uncle in Dublin used to stop lassies in O'Connell Street and say, 'Come out to Howth and I'll show you me mickey.' For no reason. Acting the bollicks. And, in the end, when they locked him up, it was because he told the doctor the television was talking to him."

"Recovered, I hope," the Canon asked.

"Oh, discharged A-one, all systems at 'go'. But now *he* talks to the television. All day, dawn till dusk, gives it the odd kick too. Christ!"

130

"Baffling," the Canon said, and remembered. "Did I see a cowboy out there, Harney?"

"Four foot and half an inch?" Harney grinned, only with his teeth. "The Maverick Flynn from Camden Town," he said. "That poisonous midge is deranged."

The Canon received the information with interest, no ripple of surprise; he watched Harney spread his tobacco on liquorice paper and expertly roll and pack his cigarette.

"You think he's mad, Harney?"

Harney emerged from a cloud of exhalation, seated himself on a crate, gazed dispassionately beyond the Canon into kaleidoscopic worlds.

"You must consider," he said, "that 'dressing–up' bit. All the gear. Spurs and plastic chaps, sidelocks, six-inch cheroots, the high-heeled gimp of him. What would be called in the profession, an escape syndrome, if you follow me?"

"Ah."

"Fortunately he needs the outward trimmings, as we'll call them, to be assured that the Last Chance Saloon and the Red River Ranch are just round the corner." Harney nodded at the Canon's compassion and smoked for a little while. "Very near the borderline, I'd say."

Harney listened for moments before he poured drinks.

"Your knowledge of these matters is a constant fascination, old friend." The Canon raised his glass. "A glimpse of another place."

Harney was pleased.

"But," the Canon said, "no doubt, to a sensitive mind, such experience is not accumulated without pain."

"Very distressing at times. The wildest animal in the world to tame. The mind." Harney's face demonstrated, only with minimal success, the attrition of mental warfare. "Take this Maverick midget, all dressed up to meet Sitting Bull and Geronimo," he said, dropping to a whispered confidence. "He needs only a very small push and he's over the top."

The Canon waited. "I'm afraid you've lost me, Harney," he said.

"Well, a sudden jolt, you see, and he won't need the

gear any more." Harney stuck a finger, like a gun muzzle, against his own forehead. "Everything will be supplied inside, matching pearl-handled forty-fives, desert dust on the boots, spurs that jingle jangle jingle. He won't even bother to get up of a morning unless someone puts a boot up his 'how's your father' . . . beg your pardon, Canon. One minute he'll be at Wounded Knee, the next at Little Bighorn, a whole world of smoke-signals, lonesome trails and the Black Hills of Dakota."

The Canon listened to the stillness. "The prairies of the mind, Harney," he said eventually. "Yes, yes, I understand," he reassured him. "Happy, of course, in the sanctuary of the bed, safe from tomahawk and flaming arrow, till someone boots him up the arse, as you say, on to the cold flagstones of reality." He leant forward, disciple to his master. "These nurses, Harney, I imagine, can be unfeeling, mindless at times."

Harney seemed to inspect a great poisonous line of them. "In need of treatment themselves, poor bastards," he said.

"Or should I call them warders?"

The Canon pleaded his inadequacy; but Harney was fired with enthusiasm. He poured more whisky.

"There's screws and nurses, Canon. Screws for security, nurses for treatment."

"Ah."

Harney smiled. "But ask a few unscheduled questions over the odds and you can get 'treatment' from the screws as well."

Harney took his drink, poured another; the Canon abstained and suddenly asked, "They treated you badly, my dear fellow?"

"Until I gave the situation a bit of study," Harney said on a rising note, cock-a-hoop, smiling, invincible. He almost winked his foxiness to the Canon; he settled himself for exposition. "You see," he said, "the whole shebang, screws, nurses, doctors, quacks, penpushers, the whole shower, they think they're clever. If you can spot that, you're home and dry."

"Astute," the Canon said.

"You're supposed to think you're not being watched at all,

see? Screws with leather belts and rings of keys strolling past you in a daydream every day, stone-bored, like they might wait and wait for Godot's bus. They don't see you. You're invisible."

"Extraordinary."

"Did you ever feel invisible, Canon?"

The Canon thought of teeming lanes down to the river, the silent world, the synchronous journeys, timeless as dreams. "I'm not sure," he said.

"A very strange sensation," Harney assured him. "A doctor goes past, the white coat flying open, hands in pockets, looking as if he has the *Times* crossword puzzle locked up in his head."

"Distressing," the Canon said.

Harney drank, smoked, waved to disperse the clouds, until the sharp outline of the Canon returned. "I stuck that crap for a week," he said. "No more. I gave it a week!"

"Adequate."

"I'm not invisible, I said to myself. But where's there a mirror, a sheet of glass? Nothing!" Harney paused. "And then, in the consultant's tinted spectacles, I looked! And there I am!"

Harney's laughter seemed to boom through this place of the dead, crash against the startled faces of the Nativity; he spilt a little whisky in his paroxysm and prodigally anointed the table.

"Yes?" the Canon said.

"Well, the next screws that come up on the horizon, I give a sudden roar like a madman. And sure enough, they look at me! I flattened the two of them." Harney demonstrated his lightning head-butt. "A nod in the teeth, that's one! Number two?" He brought up his knee like a piston to meet his fist. "Gave him the old show-stopper in the jaxie."

"In the balls?" the Canon said.

"That's it! The next thing there's screws falling out of the trees! I'm at the bottom of a loose maul, you might say, and the knuckles and boots coming in from all sides!" Harney's laughter was bellowing out in remembrance of it all; remembering the pain too. The amusement tapered off to silence. "When the chief screw calls to see me in the hospital, he's well satisfied with the surgery. 'That'll teach you to fart in church, Harney,' he says."

The Canon said, "Don't apologise, Harney."

"Thank you, Canon."

"And then?"

Harney raised his hands in a kind of alleluia. "For two months I'm the most visible man in Europe! Restored the confidence no end."

"Excellent," the Canon said with a warmth of sympathy. "There were the usual remedial consequences, repercussions, I suppose?"

Harney nodded. "Oh, tablets, the needle, all the old tricks. And of course the odd blast of electricity." Harney was momentarily agape, caught in some thunderous explosion. "You come out of that," he whispered, "like you're born thirty and died twenty-nine."

The Canon accepted a drink and they sat in silence. Outside, beyond the strip of stained glass, might be a scabrous scarified world, a flat circle of horizon. Not a sound.

The Canon said, "You decided to be an excellent fellow, Harney, let them see every day, in every way, how restored you were."

"Seven years." Harney was gazing across, past the open door of the Canon's cubicle. "Sorry about the buttons," he said.

The Canon smiled and nodded to accept such courtesy. "You killed Nancy?" he asked.

"Oh yes. Strangled her. Him too. Couldn't stand by and see her shacked up to that half-yellow limbo-dancer with a tuning fork in his gob."

"Of course, of course."

"I'll tell you a secret, Canon," Harney said. "I always wanted to be a priest, really. Would you credit that? A man of God! Me! I could have done so much. Improved mankind."

"I'm convinced of it, Harney," the Canon said. "Of course they've abolished the death sentence, you know? Humankind, that is. I think God might be getting round to it soon."

134

"God's a very funny man," Harney said.

"Indeed."

The Canon left. The sunshine and the church in warmth might even be God, he thought. Outside, the frail beautiful day survived in the walled glebeland of the vanished Dorys. He left behind the tended grass and pathways and moved out into the perished village where sunshine fell on weeds and bald compacted hillocks . . .

*. . . And then he was in the crammed riverside throng again, moving untouched in some spent soundless moments of how long past? He watched the faces he might have known, stared towards the distant frame of the land-dredger where he might see himself in sweat, knee-deep in drying sludge and rot . . .*

Catherine Delacey, as she moved about the morning care of the Rectory, upstairs, downstairs – a swift appraisal and maintenance of rooms and staircases and corridors, the broad foyer – she took with her a little sadness at the absence of Ada, gone on a last hopeful journey: she had found a path through every day and unobtrusively slipped away at the end.

"Do you believe in God?" Catherine Delacey had asked her at the beginning.

Ada had to wonder about it.

"I think so," she had said. "I suppose."

"Good."

"Not certain, of course," Ada had said.

"That's how the Dear Man left it."

There was no trace of sentiment or indifference in the pleasantness of Catherine Delacey: how many wards had she paced with identical warmth of smile and reassurance for each departing face?

"Likes to have the 'nobs' about, don't He?" Ada had rambled. "Flags and bugles in the Abbey, all them bishops' rigouts, gold and jewels and hats two foot high, gongs and smoke like bleedin' Fu Manchu . . . faces you couldn't love . . ."

"Only try."

"Shouldn't judge Him by the company He keeps, I suppose." . . .

Catherine Delacey looked down on the broad staircase, looked down at the foyer, its polished wood, the soft light that always had warmth. Paul Vincent Herlihy had given it his care; and little shuffling Lucy Dory might never have left it.

The drawing room shone in the strange morning quiet and she looked across at Ada's cabin, the drawn curtains, the river beyond it; and behind her, the childhood and gentle pictures of Dory antecedents, a vanished tribe.

She looked at her own ageing plainness in a gilded baroque mirror and remembered her youth, a moment it seemed before an infinite journey. The pitiless diasporic fifties, sixties, she remembered: the weathered-wasted car, coughing, exploding, an ancient achromatic horseless carriage, mud-encrusted – grey perhaps – that had taken her for ever from childhood . . .


. . . She was seventeen, a strapped fibre suitcase beside her, gazing through the rear-window grime at sibling and parental hands raised in farewell. Not the flute-player, of course: one hand held a doorjamb, the other gripped the strong heroic shoulder he had taken for better or for worse; his waistcoat hung open and a tin whistle bedecked each pocket. She looked at his 'crippled' leg, so firm and stout it seemed, so providentially desensitised to every cerebral command except, 'over!'

"You'll miss your father," the hackney driver said; a little unshaven man, pointed as a collie, neglected as his car. "One of the great musicians of our time."

Dear God!

The coast and its hinterland was a patchy rock-studded tundra, rare fortuitous pockets of healthy soil, glacial excrements, distanced from each other, headstoned by squat dwellings and outhouses crouched from the wind. She looked out beyond the cliffs and the rising smoke of spray, saw the Atlantic horizon gathering its dense vapour of rain for the inland sweep. A last glimpse.

"He might have been a fine dancer too but for his leg. A pity."

There were times when it could dance, she thought.

It was five miles to the village, small as a cottier's farm: a few wind-scoured streets; sand from the beach lodged at kerbs and doorways, on windowsills even; tangles of seaweed on the patched sea-wall. Mid-morning, the denizens still slumbered; a few of the élite hucksters took their shutters down on begrimed windows and vanished again. The main street, narrow enough for whispering, suddenly at its extremity splayed into a gaping delta, the venue of markets and the dung and steam of fair-days.

There the bus stood, dirty, battle-scarred, its nose pointing at almost empty miles of famished slobland.

"Off to London to make your fortune?" the hackney driver said. "I should have gone myself years ago."

She watched him drive back towards the coast-roads and cabins she thought she might see again when times were good. She was in tears, of course: everything was suddenly clothed in beauty.

It was eight hours of petrol, burning oil, body smells, blind steamed windows, to another side of the world, the Dublin quayside and its cattle-boats; and how many hours of sea-battering, the moaning death-wishes of illness, shrills of frightened livestock down near the bilges, until morning brought the Mersey and Liverpool out of the mist?

The London third-class train with strapped-up windows, sliding doors, luggage-racks, a mirror, pictures, the smell of steam heat, was a thing of grandeur, a glimpse of decadence . . .

"You're a nurse?" Ada had said.

"A nurse. A long time."

"That man, he's a doctor?"

"Dr Sinclair. A long time."

"You must thank him."

"Yes."

"Everyone." . . .

Catherine Delacey had hauled her fibre case up the ancient steps of an East End workhouse, hospital; a rechristened pile in post-war euphoric welfare, painted and scrubbed, shafted for lifts and yet dominated by its towering stone staircase and iron banisters.

Now, a neglected shell, she thought. The full circle? A workhouse soon again.

It had been the Victorian generous dustbin for aged worker and scrubber, and she felt the smell of poverty and grief still seeped from the painted brickwork. It had its wings, then, for toiling and dying, segregation of tottering male and female.

Now there were the signposted catacombs to empty spaces; sometimes, not a sound. Or perhaps a distant lift with what cargo aboard? A discarded walking-frame.

"Catherine Delacey?"

"Yes ma'am."

A handshake; and following this past-middle-aged sister tutor, endlessly at speed it seemed, to probationers' dormitories in a distant part.

"Frightened?"

"A little."

Six beds to a dormitory: a locker to each, a bedside light, a metal wardrobe, keys; a palace; linen whiter than she had ever seen, a water carafe, a glass, a wastebin, earphones for music. From the window, traffic, people down there, shop windows, church like pubs, a street market; gaps too, like missing teeth, and desolate shattered areas of war years stretching away.

She had thought for a moment of the coastal tracks, the smoke spray, the mud-painted hackney, all the roads and sea behind. She had wept a little and turned again to look at the sanctuary she had found.

"I'll send someone."

Days of shock and disbelief, compassion, fear: flesh and meaty wounds, nasal tubes, suctions, drips, flaccid genitals and limbs, suppuration, faeces, urine, descents down remote lift-shafts with sheeted corpses that had smiled perhaps at lunchtime. The preparation of the dead . . .

"Patients are people."

"Yes."

"The dead are people."

"Yes."

"We are people."

Twenty years she had spent in that formidable castle: faceless probationer, starchy nurse, 'sister' in blue, 'staff'. No further. Desks were for the ambitious, the tiring. And with each year she had moved towards those strange columbariums of the aged. Ten years stalking that geriatric limbo, souls in penny arcades, watching their loneliness on arrival, their desertion; faces and bodies with the ghostliness of an old beauty still about them; white lips, red with excitement how long ago, had pressed others? and flesh had felt flesh and minds had reeled in the final moments of love; they had been beautiful and seen beauty in each other. Now they drowned and wept in incontinency and died one interminable second to the next. They could watch each other die, await their turn in half-assuaged pain; or be poked and pricked by schoolboy housemen, practising with needles and nostrums.

Catherine Delacey talked to them, whispered, despatched them when they asked to go: watching the end of pain and battered life was more cleansing than prayer and fasting or interminable ecclesiastical silences . . .

It had been Ada's birthday on her day of arrival. She took tea with her.

"Important, am I?"

"Why not?" Catherine Delacey had said. "You look quite grand with pretty market delft, a birthday card, flowers on your table."

"Bombs tumbled everything. Only the river's the same." She had looked about her room, its fire, its curtains, its rug. "Doll's house."

"A doll's house for everyone soon. Home. Grass and trees, a church spire."

"It's good to come home."

"Yes."

"And go home." . . .

The day's beauty was ageing, a brass glint overlaying the gold; the stones, the vaults, the trees, flung out long fingers of abstraction in the shallow arc of almost winter sunlight.

The drawing room mirrored each light and shade. She turned away from her window.

"Do you love the Canon?" she had been asked once.

"Of course."

A chill was arriving with the fading brightness.

She went out of the polished foyer and walked in the churchyard, looked at the sheen of the river. It was near low-water. The first breeze of the day came, a coldness, the dry scutch of the trees. The tide would soon be on the turn.

She stopped and said aloud, "I see a cowboy, cross my heart! A garden gnome! It moves!"

Maverick Flynn was urinating against the wheel of his van when she reached him, thumbs wedged in his gun-belt while, like a performing dog, he eased himself: he put away his appendage and adjusted his dress without undue delicacy.

"Well, howdy-howdy, dear lady," he said to Catherine Delacey. "Hope I didn't shock you plumb rigid now, did I? A dazzling chick shouldn't be exposed to nature in the raw."

"I was moved to tears," Catherine Delacey said.

A strange grinning homunculus: he tilted his hat forward, set the pendant corks on its rim swinging. "To keep the flies off," he explained. He still adjusted his dress.

A thoughtful Catherine Delacey looked at a slack red gusset stitched between legs and chaps. "Unlimited, attractive accommodation, I imagine," she said. "For flies."

"Danged if the lady ain't sharp as a tack," he said. He took a plastic case from a pocket of his preciously frilled doeskin jacket, cracked a match on a high-heeled boot. He smoked a cheroot as long as a pencil.

Flies, Miss Delacey thought again: he was a near-middle-aged shrunken runt, moustached, sidelocked.

"'Maverick Flynn'," Catherine Delacey read aloud from the van, carried away in the spirit of this comic entr'acte.

"One and the same, you ripe young thing," he said. "My Riverboat Men is stakin' out the scrubland for the sweet scent of bacon and beans."

A small mountain of equipment had been off-loaded and hidden under plastic sheets.

"That's five-six grand in hi-tech," he told Catherine Delacey. "Five-six thousand, dear lady. We'll be set up in there quick as a trick. On full bellies, that is. Be safe for now in this little old churchyard. Not bandit country, is it, ma'am?"

"A graveyard," Catherine Delacey said.

He studied her from ankles up, pausing where it was sweet and lush; her plainness didn't worry him. "I'll be danged if you ain't a well-made filly," he said and blew out a great ball of smoke. "You an' me could burn a few trails, Mary Lou. Bed down night-time in the scented pinewoods."

"When you had beaned-up, no doubt," Catherine Delacey said, "and pissed on the campfire."

He called in her wake, "Tomorrow night, Mary Lou, don't you forget it! It's the big sound, honeybelle. Blow your pants off! Now that'd be a purty sight for sure."

He moved off, tipped his stetson. He was gone. Her laughter pealed out; a beautiful sound in the fading peace.


The Canon had left Harney with his booze and madness, and the perished dream of Nancy, and walked for a long way in his own madness, the silent world that could enshroud him, where all of them, somehow, might have belonged.

When it faded, sound would return; and desolation where there had been a teeming shoreline of trade and vice and poverty.

The sound that reached him now was the voice of Catherine Delacey. From the shadow of the Mortuary, where he had arrived, he saw her confronted by this hobgoblin cowboy.

A vulgar little fellow, the Canon thought, with a cheroot; and a red patch on his crotch; he watched him strut about his prestigious piled equipment, tip his hat. Then he was in his van with its forward seat and built-up pedals, lifting off in a spurt of gravel.

It was then Catherine Delacey's laughter had pealed out: the Canon, untroubled, watched her move across the churchyard into the barren ground and Ada's cabin.

141

She would keep a vigil with Ada now, sit by her until Matthew Sinclair's morticians arrived. He watched her out of sight.

The sound of the cowboy's van had faded but a fresh sound, a heavy hammering roar, was in the air. Father Jim's delivery had arrived. The brewery men were throwing open the churchyard gates and a twelve-wheel juggernaut, groaning with the burden of weekend alcohol, threaded its way to the People's Hall.

The Canon emerged from cover, came to meet them.

"Your beer, padre," the driver said.

The Canon smiled.

"Where would you like it?" A little less courteous now, faced with the Canon's unhurried complacence.

"Around the corner," the Canon said. "Can you reverse?"

"They teach us to reverse," the driver said.

"Good. Back off a bit," the Canon said professionally. "Right hand down."

The Canon moved away, a lazy progress, passed out of sight into the shrubbery.

He heard the response: the roar of open throttle, anger, the tear of abraded gravel.

Then the awful crackle and grind of the cowboy's sound system as it crumbled under twenty tons of God's goodwill in keg and bottle.

Harney heard the thunder of the brewery's truck as it crawled in, in low gear. Father Jim's special delivery, to be dropped at the rear of the Hall for Harney to do the final humping.

Brewery delivery men were snarling potbellied sloths, slugs. Harney punished them when he could.

He left the Mortuary and the church and peered carefully towards the People's Hall: there was the laden juggernaut.

There was the Canon guiding it in!

A decent skin, the Canon: the man was sane as himself. Harney went back to his mortuary seat and smoked. He drank a little, looked at the barrel where he had been stripped, held in a silent scream in its depths. He remembered the spinning awful nausea. The earphones. Jesus!

The Canon would battle them too. And lose? Sadness overlaid the anger in Harney's mind. The Canon stripped of his dignity, Harney thought, locked in some holy madhouse, gone out of reach for ever.

Harney drank again. It might be a bloody battle! The Canon would stand: to stand was the thing.

Harney had learnt, a long time ago, that in running there was no hiding-place; he could look back over decades to his teens, to desolate blighted schooldays, when for two years he had kept ahead of the attendance-men, the 'bounty hunters'. But they had nabbed him in the end, placed him in care of dedicated Brothers in holy orders who had instilled the three Rs, implanted them; instructed him in the trombone with a blackthorn stick. He had hit a flat C before the Lady Mayoress on a sports day and he could still remember the remedial horrors.

Was there an escape, he had wondered then.

Years at sea had been clean; he had fallen in love with horizons, even storms, until the randy piano-tuner had tapped his Nancy's keyboard. He looked at his hands. All accounts settled. A sojourn behind walls and doors had expiated the sin, rearranged the mind, they had told him . . .

It was at that moment the truck's roaring hammering cylinders had reached him and he had gone to espy it, and the Canon.

Now he was back in his mortuary seat, resting a while: the brewery squabs could off-load the holy booze; the humping could wait.

But Father Jim arrived.

"I was walking the riverbank, Harney, looking back at the churchyard and its 'village'. A fine piece of ground."

"Five acres, five million. A rough guess," Harney said.

Father Jim didn't discuss finance with Harney. Day-to-day truckings perhaps. But ecclesiastical millions!

He essayed amusement, disbelief. "Five million!"

In early parochial zeal, in this plot of aggrandisement, he had seen only a churchyard sitting in waste. Its location, its primeness, had hardly importance. Bazaars, booze, weekend gigs had been the earners in Father Jim's world.

"Millions?"

"A rough guess," Harney said.

"Five million?"

"Maybe ten. The Canon is a rich man."

Father Jim wondered at Harney's cunning: only in the space of the year past had he, Father Jim, been made privy to the vastness of this subterfuge.

Harney said suddenly, "We're the dummies, you and me. You don't think we're important, do you? A couple of backstage bums to keep the alleluia show on the road."

Father Jim was agape, beyond offence.

"The big battle is fought somewhere else. We're bums!"

"Harney!"

"That bishop fellow, he didn't promise you a cosy well-heeled parish when the dirty work is done, did he? And Harney is noted in high places! Ha! They'll have another dirty job for us when Bang Bang is under lock and key. Bums!"

Harney's caustic summation had the awful ring of truth, Father Jim knew at that instant. The Canon, the priceless ground, the episcopal anxiety, at once equated with reason, he knew. Enthusiasm ebbed, paled. Suddenly he glimpsed his own minuscule importance in this megaplan. A dummy. A stopgap!

He saw that Harney, nimble-witted, held him in scrutiny now, and felt a bitterness at his boozy craft. But he sidestepped into everyday trivia.

"I met Miss Delacey visiting her cabin," he said.

"Death Row," Harney nodded.

"An unsavoury business really. Hospital is the place for these people."

"Of course," Harney said.

"And Maverick Flynn has arrived, she told me. The sound system too. I had the feeling she wasn't enamoured of him. A charming little fellow. Strange."

"All kinds," Harney said. "She might fancy a Flying Nun."

Deceit, humiliation, vulgarity: the blows came from all sides. Father Jim would put on a brave face; he would keep to his task; wounds would heal; this role was not for ever. For a moment he thought again of his unimportance.

"Nunz v Narcos," he said to Harney, spun it out slowly, mouthed it for him. "Have you got it, Harney?"

"Nunz v Narcos."

"Versus narcotics, you see?"

"Very clever."

Often, and now more poignantly at moments like these, Father Jim yearned for the green grass of his ancestors: some old mouldering church without even a clustering village, only his house, the graveyard, hills, a sweeping undulation of pasture, scrub, a lake, a stream to fish in; the church empty between services where he could read his daily breviary and be close to the sanctuary. But they had sent him to this alien place where there must be treachery and connivance to keep close to salvation. The Canon and Miss Delacey, they drank port together, the parishioners whispered. Did they strip and copulate before a glowing fire? He drove the terrifying image from his mind. And this cabin of the dying. Dying? Despatched?

'Sent to judgment before God had called them.'

The Bishop's pronouncement: frightening, without forgiveness, un-Christ like.

Father Jim had begun to doubt: he could have wept. He remembered the unworldliness, the great expectations of seminarian days, and lingered until the silence was broken . . .

It was a crackle, distant, as of a great conflagration; faint voices too.

"Did you hear that, Harney?"

Harney nodded, yawned his indifference.

"What was it?" There was danger creeping into Father Jim's melancholy; choler, yellow as jaundice.

"The beer truck shunting about," Harney said. "Every foot nearer the door is a mile saved for lame dogs from the brewery."

"The *beer*, Harney?"

"The beer has arrived."

"You should be out there, Harney!"

"They'll come for a signature."

"A signature?"

"Then I'll check it, keep the bastards waiting."

"Your language, Harney!"

Expressionless, Harney considered it: Father Jim's harassment, green beneath green-studded cap, brought to him agreeable sensations. He would twist the holy gut a little. "The Canon," he said, drumming with iron fingers, very irritating. "I'm having a reassessment."

Father Jim was adjusting, but losing the battle with anger, a deadly sin. "Reassessment with who?"

"With myself."

"A bar-steward, Harney," Father Jim said, "should physically check the arrival of stock, pencil in hand. Assessments, reassessments of canons or draymen are not in the contract."

Harney was deep in thought. "I'd say the Bishop made a balls-up," he said eventually. "And sold you a dummy, Father Jim, no disrespect. A messenger boy. An ambitious young nuncio, he wanted, that's all."

Father Jim sat eyeball to eyeball with him, repeated silent seminary orisons for sufferance. He said finally, "We are all aware that the Canon is disturbed."

"Mad?"

"I prefer 'disturbed'."

"A decent man, I've come round to thinking," Harney said. "Scatters the corporal works of mercy as he goes; visits the sick, comforts the dying. Always a helping hand outstretched."

"The *beer*?" Father Jim said quietly.

"I heard the beer arriving," Harney said.

"And you sat here?"

"Well, a quick squint from the church door, to keep in touch."

"No supervision?"

"The Canon."

A few moments of silence. Father Jim said, "The Canon?"

Harney nodded. "There he is, cloak and all, like Dracula on the flight deck, flagging down a strike force of Harriers. 'Right hand down, that's it. Back off, back off, let her go!'"

Harney enhanced it, rolled his black cigarette. "All the lingo, smart as a stevedore."

Father Jim felt a chill of premonition. "Hardly his business, is it?"

"The helping hand outstretched," Harney added as if concluding his syllogism. And then, the killer-blow, soft as a prayer, "Of course the Maverick and his men came first, dropped off enough electronics out there for a moonshot."

Father Jim was on his feet, groping, fingers reaching for the table's edge.

"Musicians came first?"

"Dropped their gear, went to stuff their guts, that's the routine." Harney sent out smoke and reprobation.

"God, oh God!" Father Jim mouthed, forgot blasphemy and contrition. He recalled the crackling fire of minutes ago that had now become a splintering explosion in his mind. "Oh God!"

Harney heard him running through the church, the crash of the door at his exit. He drank a little and smoked, remembered long ago the slam of the wicket-gate when he had stepped out from his green-belt madhouse into a world that was seven years older; and had looked at, remembered, his nimble feet dancing away from the Mersey Docks to meet his Nancy, a little porcelain figure, beautiful, her purity so frightening. But she had been naked, locked arms and legs about the yellow piano-tuner when he had come with his white carnations and bonbons. He had killed them then, an iron hand on each throat, listened to them in another breathless battling passion until they were limp.

His magnificent illusion had gone; he was desolate, empty, impotent . . .

Out in the church, the door slammed again; not the sound of a hurried push; a vicious force in the ring of it now. He thought for a moment of the men in leather jackets, looked at the keg of blessed water. No more of that! He drank, put away the whisky, angled the sheath knife for battle.

There was a whingeing sound of grief out there, wandering about the church, coming to rest in the Mortuary!

Not the cleaning scrubbers, he knew: they might whinge

like rapturous satiated savages at midnight, but grief would be knocking on iron doors.

Harney crept through the passageway and peered into the emptiness of the church. He listened. The wind might be stirring again: a door gently rattled. It was darker too, the pale sunshine had been drawn into the greyness.

And then the cowl of the baptismal font moved! The Maverick Flynn's hat!

The Maverick had been whining like a wounded cur, but now he crept from cover, crouched, was on the move.

Harney was amused by the meticulous elegance of this crabbed mannikin, rhinestones and plastic, hat in a forward tilt with its swinging corks.

"Howdy," Harney said, in the spirit of things, left the black fag end hanging from his lip. He was only irked by the sounds of grief and the glare of this little stricken wart. "All down for the hoedown, bless my soul." Harney loped forward with smiling bonhomie mask.

An ugly pug face, he thought: oriental glitter of teeth and eyes, a behatted snarl, sat disproportionately on this shrunken cowboy.

The Maverick said, "Who are you, man, with all this lip and spit?"

The Carib patois, without warning, wrong-footed Harney. He tried blowing out a lot of smoke but composition failed him: he stayed with country-'n'-western.

"Mighty fine dressing-up clothes you got there, fella. Sure as shootin' you got music to match."

The Maverick spat near Harney's shoes. "Yeah?" he said.

A tentacled splash on hallowed ground. Harney looked down at it. His rancour at the visitation of Father Jim had passed and he was placable, magnanimous. He smiled. A small dog, he thought.

"You the yardman here, Uncle Tom?"

Harney's uncertainty showed.

"Tow that barge, lift that bale? You the shit-sweeper, man?"

Harney was suddenly in tune, and harmonious too. He carried it off with style and a little rumble of laughter. "Well, you could call me the head wrangler if we was being formal but we ain't. I was jes' going to ask a little favour, like," he said. "A mite presumptuous, maybe, but dang it, I got to ask."

The Maverick spat again, closer.

Harney didn't look; he said, "I got to wonderin' if in this whole crazy fireball of music, you ever got to playing 'Springtime in the Rockies'? Without sound, that is."

Harney hadn't seen the battered microphone and a torn yard of flex in the Maverick's hand; he heard the whirr of it, like a bolas.

Consciousness was lost in a white surf of light. Its absence was for moments only; as he raised himself from the cold flags the door was crashing shut in the wake of the Maverick. He felt his forehead, explored, brought away a bloodied hand: the world was in a slow dance; he was on tilting shifting ground.

The warm clasp of a drink, he thought.

He half tottered, trotted, to the Mortuary. Without care he took a bottle and drank. Nausea hovered and faded; warmth and measured breath returned; the blood trickled on his face. The cowboy! The cowboy, the performing flea with a hat and rhinestones, was *dead*, he decided. And who had sent him?

In a triangle of broken mirror from the shelf he looked and beheld the man! The bloodied ridge across his hairline had the spiky sanctity of a crown. He took the linen veil from the Virgin in the crib and with blessed water and whisky cleansed and purified the wound. Then, like a Lascar deck hand, he twisted himself a turban.

For a while, scrambled, drowsing, awaking, he remembered the old times: the screws, the boots, the keys, the needles, the rubber wedge. He made a cigarette, drank again: the ache receded, he drowsed. He drifted back to trombone days and the holy Brothers . . .

. . . Once, before his schooldays' capture and sequestration, he had watched the great Dorsey on 'celluloid', had heard the golden trombone, had been borne heavenwards on 'Song of India'. In captivity, it had returned: he had crept to the

149

band-room, mute in hand, to strive for such beauty. But a saintly Brother Benignus, slithering like a Bombay thug, had, with a flailing palm, left him almost in paralysis.

"Music, you call it! Music!" Ears ringing with each clattering swipe. ". . . ravings of diseased and degenerate minds!"

In further enlightened punishment, for four weeks, he had played prescribed dirges of sacred tonelessness. Again, again, again!

He had thought there was no escape from this 'prison' but inspiration had sprung from the atonal agonies of his days.

Carnal knowledge of Agnes Mullane, scullery-maid and skiv, was beyond even the tolerance and forgiveness of this reformatory and its celibate anointed screws.

They had expelled, expunged him. Escape!

He had never known her name till then. She had been the 'ginger piece' in the kitchen. He had climbed through her window and when he had been at the very moment of ineffable joy, she had 'resigned' herself to ecstasy and squared herself with God. "If you do this to me," she had said, hoarse as a crow, "you won't have a day's luck for it." . . .

Funny, Harney thought, he never had. He ground out his cigarette, took his whisky again, and locked himself in the Canon's cubicle. There was a light-switch but he knelt on the prie-dieu in darkness. There was almost peace from a pulsating dome of forehead; he slept.

Not for long.

Awful inhuman screamings, the ravings of Mrs Murphy, mother of groin-stricken Francis Xavier, curator of the altar, its brass and linen and all things holy, ripped the church air with explosive terror.

Harney drank, raised his bottle again, again. Maybe, he thought in hope, she'd broken a leg dusting her statues and brass candlesticks.

Silence: then the sound of the scrubbers, Doll and Flo: mynah-bird squawks and screeches. It was a babble of sound and crosstalk, banging of doors, clashing, colliding in the hollow church. Endless, unbearable. Harney's watch was in the darkness of the cubicle; and he needed darkness. But he began his countdown. Two minutes would be blast-off. He'd clear the house. The uproar beat on his wounded head!

There was the final crash and bellowing; and then, the diminishing bovine groans of Mrs Murphy rushing into the distance and silence.

Harney wondered about the confusion of the world, people locked in madhouses, people locked out of them. Peace was returning but so were Doll and Flo. Oh Christ! he thought. With heels hammering like pistons they arrived in the Mortuary. He opened the door a paper-thin crack to watch them.

"Fuck my old boots," Doll said.

Flo nodded. "A madhouse, a madhouse, we're in a madhouse!"

"Deadhouse."

They sat at the table. "Don't know about you, love, but Dolly Durkin's having a blow."

They smoked long gold-banded cigarettes, heads nodding, tipping, tilting, like jumpy hens in a farmyard. Silence. It was – for them – strange.

Suddenly Flo said in a voice, off-key, hardly her own, "She said it was the *Canon* but couldn't see him proper. A black shadow flying round the church! Ten foot off the ground!" Flo rapped the table. "That's what she said, that Murphy mare, the Canon flying round the church, ten foot off the ground! Stick a pin in me, love, will you?"

"Black shadows, madhouses, deadhouses, Harney in heat, that Father Jim, in his cap, squinting round corners. Cold enough in here to store corpses."

Flo settled herself in a vicious anticipation of further thunderbolts. "That Harney slug," she said, "there's something not right about him, you know. Something odd."

Doll went to Harney's boxes and brought back whisky. "Something serious, I hope," she said; she slopped prodigal measures in the teacups.

They drank.

"All that booze in his belly," Flo said, "and ringing his bells up there like ding-dong on an ice-cream van."

There was silence: Doll replaced the whisky bottle, they

151

smoked, waited to emerge from this fairground chamber of horrors.

"Naw!" Flo said with a suddenness that rocked Harney on his prie-dieu. "The Canon couldn't do nothing like that!" She looked to Doll for some screech of wild derision; or smoke, or profanity. "Could he, love? All eleven stone of him flying round the church, touching up Mrs Francis Xavier Murphy, swooping away with her stepladder in his beak . . ."

But Doll was frozen in pragmatism. "Leaves the ladder out on the gravel, love, don't forget. Couldn't have walked, could it?"

Harney, turbaned, flung open the door of the cubicle, surveyed them, said with a soft lilt, "Afternoon, me old scrubbers." He smiled his professional smile. "Overwork is what does it, overtaxing them little scraps of brain God had left over, leads to sleepless nights, hallucinations, and 'the bottle' in the end, you couple of thieving over-the-top sparrow-farts. If I wasn't in a hurry and the ground conse-crated, I'd have the two of you on the table before you could screech for hustler Jim and the Temple Traders' Association!"

Doll and Flo were on their feet, crouched and poised for combat.

"Don't touch me, you rapist!" Doll said. "Coming out of that box like Doctor Who with the clap." She gazed at his head. "Fancy dress, is it? Like one of them jossers in the crib. A Wise King, maybe?"

Flo showed him her scarlet nails. "More like that dozy sheep with the busted leg."

Harney shut it out, pointed to the whisky stock.

Very quietly he said, "No more. Never again, remember it?" He took a delicate swig himself. "Sit!" he told them. "Remember, won't you? Remember! You look like you might break wind, or worse." He thought about it. "Maybe it was you flashing round the church, eh? Broomstick pilots, touching up Mrs Murphy's clouts." He said to Doll, "En-joyed having a mid-air grope, did you?" . . .

But Father Jim, at speed, had come through the church unheard; he stood breathless in the archway.

"Harney?"

They stared at him.

"The Canon!" he shouted. "Have you seen him?"

"I'm getting confused with this Canon situation."

"Harney! Thousands, thousands of pounds! A whole fragile system of amplification ground to dust! The beer truck, Harney, the beer truck! The Canon in charge, remember, Harney?"

Father Jim's lips trembled, he might have prayed.

Harney's mind throbbed in the confusion, the scar ached, the tightness was a long tumescent ridge. He pointed to it and was ignored, commanded to silence.

"The beer truck!" Father Jim roared at him.

Behind the contrite mask that psychiatry and walls and bars had patiently fashioned, bequeathed him, Harney's homicide grin was hiding.

"Well," he said with a calmness to infuriate, "a heavy-duty twelve-wheeler, steel body, full load-up, coming fast in reverse . . ."

Father Jim was seized in a convulsion of rage. "I'll crucify him, crucify him, that sacrilegious godless maniac! And *you*, Harney, you drunken wretch! The Canon? Where is he?"

Doll said, "Mrs Francis Xavier Murphy says she seen him flying round the church like a model aeroplane."

The silence was a thunderclap: Father Jim thought he might strike her; he paced the length of the Mortuary once, twice, a dozen times, gathering shreds of composure.

"The Canon?" he said eventually to Doll.

Doll, with outstretched arms, made a rolling Spitfire motion. "Flying round the church, like I said, ten foot off the ground."

Father Jim resumed his pacing. Harney, unperturbed, a show of contempt, drank a slug from his bottle. Minutes passed. The outside stillness seeped into them, an uneasy pause, it seemed, at the onset of fresh irruptions.

Father Jim stood, addressed them, a strange formality about it all.

"Mrs Murphy," he said, "has had a severe shock. The grievous injury inflicted on her son's . . ."

He was in search of euphemism.

"His thingy," Doll said.

"Little waterworks, Father Jim," Flo atoned at once, made a twitching moue of distress.

Father Jim began to find horror in their glittering faces. Once more, only once, he paced the Mortuary: clipboard held like a swagger stick, he halted before them. "Yes!" he said in a high key of incisiveness. "And *now* this alleged incident in the church."

"On the statue it was really," Doll said. "Up on St Anthony it was."

"Church, statue, Rectory rooftop, whatever, wherever!" Father Jim snapped her into silence. "Mrs Murphy is quite overwrought. We must forget these emotional outbursts. In her disturbed state she is not responsible. Do I make myself clear? Understood?" He paused, waited for nods of submission. "Now, ladies, I want facts. *Facts!*"

There was a whispered consultation, the lighting of cigarettes, and Flo commenced.

"Well, we comes into the church, Father Jim, to dust the seats and disinfect the confession-boxes, and it's dark, like, with them stained-glass windows, and the weather, and only one light on so you can save the electricity . . ."

Father Jim clung to the remnants of restraint. "Yes, yes?"

"Then of a sudden there's this sound! A moan, I thought, like the wind. Doll hears it first."

Doll said, "Yeah, more like a ship lost on the river, really."

Flo nodded. "That's right, love, that was it! A ship lost in the fog."

Hands to her mouth, like a conch, Doll made a foghorn sound. "Like that."

Agreement was reached.

Harney said, "Try not to make a production out of it. Twenty-four hours in one day, seven days in one week."

Narration ceased at once: poker faces, billows of smoke.

Father Jim gimleted Harney. "You'll put that whisky away at once, do you hear? And hold your tongue. These ladies are not in your charge. I'll deal with *you* later."

There was a generous dram of whisky left and Harney

'put it away' with a great beaming smile. He dropped the empty bottle at his feet.

Stillness was like a portent.

Father Jim prompted, "You heard noise, a sound, a moan? And then?"

They were in surly mood now.

"And then?"

Doll relented. "Well, it was the other side of the crowd barrier, see?"

"The *communion rail*? The other side of the communion rail?"

"That's it, the communion rail. I always think of it as a crowd barrier, somehow, holding back the people from God, you know?"

Flo was suddenly upstage. "The side-altar of St Anthony, to be precise, Father Jim," she said. "There's St Anthony, large as life, ten foot up on his pedestal, and Mrs Murphy too, stuck to him, one leg cocked, like something on a wall in India."

They stood up to enact it for Father Jim but he quelled them.

"There was no ladder?"

"Oh no ladder! Out on the gravel you'll find the ladder! She's ten foot up there all right but no ladder!"

Doll said, "We was stood there stupefied, Father Jim."

"That's it, stupefied," Flo confirmed. "I mean, she's high as a Globetrotter, we know, but she couldn't jump ten foot up in the air and land on one leg beside St Anthony."

Father Jim's faith and assurance were tottering. "No," he said. "She couldn't jump up in the air."

"Or down," Doll said.

Father Jim awaited silence again, pointed towards the sanctuary. "There was a rope too," he said. "Flung across the ironwork out there, the satin rope from around the baptismal font."

Doll said, "Well, I told her to swing, didn't I?"

"Swing?" The vision of his distant ageing church in Atlantic poverty, peaceful fields, the sounds of tankards and cattle, so remote, assailed Father Jim again . . .

Flo was expatiating. "What you said was 'Now, like Tarzan in the trees, come to Doll'. That's what you said, wasn't it?"

"Yeah," Doll said. "'Come on, come on', I keep at her. 'Flo and me'll grab you.' But she gets the rope a bit low down and never clears the fence. The crowd barrier!"

"The communion rail!" Father Jim barely found voice.

"The communion rail," Doll amended. "She didn't clear it, Father Jim. Does a half-somersault and hits the deck. 'The Canon can fly!' she says, a kind of rattle, like she's knackered, fit to drop. 'He can fly, he's a bird!'"

Delicacy had a moment of restraint. "Even . . . touched her . . . she said . . ."

"Yes!" Father Jim halted it.

Flo released symbolic smoke. "And suddenly he's gone. Ladder and all, out in the graveyard. That's what she said. One minute it's a bird, the next it's the Canon with wings. No holding her, she's off, hopping on one leg out of the door, on to the gravel, and trips over . . . guess what?"

"Yes, yes, the ladder," Father Jim concluded it.

He must flee from them, he thought.

"Her son's disfigurement, remember, passing though it is, has distressed her," he said. "Rest and sedation for a day or two, that's all." This time he encompassed Harney. "Now, has *anyone* seen the Canon?"

Doll said, "Not since he's larking about with them brewery slobs and they backs into all that rubbish the musicians leave."

From the archway, Father Jim said, "Miss Durkin, Miss Rorke!"

The sudden enunciation of surnames left them wide-eyed, agog.

"To the Hall at once, please, without delay. A lot of neglected work, shoddy work." He paused. "For *you*, Harney, I'll draw up a rota. Come and see me later. And take that ridiculous thing off your head!"

Harney was silent.

"Do you hear me, Harney?"

With strange humility Harney said, "Loud and clear, Father Jim."

"Good."

A breath of wind came and went, a stray moment of yesterday. Stillness again. "Wind and rain," Harney said. "I lived in storms once. She'll blow again tomorrow. Slates flying like razor-blades. The man in his cloak in the midst of it." He intoned, "Take care, take care . . . she'll blow again."

They listened to Father Jim's echoing footfalls through the church, the anger, the crash of the door.

"That's one up yours, Biggles," Doll said.

Flo's amusement lit up her glittering spectacles.

"Move!" Harney said.

They put on high boots, coats, plastic headgear.

"Touch them bottles again," he told them, "and you'll be swimming home in your little goose-pimpled skins with Harney coming up behind like Dinky the dolphin. Get it?"

"Filthy bugger," Doll said. "Wonder God don't strike you."

"I often think about that," Flo said. "He don't strike nobody nowadays. Going back a bit, reading about it, you know, it wasn't bleedin' safe to put your head outside the door. Burning bushes, flaming swords, pillars of salt . . ."

"Foolish virgins," Harney said. "The Man is tired watching us. Getting old, maybe, losing His marbles like the Canon." He drank from his own whisky bottle, stood motionless in a kind of catatonic freeze, staring at the knife-wounds in the table.

Doll and Flo tiptoed away.

In a little while, Harney, in turban, a battered Magus, head bowed in penitence, found Father Jim and the Maverick standing over a transistorised scatter of dead technology.

The Maverick's bolas swung gently, like a pendulum; he watched the approach of Harney, his arrival. They stood in silence.

Father Jim said, "I don't remember sending for you, Harney."

The Maverick cleared his throat and spat: a gob of phlegmy

mucus spread itself on the toe of Harney's polished brogue.

"I'm guilty," Harney said. "Desertion of duty."

"The Canon . . ." Father Jim began.

"The Canon," Harney said, "waits in the Mortuary."

They followed him.

The Mortuary was empty.

With a backswing and bare knuckles, Harney knocked the little Maverick senseless. He strangled Father Jim first, and then the wizened cowboy. He wrapped them in the lime-splashed tarpaulins of the Christmas crib, brought cable in from the debris to bind them: neat compact 'mummies' to be consigned to the deep. On Father Jim he fastened the cap with its sea-green button; on the Maverick, his tall stetson. He laid them temporarily to rest, out of sight, beneath his pyramid of spirit cases.

When the Riverboat Men arrived, Harney said, "An accident. The ambulance took him."

"What hospital?"

"Christ knows. Ask Father Jim."

"Where is *he*?"

"He might have gone in the ambulance."

"What about you?"

"I wasn't here," Harney said.

It was time to roll tobacco, he thought, to smoke, to drink. A great warmth of peace surrounded him.

A decent shipmate, the Canon.

Fast in his chair at the Rectory, hidden in its depths and enveloping wings, the Canon considered with a trace of regret the pulverisation of the great Maverick's sound machine, the very soul of latter-day musicians.

Discourtesy to Catherine Delacey, however competently dealt with by her goodself, was hardly forgivable, he thought: action and reaction, quid pro quo, crime and punishment. Licence to asperse, affront, for irreverence, innuendo, had a price-tag: a sliding scale of vendetta.

A happy, perhaps boorish, breed had been the afterbirth

of wartime: unimpinging boorishness of course among the boorish, in their created milieu. But not for the Canon and his diminishing peers. 'Shock' had been coined a holy word. But it had always been a holy word in the Canon's dogma. The sudden catharsis of a blow well-placed was absolution indeed.

That little cowboy would be absolved. The sonar blowing-away of Catherine Delacey's bloomers, the concept, however in jest, was distasteful, offensive. Well, the hurricane weapon of technology had been spent . . .

. . . Once, in preordination retreat, a saintly divine had counselled Paul Vincent Herlihy: "The flesh, the flesh, it will trouble us to our last days, even to senility, to the very last moments when suspiring desire makes a last stand. Celibacy is a heroic cross to bear."

Almost a song.

"Have you seen it?" the Canon asked.

"Celibacy?"

"Copulation."

An upheld hand for silence.

"I was a foster child," the Canon told him. "Purchased, you could say."

The Canon remembered his vendors, the day, the moment of exchange, a 'donation' in gratitude, arrival in the bleak flatness of border lake country where Ulster Masonry crept into the tight-fenced Catholic fields. A barren couple they were, in seed and sentiment: a bow-legged prognathous male, a female of prodigious legs and buttocks, lightly moustached; a remarkable absence of mammaries. On the wall, a picture of Christ, with a bleeding sword-pierced heart, dominated the spartan kitchen.

"I was fostered," he said again. "I used to watch them, listen to them, shagging like animals."

"Herlihy, Herlihy, there are better words . . . other words."

"Are there?"

A silence.

"You were shocked, my boy."

159

Shocked, the Canon thought. Astounded, appalled, unmanned. A battle of dinosaurs and never a wink or a drip of blood from God's picture . . .

He thought of Catherine Delacey and her fine inviolable dignity. They looked at naked bodies together, washed them, prepared them for the journey, saw a little sadness in each other across the precious remains, the disfigurements, the ugliness. They loved each other: gentleness, a clasp of hands, immense unspoken approbation: that was love.

The cowboy, he thought; the lignum vitae rod in the foyer: '*Ich kann nicht anders*'. Catherine sitting with the dead; the smoked-glass van coming for its freight. He stood, went to the window, looked at the almost unruffled flow of the river . . .

. . . He had sat seven nights with the dying prognathous foster parent, in the dim light, in the thunderous breathing that could diminish to a sigh and suddenly erupt again. The great female would sleep the night and weep in daytime for visiting kin and fellow smallholders.

He had died at midday, a blessed sign, and the Angelus was said about him. A priest came with the last holy oils; the corpse-woman for the laying-out.

People were coming again, always people in clusters of whispering; tea and cold meat; rosaries recited. But he was hardly cold when there was a spectral silence.

A lamp, from its secure shelf, crashed to the ground. On a still day, the windows rattled.

A pale nervous silence; then mutterings and signs of the cross.

"The spirit leaving the body," the corpse-woman said.

And in weeks he had fled himself, travelled the roads for weeks, took work at tillage in a seminary. A strange journey to priesthood . . .

He went back to his chair in the drawing room and listened to the stir of the wind, the end-of-autumn rustle in the trees: the evening would close in now with a depth of darkness and rain creeping up from the estuary. It would be a strange evening; it had been a strange day. Lottie and her midnight homicide was ahead; Stan-Stan-the-Pianoman, the lover in fear. The Maverick Flynn, the Riverboat Men; Catherine alone with the dead; unhappy Father Jim; Harney blessed with madness; Sinclair; the leather jackets and their paymasters. The Canon wandered among them, saw approaching battles. Sulvan? And the end?

He stood again, a restlessness, moved about, seemed drawn to his window to look across the open ground. For a moment he might have seen the cowboy and Father Jim, arm-in-arm on the riverbank, and then they were out of sight. They moved with the smoothness of shadows.

The house was in silence; only the sound of the fire. He looked at the lovers' chair where Lucy and her poet must have sat to gaze at each other in such happiness; and the shelf of Dory logs and diaries; and leather-bound books of piety.

At parting, on his slim monograph of love for Lucy, the poet had inscribed, let the Cavalier speak it for him:

> Yet this inconstancy is such,
> As you too shall adore;
> I could not love thee (Dear) so much,
> Lov'd I not honour more.

It was darkening, the bruised darkness of winter before its time, a cold vapour.

He missed Catherine's footsteps, the softness of talk and laughter, too long in absence . . .

*. . . He watched almost in drowsiness: the old silent frames were shifting again. Beyond the walls and gates, the crowded streets were forming for him, the wharves, the jetties, the packed gut of moored and crawling traffic on the river; the silence. It was night-time. In the street-lights, tapered iron-cast lanterns straddled corner brickwork, the oil-lamps flickered, smoked; port and starboard reds and greens stirred on the river too, pale mast-lights. And movement was diminishing now: a gathering.*

*Distant, at the end of convergence, he saw the flare of torches*

161

held high, coming from the riverside, the quays, the strips of foreshore.

Outside his gate, the churchyard iron gate and wicket, a long rectangle of cobblestones had been prised loose, arranged with care by the pitiable hobbling midget that was the Maverick; men, Kilmartin and Harney, had dug themselves shoulder-deep into the roadway. He could see the rise and fall of picks, the follow-through of spades.

A grave. A grave at his gateway.

The blaze of torches, nearer now, a tide of waving fists pushing a concourse before them, dragging it in their wake. The crush poured out as from a bottleneck, gathered and settled about the men and the deepening grave: a changing sea of physiognomy, a terrifying sea.

The multitude opened out before the arriving torches; and a silent dray, silent to the Canon even on iron-shod wheels, pushed by seamen, rabble, scruff, whores Doll and Flo, tussling, battling squads, was butted forward. The shafts were lowered, the floor and its contents tilted, exposed: a body, naked, bleached, cockled ecru skin, the hangman's rope like a ring of marquetry sunk in the flesh, the loose end sprawling along chest and groin. Rats had chewed at feet and hands and genitals and eyes, while it had hung over the jetty to be embraced and left cold in the comings and goings of tides.

The grave-diggers were out, the torches flared. The face with ravaged sockets was Sulvan's. He was hauled to the grave's edge and booted, hacked out of sight into his pit. The backfilling of the roadside hole had begun.

The Canon looked out beyond the white blobs and open mouths that must be sending out a thunder of applause, to a raised lantern-illuminated platform where the High Constable and borough dignitaries watched the burial in damnation of this savage. Sinclair sat among them.

And far beyond the converging street, across the marshes, there the gallows and its gantry sat above the water.

Sulvan's grave . . .

Catherine Delacey and Sinclair, returning from Ada's room, rattled the gate, in a single moment banished the past.

He remained at the window.

"You were watching Ada taking her leave?" Catherine Delacey said.

He turned.

"The van," she said. "It passed the gate. You saw it?"

He smiled.

Sinclair had stood on the threshold; now he closed the door, in light-infantry measure marched to the fire. His back to it, he surveyed the room.

"They had good taste," he said; it was his changeless opening sally.

"Comfort is good taste," the Canon said.

"Artists were artisans then, you see." Sinclair left Ada's certificates of death and cremation on the table. A picture above him at the fireplace had shadowed faces, glances of caution, soft light falling across furniture and fabric. He turned to it, peered at the ageing varnish, its shrinkage.

"Painting is illiterate handwriting now," Catherine Delacey said. "I'll make some tea. Smudges, blobs and all." She smiled, determined to be outrageous, thought of Ada. "If you can't read it, you're dull."

"Dull?"

"Excrements of paints."

"Coprology," Sinclair said. "Brown studies." When he laughed there was a kind of 'wickedness' about it.

He looked at home there, the Canon thought; or an actor on some manorial set of the thirties, discretion in the greyness of his suit, pale cashmere waistcoat, the Burberry.

"I'm going racing," he told the Canon.

"Now?"

"Travelling now."

Sinclair liked to wake in the bustle of small racing towns, see from his window the stands and white rails, pastures and woodland reaching away to the skyline: if there was peace for Sinclair, this was close to it.

"Racing, tomorrow," he said.

He was wearing heavy shoes, the Canon saw; gloves and a cap stuck from his pocket. He had left a Gladstone in the hall.

"You'll take tea with Catherine first?" the Canon said. "Then your train."

"And you?" Sinclair asked.

The Canon said, "I have a busy night." He looked at Catherine Delacey. "A lot of business tonight."

She brought him his cloak and beret and stick in the foyer, stood with him a while. The web of mist, lost in darkness, was cold on his skin; light from the open door caught the leaves of a shrub gathering tiny glistening wells and losing them.

He crossed the churchyard, stood at the gateway and looked down at the cobbled track that still survived. At his feet was Sulvan's grave; out on the river there had been raised mud and marshland and a gallows overhanging the flow.

He looked across at the lighted windows: Sulvan's house straddling the frozen dead from the immigrant brigs. And Sulvan would be met again at midnight; he looked across the open ground between rubble and weedy hassocks. And at Sulvan's again. He strode away towards it. From the drawing room Sinclair had called his farewell.

"Till Monday, old friend. Till Monday."

Catherine Delacey watched a moment or two and shut out the weeping darkness. She left Sinclair at the fire.

"I'll bring some tea, Matthew."

Sinclair, a countryman, two generations of doctors before him, liked to walk about the Dory drawing room, feeling the warmth, the polished wood, the great walls that should be built about possessions and the dignity they brought. Sinclair had grown up inside walls like these. There were steps, polished brass plate and door furnishings, the lead-embedded shoe-scraper, a fanlight of delicate beauty that showed racing prints, a mirrored hall stand with its drip-trays and canes . . .

. . . Once, the young Sinclair had fallen, gashed his forehead on the scraper blade. His mother, beloved, heroic, cast for moments of high drama, was in quavering contralto. "My God! my God! he's lacerated, his beautiful face disfigured for ever, for ever . . ."

"Don't coddle him, my dear. Have some tea or something.

Rest, take an aspirin . . ." He was a sturdy humorous man, balding a little: the three-piece suit, 'pepper and salt' serge, watch chain and fob, polished brogues, gold-framed spectacles. Two stitches pulled the wound together; sticking-plaster and a patch of lint was the closure of this surgical emergency.

"All right?"

"Yes."

A pat on the shoulder. "We'll go to Cheltenham on Saturday, eh? Break the 'books'?"

"Yes."

Sinclair looked at pictures of the Dory ancestry: dour, well-dressed peasant men. Horatio Samuel Taylor Catchpole's graduation-day pose too, with scroll and gown and mortar-board. It brought to mind always his own emergence from Edinburgh: Matthew Luke Sinclair, MB BCh BAO . . .

"We'll go to Cheltenham on Saturday."

The world was at war.

They sent him to sit in colonial airless garrisons: the Gold Coast mines, Sierra Leone, Nigeria. No visible enemy. Only the silent female mosquito, the tsetse, malaria, blackwater fever, alcoholism, madness.

But in Nigeria, deep in the bush, he had met Connel, a struck-off man of medicine. Connel, with African wives and their progeny, drank palm wine, whisky when he could get it, had raised a corrugated-iron hospice for lepers or worse.

"Lepers?"

"They come here to die."

"You put them to sleep?"

"Journey's end."

"Lepers?"

"Rabies too. Water, the sound of it even, to make inhuman screams of agony. 'Animals'. Mad. A scratch, a spit, you're a mad dog in the making. If they run wild, I shoot them."

"Shoot?"

"They come here to die."

And Connel too, Sinclair had thought, compassionate, a gentle drunken man, had come here to die . . .

Sinclair, when all the world's blood had been let and the

165

burning done, pieces of paper signed, had come back to the brave new world. The unforgettable house had been gambled away; and he saw where they had died together, side by side, in magnificent winged armchairs, hands clasped together as on a wedding day.

He had fled to London. A side street, 'SURGERY' painted on an aged shop window, second-hand chairs to line the walls; what might have been a scullery, his reception room. Tap, tap on the bell . . . next . . . next . . . next . . .

In a journal for country gentlewomen, a two-line personal entry had said: 'Needed. Private Doctor'. A box number. He had met Lucy Dory-Catchpole . . .

He was looking at her picture when Catherine Delacey entered.

"We'll eat by the fire, Matthew. Comfortable."

He smiled.

"You knew her a lot of years."

"Near thirty."

"Not always ill?"

"The end only. She wasn't meant for waiting-rooms. Even good ones."

"Nor you, Matthew."

Sinclair smiled again.

Stan, at ground-level now, a drink on the stageside table before him, the floodlight spilling out to catch him and soak into the darkness of the lounge. Lottie stood above him, on the stage, silent for the Canon's arrival.

"I'll bring you a drink," she said to the Canon, was glad to escape.

The Canon listened.

Stan said, "It's still tonight. Mist and stillness."

"The singing," the Canon said; in the rambling house he could hear the faint thread of melody.

"Cracks and flues, I told you. Like stops on a penny whistle."

The Canon sat. "Yes, stillness tonight," he said. "Not a breath to push against a window-pane up there. Or sway a curtain."

Stan was silent.

"Like a warning, isn't it?"

"A warning?"

"The singing," the Canon said.

Lottie came with the Canon's drink, silently, too silently: she had been listening.

"Late, isn't he? Sulvan, he's late."

She had gathered and penned her courage: the dread now was that opportunity might slip.

The Canon had watched Stan, the sutured face, the scar-web, so pale and convex, laid on it.

Lottie said, "When he goes he might stay a week, a month."

"Sometimes," the Canon said.

"Then, he's back!" There was anger and fear. "The same, never a slower step. The same, always the same. Somebody else."

The Canon watched her.

"Once I thought he was dead," Lottie remembered. "Heard the door, his footstep on the stairs but there was nothing."

"Old houses talking to themselves," the Canon said. "Sometimes I hear singing up there in the corridors." He looked at Stan.

"I never saw him for ten when I 'went down'," Stan said.

"You get old in ten."

"Not him. I come out. There he is."

"You get old in ten," the Canon said again.

Stan nodded, looked at his hands; Lottie watched her faltering Pianoman.

"Who knew Sulvan, young or old?" Stan said.

"Or Sulvan dead?" the Canon wondered.

Lottie's knees and stomach tightened in foreboding, but anger was a sheet anchor. "He's not a bloody ghost!" she said . . .

Beyond the bar and storerooms, the main house door had opened: there was the sound of feet, a shuffling. How many?

"It's him," Lottie said: relief for a moment, then wavering resolution.

"More than *one*," the Pianoman said. "Visitors."

They listened to the sounds on the stairs, pauses, movement, the final solid emplacement of Sulvan's door.

Lottie had ears only for Sulvan's footfalls. Doughtiness returned. "It's him. He's back." She held Stan in her gaze until he raised his eyes to meet hers.

"Yes," he said.

It was moving into evening. She switched on the lounge lights and amber and yellow warmth fell on tables, on carpet and upholstery. Gold brocade curtains on the riverside wall became priceless fabric: the shut-out drizzling dark spaced an infinite distance from reality. Lottie stepped down and went on her round of dusting and arranging. Stan's tape recorder spun and his entr'acte medley was cued for action: "This is Stan-Stan, the thirsty man . . ." He sat on his stool, stretched his punished fingers, sent chords out to the warmth, made imperceptible adjustments to an amplifier. Everything was in readiness. He stood and waited for Lottie.

"There's food," she told the Canon.

"Nothing." The Canon thanked her, listened to their muted exit through the bar and hallway. Distantly he could hear her laughter: an excitement, a sweetness. Love. Killing for it had some strange mitigation, a ghostly shadow of honour? Death was a moment's suspension from laughter.

Once, in requiem prayers in his ramshackle church, his own words of *de Profundis*, long ago, had been drowned in the laughter and screech of children in the streets. He had thought of the ephemeral grief of mourners; laughter fading, laughter gone, safe in the varnished box with handles and breastplate of plastic 'brass'.

He looked up. Sulvan was standing at the curtains.

"Park Lane," Sulvan said, "is a greedy hill to Marble Arch."

"It had a gallows tree once."

"Once I saw sixty-five paupers hanged on a bridge," Sulvan said and paused. "I brought your visitor."

"The Bishop's man?" The Canon waited.

"Hand-tailored, hand-shod, not a button misplaced. Park Lane at his feet."

"You frightened him a little?"

"A little for now."

The Canon pushed his drink aside. "The leather jackets?" he asked.

"Soon. They'll come soon."

Sulvan sat with the Canon; the drink was untouched. "Don't kill him," the Canon said.

Sulvan nodded.

"Frighten him."

"A little more," Sulvan said.

"And give him to *me*."

Sulvan thought about it for only a moment or two. "I'll send him to you, Bang Bang. In the small hours. To your doorstep."

"My doorstep?"

"Your gateway. The cobbles."

"I was at your burial today," the Canon said.

"A long journey from the river mud."

"A long journey."

"You saw me there?" Sulvan said.

"A corpse."

"A mourner too."

"A pit dug in the darkness," the Canon said.

"Dead of night."

"In the cobbled road."

"Naked."

"Dishonoured?" the Canon said.

"Yes."

Sulvan walked down through the warm pale gold of the lounge, held back a curtain for a moment: it had turned low-water, the wind spent, a veil of drizzle hung and swayed over the river. He came back to sit with the Canon.

"There was a marsh out there once."

"A gallows above the water?"

The Canon thought of the ship's cabin, the slaughter, dismembered hands: Maxwell, Dowty's fustian tunic, the head cleft with a single blow. Did Sulvan remember?

169

Did he remember the long trudge to death, the almost Christlike stations to the gallows; barefoot, stripped to the waist, along narrow streets, beaten, scourged from yard to yard; the tarred rope-ends of seamen tearing flesh like paper, the nails of outraged whores; the Dolls and Flos, the rabble opening like a mouth before him, opening, closing, the awful terrible beating: torn lips hanging down, hair ripped from its scalp, blood oozing from it? They had hauled him, legs first, the height of the gantry to where McMorrow, the hangman, stood: white shirt, rolled sleeves, fair hair tied at the nape; a black headband, jet against his forehead. There they held him erect; and McMorrow, with a sudden savage elbow, sent him dropping down from the gallows hook. A stout rope, too stout, a ravaged perished body in its noose: death took an hour to creep over him.

And he had stood and watched it, somehow resurrected in hate, restored in flesh and mind: roadworn boots, mud-embedded trousers of frieze, kerchief, shirt, brimmed hat: he might have been tramp or journeyman; a pipe too, his lips tight over it; and lips tight over the shibboleth lilt of Gaelic English. He had watched himself kicking to death: crucified eyes, tongue pushed out like the birth of some skinless rodent.

Until they cut him down, he had come each day to see the tide rise above him and the ebb leave him paler, gnawed, frayed.

Sulvan remembered.

"They brought you in a dray," the Canon said. "Except what the rats had taken."

"Pit and quicklime."

"In darkness."

"Fit for the damned," Sulvan said quietly. "A Master and his bosun. Their poisoned blood for my woman frozen to the deck. Fair. A child too, maybe."

"For love or hate?" the Canon said.

"Hate," Sulvan said. "It doesn't die." He looked at the polished floor beneath his feet. "Down there, what's left. This is a headstone."

The Canon said, "Lottie will kill for *love*. This is her night."

"Kill? . . ."

Staying old was the punishment, the Canon thought; death only the last fleeting moment. Death. Youth went in fear of death, age in fear of living. He looked at Sulvan, saw the empty sockets, the shreds of tongue for a moment. He borrowed a heavy oilskin that came to his ankles.

"I'm going to walk for a long time," he told Sulvan.

"Stand on my grave. Walk down to the empty river, look out to where the gallows stood."

At the end of the hallway the Canon held open the door and looked at the night, stretched out a hand to touch the wetness. There was the stairs climbing away from him; the soft distant singing; or draughts perhaps wandering astray in the massive stonework.

He crunched his way into the darkness, stick shouldered like a rifle.

"I saw sixty-five paupers hanged on a bridge," Sulvan had said.

The Canon walked on through the motionless curtain of drizzle, the perishing stubs and skeletons of industry and vanished skill and artefact. Victory had gone to the screens and robots; up there beyond the twists of the river, the great glare of 'campfires' climbed high up along the crystal threads of rain from the towering City: the world was a printed circuit of nods and winks, a language of tick-tack; invisible boundless wealth was staked and lost and won how many times in a timeless day?

But 'pop' heroes sang for the suppers of starving savages.

"Sixty-five paupers hanged on a bridge."

That was Wexford Bridge of history and ballad-sheets, the Canon knew: the year of Our Lord seventeen ninety-eight. Wexford Town looking across St George's Channel at England's kingdom of Wales from where the swallow-tailed redcoats embarked with guns and bayonets and bullwhips. Now a need for flags and hurrahs again: so soon since Britannia had

171

raised her skirts and fled at Saratoga; Bonaparte tumbling across Europe.

It was time to lock and bar once more the immemorial Irish back door to the Empire's back yard, dowse the last flare of 'ninety-eight's rebellion, punish brutes with brutality.

"Who fears to speak of Ninety-Eight?

Who blushes at the name?"

The Canon sat in the shelter of a coal-hopper and looked out at the impenetrable blackness of the river's midstream. He was seeing the bloody end of its slaughter . . .

. . . *An army of paddy-paupers, destitute, twelve-foot pikes on the shoulder, the pitchfork, the haphazard long-barrelled gun, against fine, entrenched, battle-wise soldiery. The town's houses of implanted loyalists were intact, fortified even, their residents safe, afloat on ships in the harbour; the native peasant houses in flames; women and children stumbled in terror across the fields to find some dirt-road to safety; or to be clubbed and ravished and left to rot.*

*The pikemen were charging now: fusillades from hidden dug-in rifles, ahead, at the flanks, cut them like brittle winter stalks.*

*And he saw Sulvan, powerful, wild-faced, holding aloft his pike, a redcoat squirming like a fish on its point.*

*The Canon looked beyond at the untroubled fields: leaves, the sound of water, shadows on hills; and then at the blaze and obscenity of the town clustered at the estuary.*

*An army of paupers, a pitiable rabble, wavered, rallied, wavered, rallied, fled. The horse and foot of all the King's men drove them deep into death, deep down in the green fields that had once been their own. The Canon wept.*

*Sulvan, lying for dead, slid into cover now.*

*Down at the bridge, sixty-five ropes were noosed for sixty-five shrunken necks. The burning houses were victory bonfires. The bodies dropped and swung like scarecrows. The awful horror of screams of death and fear and anger was like God's punishment for the damned.*

*"Who fears to speak of Ninety-Eight?"*

*Dusk crept into the pall of a dying conflagration; and darkness fell like a lid. Sulvan belly-crawled down to the smoke and smell* of tumbled masonry, close enough to hear the singsong Welsh of English conquerors, laughter of 'brave' men, the smashing of bottles: an endless inch-by-inch crawl to reach the burnt-out deserted rebel ghetto. He reached his forge first, the tumbled walls of it, the roof about his feet. The tools of his trade, even the anvil, were gone, to be dumped in the deep channel of the harbour; the hand-bellows had been slashed, shattered, set alight. He had been O'Sullivan the blacksmith then, and smiths made pikes, smiths were special. He went to the ruin of his back-to-back dwelling. He saw his naked wife first: ravished, mutilated, slashed, her eyes and mouth frozen open in terror: some rebel pike had been found to pin her to the floor. He closed her parted legs and covered her, buried her in stone and rubble.

She had hidden her children; he found them in a wall-cage with fodder, soundless, emaciated to weakness. He took a wheelbarrow and straw to bed and cover them, following the coast, pushed on into the night. When the first light crept up behind him he was eight miles from the burned town. He sat on a road that was hardly a track and looked back east at the dawn, watched the darkness brushed away across countless acres of pasture and woodland, proliferous, shimmering in morning damp; distant herds, bloodstock for sporting days; gourmand nights at the great houses of lords and land agents. And to every land agent, his land agent: five, six, eight? How many? And the peasant pauper on a rented acre paid them all, survived on base potato seed and refuse. And the manor lord? Some great scion across the Channel, seed of noble house, whose bequest or bribe it was, a thousand acres from a grateful Monarch; and the rewarded would never set foot on it, nor his inheriting breed. Only the eroded sack of rent from exacting agent, on his pyramid of agents, would cross water, a mere pourboire, swallowed in London splendour.

Sulvan had turned away from the sun, knelt between the shafts of his barrow, drooped forward like a penitent. He had belonged in a house once: he remembered the naked body, the parted legs, the eyes glaring, the laughter of the King's army. Jesus! he slumped into an overpowering sleep . . .

. . . Consciousness returned with an explosion of pain: a rifle-butt had fallen like a mace across his back. He could focus on them now:

173

*four redcoat cavalry. Three rankers and a gaudy young cornet, a peacock in his uniform, an empire in his face.*

*The cornet said, "Get him up!"*

*They kicked him until he stood and balanced; felled him and kicked again. He crawled to a roadside tree, hauled himself upright and lay with his back to it.*

*"Yes," the cornet said. "A big one, by God."*

*A ranker held a sabre with both hands across his throat. "Who are you, you pox?"*

*Sulvan looked past him at the countryside, hills, clouds piped along the skyline.*

*"Who are you, pox?"*

*Sulvan knew their language but he spoke in Gaelic. "I am a man in his own country."*

*They spun him, saw blood on his shirt, his forearms, blood matted in his hair.*

*The mounted cornet smiled. "Black hands, hasn't he?"*

*The hands were gripped, held out for inspection: the blackened hands and nails of his trade; forge-dust, case-hardened with fire and bellows.*

*"Smell his clothes," the cornet said.*

*"A blacksmith, sir! Limping Jesus, a pike-maker!"*

*"Make him a cap," the cornet said.*

*They were equipped for sport. Sulvan's hands were strapped behind the tree, his scalp kneaded with pitch; his ripped-off shirt was pitch-soaked too, shaped into a skullcap, set alight. When it was ablaze, it was raised with a sabre and dropped on his head.*

*Sulvan's screams echoed across the empty countryside, agonising, horrendous, unbearable.*

*"Filthy lice," the cornet said. They galloped down the winding track, out of sight, out of hearing . . .*

*Sulvan's consciousness was on the brink, and madness flickered in his mind. There must be a last effort, or death. He gathered air into his lungs, tightened every muscle, and his shout must have been heard in the farthest hills. The strap had snapped! He fell on his knees, with his hands tore off the burning cap, taking long strips of scalp and hair with it. He held his head in the roadside ditch to dowse the flaming, burning mess, tried to crawl to his barrow. Consciousness slipped away.*

*The day and the night had passed when he awoke. He had been lodged carefully in a dry dyke, hidden away, his barrow with him. Pain was a blinding throb, unending. Some salve had been painted on his wounds and he could feel the tightness of a bandage and a hat pulled low on his head; a ragged jerkin hung on his shoulders. There was no sound: morning fields, hills, herds, bloodstock. People were locked out of sight. The Samaritans had come and vanished: succour for rebels earned the 'rope' or a cabin knocked about one's feet.*

*He raised himself up, joint by joint: ankles, knees, hips, hands spread apart for balance.*

*A cloth had been placed on the barrow too, a white laundered cloth. The children were dead. With his hands he scooped a shallow bowl in a gravel patch and tipped them into it, backfilled with his feet. Bodies were the slough of death.*

*When darkness came he moved away into the night . . .*

. . . The Canon saw the river again, the webbed miles of drizzle, rectory windows. An hour passed, or minutes or years.

How many years had Sulvan tramped the roads, taken a ghostly woman, and then, for a mud windowless cabin, a piece of sour ground, tied himself to a master? The Canon saw him, hard, gaunt, hair longer, covering the shiny barren stripes on his scalp.

*Soldiers again now and fashionable men on horseback watched Sulvan's cabin pounded to rubble. There was his crawling pregnant woman. They were pushed on the road, watched out of sight. Cottiers and tillage were troublesome; cattle grazed, there was money in beef . . .*

*It took ten days to reach the fair port of Cork where a Dory Master and bosun loaded to the gunwales with emigrant 'ballast'. Once, travelling empty to London was a debit on the ledger, now flesh and bone was a valuable ballast; and what lay sprawled on the open deck was bunce for the Master.*

*It was winter. Sulvan's bellied woman, a wraith, perished, frozen to the deck. A mile downriver from Dory's, careful of the decking, they chipped loose the brittle body with axes, piece by piece: arms, legs, torso, made a hessian parcel to dump with filth and waste in the sludge by the jetty marshland where Sulvan built the first room of his brothel.*

"In the year of Our Lord, 1806" . . .

The Canon moved from his shelter, saw the great towering monument of Sulvan's now, the churchyard, a light here and there starlike in the drizzle. He looked for a moment at the river. Only blackness now. He began to walk towards the Mortuary with its faint glimmer of stained glass.

The Canon in oilskins and beret was a shadow moving into the churchyard. He stood on the grass and sodden leaves where Lucy Dory-Catchpole and her warrior-poet, Horatio, so often brought their own orb of summer; he touched the jagged stone that marked the grave . . .

. . . He was remembering again his totter's pushcart at the gate, the walk to her doorstep where she was waiting, with dead Horatio, to receive him. A rag-and-bone man to tea. Had she sent for him or had he been drawn back to where the land-dredger had stood and he might have been hip-deep in river muck? Had he died out there under the great poisoned befouled river that gave him solace now? Had Sulvan sent?

Lucy Dory-Catchpole's face had always been beautiful, he remembered, in the last months of distress even, reassuring him day by day.

"Why?" he had asked her.

"I can leave when I please. I'm not imprisoned."

"Age is imprisonment?"

"The door is never locked."

Lucy's smiling God could have no doubts Himself. The Canon took a wet leaf from the grave, a talisman, and pushed it into the coarse pocket of the oilskin . . .

There was light from the drawing-room windows where Catherine would be sitting; and, more distant, the faintest

176

glimmer from beneath the eaves of the Mortuary. The Dory bookshelves had their dedicated tomes of outdated encyclopaedic knowledge, diaries of males and females of Victorian conquest and derring-do; ramblings of Empire-builders; the logs.

A long-forgotten estimable lady from St Albans had recorded; and Catherine had read aloud.

'I spent Autumn with N and H in western Ireland. What beauty they have created within their magnificent home and its countless surrounding acres of grass and woodland. N has an ice house to keep his salmon fresh, magnificent beagles and horseflesh. He is so capable and ingenious. H adores it all. But not more than a mile from all this bliss one finds surely the most tattered and retarded humans imaginable. They are quite impossible. N despairs at their improvidence and prays that perhaps this present wave of self-imposed hardship may disperse them to other climes. I take him to task about this. Our seaports of England, I tell him, are becoming infested with the creatures, bringing vice and disease with them. He was all apologies and H laughed so much to see him bested . . .'

Catherine had added, "And after dinner the men had pisspots in the dining room. Droit de seigneur."

Recalling it, the Canon could laugh; but he thought too of Sulvan and his frozen corpse, infested creatures, vice, disease . . .

Harney was in the Mortuary; smoke hung on the air, in drifts, in motionless banks. He was drinking but there were neither traces of elation nor drowsiness. He was sober. The Canon's arrival was a blessed epiphany.

He stood up and shouted, "God!"

"My dear fellow," the Canon said. "Let me see."

Harney's turban had slipped from his head and the garment hung about his shoulders. The scar was a long jagged tear where the Maverick had caught him with his bolas. The blood had congealed in scabrous humps and there was swelling too: a pale blue tumescence like smudges of eyeshadow.

The Canon seated him gently and brought a first-aid box from his cubicle, wooden, brass-hinged, with a tray on top, a drawer beneath: another Dory utility that had sailed the seas. The Canon had restocked it.

With lint and antiseptic, he carefully cleaned and tidied the damage, covered it with overlapping strips of dressing. He sponged the blood from Harney's hair, dried it; brought him his cap and arranged it.

"Now," he said, holding up the spotted triangle of mirror, "you're in charge again."

Harney was crying. "Jesus," he said, "I was never helped like that before."

"Did you fall?" the Canon asked.

"I was dive-bombed," Harney told him.

"Dive-bombed?"

"Poleaxed."

"Ah."

"The little pox-ridden cowboy."

"The Maverick!" The Canon thought of the scattered debris and wailing rage. "My poor fellow."

Harney steadied himself, was a little abashed by the sudden rush of tears.

The Canon poured him a drink.

"Small people. Sometimes very vindictive, you see."

"Bastard little midget!"

The Canon waived apologies.

"Could have killed me."

"Possessions," the Canon said.

Harney nodded. A decent man, the Canon.

He drank; he could stretch out his legs and feel the canvassed 'mummies' in their hiding-place. He was pleased.

The Canon waited.

"Do you ever play 'Springtime in the Rockies'? I asked him. That's all! 'Springtime in the Rockies'. And like a hammer-thrower, he swings a microphone, leaves me stretched on the flags."

178

"Father Jim will deal with him, I'm sure." The Canon breathed out peace.

Harney showed his displeasure. "I'm a 'drunken wretch' in that man's little book! His little holy book!"

"Drunken?"

"I don't like that word 'wretch', you see."

"Well, they're probably repenting now," the Canon said. "Anxious for placid waters."

"Or lying low," Harney said, touching their canvas grave clothes again with his feet.

There was silence, not a stir; the Canon listened. "The wind has dropped, hardly a blow. But a drizzle. Strange weather."

"Calms before storms," Harney said. "Ask a deep-sea man."

"Bring your bottle," the Canon told him. "We can walk. The river heals, you know."

"Do you find it like that?"

"Yes," the Canon said.

Harney wore pull-ups, a tarred reefer, a sou'wester hat: a Dickensian ghost from the Norfolk beaches. They went across the open ground towards the riverside, past Ada's empty cabin.

The night was black. Shore-lights, distantly spaced, charted the river. Only in the near distance, the glare of London's money-city, the little sleepless patch, filtered into the drizzle and hung like a shroud.

"El Dorado," Harney said.

"Yes."

"All that fragile glass."

"Fragile?"

"Watch your step," Harney said. "They're going to lock you up."

"Well, I'm mad, you see," the Canon said.

"Mad! Dear Christ!" Harney laughed. "Shipmate," he said, "you're sound as myself. As a bell."

They walked along the desolate granite quaysides: corroded ironwork, rotted timbers, shells of stores and dwellings.

"What brought you here?" Harney asked; he watched the Canon for moments, drank from his bottle.

"I don't know," the Canon said.

"I was coming here all my life," Harney said. "I was expected."

The Canon looked out to where the mud flats had been.

"We all come for something, I suppose."

"Yes," the Canon said.

Harney suddenly whispered, "We're on haunted ground. Up there on the High Road, a half a mile, is it, is another place. There's no escape."

"None," the Canon said.

They stood a moment, looked back at the single cabin in its wilderness; and beyond it, the gateway, the churchyard trees, motionless sentinels in the darkness. Sulvan's pile hung over the river; and his balcony, scarcely visible against the jet shine of the water and distant lights.

"He stands there sometimes till daylight," Harney said. "I watched him once. Never a move. He could be dead."

"You walk at night-time?" the Canon asked.

"I hardly sleep," Harney said.

"You walk the riverbank?"

"Your village," Harney said. "Build your wall first. A high wall," he said; he was looking at the City's glare in the sky. "Keep out the creeping pox. I'll be your doorman."

"A monastery garden," the Canon said.

"'Monastery Garden'!" Harney was breathless, singing now, hands flung out to conduct an unseen mass in the drizzle and darkness. "A great man, Ketelby. I used to do him on the trombone. And 'Bells Across the Meadow'. Ah, dear Christ! . . ."

"Very beautiful," the Canon said.

"Build your wall high," he said again. "And then your narrow winding street." Harney stopped, envisaged it.

"Small windows, eight panes to a frame?"

The Canon nodded.

"Front doors, chamfered laths with iron knobs and thumb-latches?"

"Yes."

"Tall chimneys?"

"Yes."

"How did I know?"

The Canon wondered.

"You'll buy old bricks too, and heavy slate. Nothing new.
And street-lanterns on the brickwork. I knew streets like that,
whole towns of them. Places to live."

"And die," the Canon said.

The tide was rising, seeming to slow the sweep of the
river. Caught in pockets and angles were thick skins of
refuse and scum; scum hugged the river wall too, moving
a while with the flow, then, caught in the tide, eddying back
to its starting-point.

"A man told me once," Harney said, "that up in Barking
his father's father ran across the fields at Creekmouth and
dived in clear water, would you believe it?"

"No," the Canon said.

They were walking now. Harney knew the gaps in high
barriers from wharf to wharf, the fallen jetties, the stubby
fingers of creekland. The mist, hardly a vapour, was a sweat
on their faces.

"Listen!" Harney said.

They were in the shelter of a wartime Nissen, smashed,
eroded to a single arc. There was silence.

"Always something moving here in the darkness," Harney
whispered.

A thud, dull, heavy, muted, reached them.

"That's it," Harney said.

"Late workers."

"In rain and darkness?" Harney grinned.

He was moving with caution now, the Canon in his wake;
he knew the twists and turns everywhere.

"You're an old hand," the Canon said.

The ground rose a little and, at its crest, remnants of a
fence, long in decay, made gaps of concealment.

"See?" Harney said; he pointed down.

Not a glimmer of light. It was a derelict jetty, small even
in its prime. A forty-footer, old, patched, pulled out of some

scrap basin, was berthed, its stern decking padded with foam and tarpaulin. Steel drums, rows of them, ribbed for strength, had been loaded. The last, hung a moment in mid-air, was lowered aboard, hand-winched for silence.

"Engines make noise," Harney whispered.

They watched the silent crew: the load tied down, hidden beneath plastic sheets.

"She'll go with the tide," Harney said.

He drank from his bottle. Sure-footed, steady, he led the way back to the Dory riverside.

"Ten thousand a week she can clear when the time and tide is right."

"Very good," the Canon said.

"A couple of trips when the tide's on the run and it's black enough. Big men somewhere." Harney looked back at the City.

"Tar barrels?" the Canon said.

Harney laughed. "On the heavy side for tar," he said. "You wouldn't slam them down on deck like kegs of beer for a pub, would you? But what's in them, eh?"

"Liquor of some value," the Canon guessed.

"Or dangerous," Harney wondered.

"Dumping?" the Canon said.

Harney was pleased with him. "Dumping, dumping, that's the game! You got it in one. Ten barrels a trip, that's all they load. I counted them."

"To sea, to the bottomless depths," the Canon said.

"Bottomless depths, my arse!" Harney said and forgot to apologise. "They're still looking back at Southend Pier, and Margate starboard ahead, when the drop is made. Or they might go past Dungeness by mistake. One of these days, one of these days! . . ." Harney warned. "The sea can puke too. A bloody volcano."

The Canon looked at the swollen forehead. "I can see you've improved no end," he said.

Harney drank, held his face up to black mist and exhaled. "God's in His Heaven," he concluded.

They walked back to the churchyard. Harney looked down the river. "A lot of 'tar barrels' out there. I stand in the pulpit and watch the river. And I count. There's a thousand canisters out there, or I'm mad!"

The Canon patted his shoulder. "I believe it," he said. "Rest will restore you now. Be kind to Father Jim."

"I won't disturb him," Harney said.

The Canon listened to his light strut along the gravel path; the sound of the church door came back through the darkness; and then, the return of stillness to Dory's Jetty; only the faint fall of drizzle on grass and shrubs. For a moment, the Canon thought he could hear Harney's laughter. Or was it pain? It faded.

The Canon crossed down to Sulvan's. In the foyer now there was a 'soldier' to take his oilskin and beret. But not the stick.

"A bad night for anything, padre," the soldier said.

The Canon smiled.

The lounge was a bright flash in a storm sky; a place of reassurance to lock out bitter days and nights; or airless glaring summers too, dust and yellow papers. People of style sat at the tables: expensive, reserved, groomed, inculpable men; women of beauty.

Lottie would be in her bar, perched at her till, with staff to dispense, to keep the trays of liquor flowing.

He saw Sulvan.

Sulvan took his presence, quiet, laconic, haphazardly from table to table. When he reached the Canon, he said, "The river will wash away the sins of Mr McMorrow, Bang Bang. Lottie's too. And the Bishop's."

He moved on. A pretty girl brought the Canon a drink.

Stan, old trouper up there, nursed his way gently through the last hour, adorned his mini-stage, an incongruous battered artiste, hobbling across old tunes, loud enough only to raise barriers between table and table, to create pools of privacy. And then suddenly he would hustle them from talk of love or whatever . . . "My lords . . . ladies . . . and gentle . . . men!"

183

He could shoot out a volley of one-liners, hacked as himself, to raise a laugh; or call up a tone-deaf ageing crooner, happy to play gommy 'feed' to Stan-Stan-the-Pianoman. Stan, sadly, would accompany, hold up printed legends behind the quaver and discord: 'PISSED', 'BLOODY AWFUL, AIN'T IT?', 'DON'T APPLAUD'. Moments of an amusing changeless game. And then, standing applause . . .

He drank from his beer jug, half spiked with whisky, watched Sulvan move through the lounge. Out on the river now it was past high-water, the current and ebb would join forces in a great sweep of forty miles to the estuary.

Sulvan raised his glass to him.

"Jesus," Stan said aloud; he looked and saw Lottie at the curtains to the bar: fear had tightened the skin of her face, years had fallen from it. "I love you," she mouthed at him, needing to be loved too.

He nodded, looked down at the yellowed keys, the gnarled fingerjoints. He was singing, and they always listened to Stan, close to his 'mike', talking his songs: the end of an evening. "Oh yes!" he invited them . . .

> ". . . the magic of our singing,
> Of the song we love so well . . ."

Sulvan floating weightless to the sea, he thought. Sulvan, never old, never young. Never dead, the Canon said.

> ". . . Damned from here to eternity,
> Lord have mercy on such as we . . ."

They were standing again now for the last hammering chords, the harmony.

Stan took his applause; his hands were wet . . .

The Canon stood and watched the dispersal, Sulvan moving among them like a pontiff: a word here and there, a nod.

Stan was a graven image at his piano.

When the Canon turned back, the lounge was empty, Sulvan had gone.

The Canon took his beret and oilskin and went out into the ceaseless drizzle. From the riverside, he looked back and upwards at Sulvan's balcony perched high above the sweep

184

of the current. A glimmer of light shone. He found what shelter he could, and waited . . .

Sulvan had brought a drink to Stan, had raised a glass to him.

"You worry too much, Pianoman. Take the day, every day, and what you can get. We all do."

He was looking down the smoky lounge. Maybe far beyond it, at the glass pinnacles of the City.

"Drink."

"I owe you . . ." Stan commenced: the brink of confession.

"You never owe."

Sulvan had moved out of sight beyond the curtains, watched wary staff put the last steaming glasses to drain, to hurry away to lovers and studs. They might have been afraid of him.

Lottie smoothed notes, made pillars of coin that she could pick and slip into plastic bags. She fumbled them now.

"Why don't you marry the Pianoman?" he said; he brought her a glass. "Afraid?"

For a moment he might have sparked whatever anger she needed. "Bring the cash," he said; she listened to his footsteps in the hallway, and high up on the wooden steps to his room.

"Soon," she said, when he had gone . . .

In Sulvan's room, the prisoner, McMorrow, sat upright in an easy chair, expensively wrapped. But his boyish face had aged: for moments it was slack-jawed, misshapen; the glaze of dread was like illness.

His gaolers, expressionless, fleshy, mute, seemed unaware of him. They sat in guard: at the door, one on a tilted chair; the other by the balconied window where the curtains had been drawn. At the sound of Sulvan's keys, they stood to receive him.

He nodded, held open the door and in a moment they had vanished, not a sound on the stairway, a creak or the groan of a timber. He left the room door ajar, less than an inch, the keys in it.

"Courage."

He poured a measure, a brimming one, for McMorrow.

"You'll need it where you're going. Don't slop it, drink it!"

McMorrow drank; he felt not even the warmth of it.

Sulvan unlocked his safe, took a leather attaché case, put a hundred thousand in it. He left it on the floor by his desk, threw open the lid.

He locked the safe again, took hold of McMorrow by his moulded collar. "I must talk with you." He took him through the curtains, on to the ironwork perch above the river.

"Listening?"

"Yes."

"That next green island across the way, where I was banished, brother, a stepping-stone from there to here, wouldn't you say, to this, my neighbour's ground. They sent cheapjack squires to take men's places, to ship us out whatever way the wind was blowing." He twisted McMorrow's face at the gathering ebb. "We sailed up there two hundred years ago, dead or alive. You're standing on holy ground. There's fifty men's bones and their women's down there in the dirt. Mad poxed German kings, a little randy prissy queen and her diary, didn't care much for them or me. But I'll never die. You and your aping breed will."

The faint light coming through the curtains caught shifting margarite arcs of mist on the silky hair of McMorrow. He stood in terror . . .

Sulvan listened.

With her till and stacked takings, Lottie came from the corridor, pushed open the door with a feather touch: the faint stir of air pushed the curtains to outline McMorrow's figure on the balcony. She squatted to lay the till soundlessly on the carpet, saw the attaché case of wealth. Shock and excitement fused. Slowly she raised herself erect: arms, shoulders, flat palms, she struck at the curtains. She heard the choked small thread of terror as McMorrow tumbled into the darkness.

Then she was at the door, calling for Stan: a weeping call, a whisper.

He had come running, caught her, muffled her, held her until the sobbing had ended.

"I couldn't see you up there for ever. Up at that piano for

186

ever and ever. Stan-Stan-the-Weekend-Man, fool on a stool, older and older. And me, the bar-room skiv!"

Stan looked at the curtains, hardly moving, the locked safe, the stacked-up case of twenties; they had been left there, he knew.

He went to the window, threw back its curtains. An empty balcony, the pitch-black of mist and darkness.

He said, "*I* should've done it, shouldn't I?"

"We did it," she said.

Stan shook his head.

"*You* won't be different?" she said; she saw his trembling hands, took them and kissed them.

They went downstairs to the empty locked and bolted house. He went to the bar. She sat alone at his keyboard, read his funny-man cards on the rack, tore them, one by one, dropped them at her feet.

Suddenly Sulvan was there.

She was unable to move, to shape a word or a scream.

Sulvan said, "Your taxi's out there. Your money on the deck. You'll make a mark, Lottie girl."

He was gone. Not a sound until Stan came with a tray and rattling glasses.

"You met him?" she said.

"Met who?"

They drank.

"Met who?"

Lottie brought coats and money; the taxi's diesel hammered outside.

"For us," she said. "This is the move."


The Canon, all in black, had dissolved in the riverside night: the high collar of his oilskin shrouded his face, the pulled-forward beret bent down to meet it. Motionless – for how long, he wondered – he peered out from the single slot of his 'visor'. Downstream, the brickwork of Sulvan's house had become visible, the race of water past it, swinging out to midstream. There was the shadow of a boat lashed at

187

the steps. And somewhere, figures too, big men, the Canon thought, motionless, invisible as himself.

He looked back at Catherine's window and the Rectory, a single tablet of warmth, somehow distant, smaller. She had asked him once, looking at Christ's image above the pediment of the church doors, "Do you feel He's offended?"

"We must ask Him."

"When we find Him?"

"Yes."

"Search parties we need," she had said. "Not sanctuaries." . . .

The curtains of Sulvan's window stirred, a wedge of light escaped and there was darkness again. Now McMorrow's image was there and beyond him, more insubstantial, Sulvan. Sulvan pointed downriver, stood in the deepest shadow.

Only moments passed. McMorrow was flung forward. He turned, balanced supine on the iron handrail for an instant, and dropped in a long scream to the water. The amorphous boat and its crew were already in motion. They would half-drown him first; the rescue then, the Canon knew.

He walked up from the river now to the rectory wall, the gate. He stood on Sulvan's cobbled grave until the car came. McMorrow was encased in filth, a caul of river muck. It dripped from his face and scalp, bled into the texture of his clothing; he retched, hung, ugly, agape, between his minders. The Canon went to the driver, gave him the Bishop's address. "Deliver him," he said, "person to person. No messages, sender unknown."

# Saturday

It was after seven, morning light, when Dowty and Maxwell
pushed along what were now studied back-streets, touching
the riverside at times and then working along the lee of the
crumbling dockland ghost-world. The mist had been drawn
away with the ebbing tide, the starkness uncovered again.
East wind could bleach the ground with the suddenness of
its arrival, in half a morning flail it to dust and motion again:
the river was a turmoil, driven upstream before the rush,
boosted to spread and drown the low-water mudbanks.

They wore their leather jackets.

"Weather," Maxwell said; he gave it a smear and redolence
of raw filth. He switched off the heater, opened his window
and the rush of wind filled and juddered the car.

Dowty leant on the steering-wheel. "Close it," he said.

"Oxygen," Maxwell told him.

"Close it."

Maxwell wound it up: it was like a sudden stillness.

"And no balls-ups this time," Dowty said. "For another
fifteen, no balls-ups."

"For three days' work, duckie? Half a week. We're working cheap."

"Five hundred we have," Dowty told him. "Fifteen to
come. Two grand apiece."

"A piece of Thursday, most of Friday, today is Saturday,"
Maxwell said. "A half-hour's work was the deal, remember?"

"Tomorrow is Sunday," Dowty said. "A day of rest." He
saw the chassis of a giant crane ahead on rusted clay-caulked
rails. The jib and windowed cab were long gone.

He parked out of sight, between the splayed legs, behind
a wind-baffle of debris piled up by a decade of dossers.

"We walk from here," he said.

189

"A mile?" Maxwell looked at the littered ground, the east-wind morning.

"About that."

"A poxy mile."

In a pattern of tacks, following buttressed brick, piled detritus, barns, entrepôts, vestiges of alleys, a moribund world, they came within sight of the church, the Rectory, the People's Hall.

Dowty's face was without pity. "This is a daylight creep," he said. "I'd be very careful, Maxie. You know?"

They reached the wall of the churchyard glebe, and hugging close, ran at speed – black soundless mastiffs – until the church had hidden them from the Rectory. A grip, a foothold, a single swing and they were inside.

"Jesus, that wind," Maxwell said.

Their faces were wet; weeping eyes from the wind and dust-sweep. At the church door, patient, noiseless, they turned the heavy ring and, inside, with the same unwavering patience, secured it.

But, in the Mortuary, Harney was alerted. The cold draught brushed his face. From the archway he listened.

"If he's not in this deadhouse? . . ." He could hear Maxwell, even his whispering.

"We find him. We know what he looks like." Dowty gazed at a snapshot picture again, a signature, 'Paul Vincent Herlihy', appended. He zipped it back in his leather jacket. "We know what he looks like." . . .

The voices.

Harney took the sheath knife from his waist. Murderous bastards! A chance, maybe. A chance.

On the floor, he slid in to lie with the corpses of Father Jim and the Maverick; he drew up the spirit cases to seal his 'tomb'.

Almost in stillness they arrived.

"Nothing," Maxwell said. "The same shit and rubbish we left. Not even the boozy slob we shoved in the barrel."

"We should've listened," Dowty said. "The 'boozy slob' had it right."

Maxwell said, "Micks are thick as planks."

"Not long gone," Dowty said. There was a pause. "You can smell the fags and liquor. But," he said softly to Maxwell, "we don't want *him*, do we? We want Paul Vincent Herlihy." He tapped his pocket. "Paul Vincent Herlihy."

"And if we meet that boozy beer-bag again?"

"Screw him."

Maxwell laughed, nodded. "He's mine?"

"Yours."

Harney could smell the dead unwashed bodies beside him. He listened to the retreating footsteps, the progress through the church. Then silence for minutes.

When he began his inch-by-inch exit he was a dangerous wary prowler, listening to the darkness. There was ordure and a faint sweetness in the air about him. Heat too: he was sweating. He pushed away the enclosing spirit cases; each, a glacial movement, a listening pause, again and again, tirelessly repeated.

The church door was open; the sweat on his face caught the bitter chill of it. Sweat was a blessed unction now. The wind was rising again; he could hear it in the trees and shrubs, the rustle of driven leaves, the hollow sound it made in the church. In the dying moments he could hear the shuffle of Dowty and Maxwell.

They waited, Harney thought, for his shipmate, Paul Vincent Herlihy, who had cleansed and bandaged him, even brought to him his cap and mirror. "Now, you're in charge again."

A decent man.

With the same meticulous care he raised himself, looked at the edged blade of the knife in his hand, its needle point; and then remembered the screaming suffocating seconds in the stale butt of holy water, his nakedness, his genitals dowsed in spirit, ready for ignition.

Harney had sat naked in madhouse cells, nursing pain for the yellowskin bastard who had mounted his Nancy. But the Canon! Paul Vincent Herlihy abased, diminished, stripped maybe, that numinous presence that could watch the river and knew how it healed. Jesus! Harney thought.

The odour of corpses reached him again and he opened

a bottle of whisky, poured it over the tarpaulin shrouds. He pushed back the cases to seal the vault again. He smelt his clothes, drank a great mouthful of whisky, and then generously sprinkled himself with it. Everything done with painstaking care.

'Not even the boozy slob we shoved in the barrel', that Jock animal had said.

Harney moved wraithlike to the archway, along the passage to the squint, and from that narrow oblique cleft viewed the church.

The door was held barely ajar and the pair waited, stood in watch. The wind gathered and spent itself, sweeping in from the river. Maxwell's shoe jammed the door but sudden gusts almost dislodged it and the rolling gratuitous slime of blasphemy offended Harney. Interminably, they waited, watched, leather jackets at the door, Harney at the squint.

Maxwell said, "We're a pair of spares in a brothel."

"That's right."

"He's out there somewhere."

"That's right."

"We get him, give him his ballpoint, make a corkscrew of his nuts, and that's it!"

"Quick, tidy, expert," Dowty reminded.

Maxwell smiled. "Professionals!"

"That's right," Dowty told him. "We get paid."

Harney's body felt cold, he shivered; only the ridge of torn flesh on his forehead pulsed with heat. He took his own half-bottle from his jacket. Hands apart, knife held vertical, the bottle, the taped wound: he was a comic assassin from some abandoned road-show waxworks. He drank and listened to the wind. A rising wind, a waiting wind; and it was darkening, the morning light had hardly gathered and it was taking flight again.

Maxwell, in a single syllable of blasphemy, alerted him. He focused on them. A quarry in sight? He heard the hardly soundless closing of the door in their hurry. They were gone.

Harney hurried into the church, climbed the pulpit, his old coign of vantage from where he could view the river night-time traffic, the walled churchland, the razed village, Sulvan's, the waterfront.

He saw Catherine Delacey wrapped against the wind. She had left the churchyard and moved across, pushed and halted by sudden gusts, to the empty cabin where death came and went.

Maxwell and Dowty had vanished.

Harney's gaze ranged the boundary wall, the vaults, the trees, the shrubs, sweeps of leaves, grass lying flat, frantic half-naked branches. No other stir of life.

He went out, running, half crouched, knife in hand, skirted the walls and buildings, the sheltered side of monuments, parted shrubs and prodded deep into them. He stood in an empty world: the churchyard, the village, the waterfront. Only the wind made noise and movement.

He stood by Lucy Dory-Catchpole's gravestone, held tight to its jagged edges. He had walked the perimeter of the Rectory: not a window broken or raised, not a door unlocked. Catherine Delacey, he thought.

Death Row!

He left the churchyard and moved across the open space, unknowingly spied upon from two windows: the Canon watched him from the Rectory; Maxwell, from Ada's cabin.

Harney's searching wary face, the knife. Bloody signs, the Canon knew . . .

At Ada's Dowty arranged a bedside locker for a table, put envelope and pen on it, awaiting the signature. Catherine Delacey lay on Ada's hardly disturbed death-sheets she had come to change. Dowty stood over her. "He'll be looking for *this* soon," he said.

"I wouldn't."

Dowty looked at him without humour.

"I wouldn't with yours," Maxwell said.

Catherine Delacey was in no distress but a little angry. She wore a deep blue belted smock; her cuffed white linen sleeves shone against it. She could study these berserkers: fingers, lips, eyes. Very efficient, she thought; without compassion.

Maxwell held back an edge of the drawn curtains; he said,

"The bog-trotter from the deadhouse is coming our way. Knife and all, by Christ! We missed him."

Dowty said, "Real slow he'll push open the door . . . are you listening?"

Maxwell nodded.

"You know the rest. You know the game."

He said to Catherine Delacey, "You won't make a sound, will you?" He held a chopping-edge hand resting almost on her throat . . .

Like a weather-eyed thief, Harney did inch open the door and was suddenly in motion, as if sucked in a vacuum: in a single strike, Maxwell had pulled, and sunk a fist in him, left him airless. The knife clattered on the tiles. Harney was a shapeless bundle in the corner; his fingers trembled, his mouth gaped in agony for breath that wouldn't come. When it did, it grated like a death-rattle in his throat, and in a sudden eructation brought food and drink with it. He seemed to drowse.

"He could choke," Catherine Delacey said.

"With luck."

Now Maxwell could see the Canon coming from the churchyard gate: beret, hands hidden beneath his cloak, wrapping it tight about himself, against sudden squalls from the river.

He said, "He's here! The big one!"

He gently released the edge of the curtain, stood, long-armed, ape-like, at the blind edge of the door.

Dowty glanced at him.

The Canon entered.

Dowty said, "Paul Vincent Herlihy. My pleasure."

With his buttocks Maxwell slammed the door, spread his shoulders across it, a great smiling sentinel.

The Canon looked at Catherine Delacey. "My dear?" he said. "You haven't been upset by our visitors, I hope."

Maxwell said, "Not for the moment, padre." He kicked Harney's knife against the skirting-boards.

Harney stirred, made a retching sound, and lost the battle against recovery.

Catherine Delacey, Harney, his vomit, the leather jackets: the Canon surveyed it all, reconstructed it.

Harney, man of honour, madman, he pondered. He looked at his helpless squat.

"We thought you'd come sniffing your mare on the bed," Maxwell said. "You like a little morning rattle, do you, padre?"

The Canon said, "We take care of old people here. Miss Delacey is a nurse." He showed great courtesy to Maxwell.

"But special," Dowty said.

"Oh yes."

"Very special."

"Indeed."

"Little cowboys and kinky knickers. Not nice, is it?" Harney stirred again and was booted. "All that busted gear out there. Shame." Maxwell was in high humour. "Did a recce yesterday, padre. Got it right this time, didn't we?"

The Canon said, "I usually punish people for that kind of thing."

Maxwell had solid pillars of teeth but when he laughed he exposed gums too and parted an ugly gash.

"Shut up!" Dowty told him; he said to the Canon, "We need your signature, Reverend." He pointed to the envelope and pen. "Ten seconds, no fuss."

"No fuss."

"Unless I say so," Dowty said. "My colleague, you can imagine, might offend Miss . . ."

"Delacey," the Canon said.

"Might offend Miss Delacey. Physically, I mean. He dislikes women."

"That would be unfortunate," the Canon said.

"Wouldn't it?"

"Extremely."

Dowty turned to the makeshift table. "A signature, that's all. Your usual signature. 'Paul Vincent Herlihy'." He produced the picture and its specimen. "No canons or padres or holy fathers, just Paul Vincent Herlihy."

"What am I signing?" the Canon asked.

"Think of us as messenger boys," Dowty said. "Collect, deliver. Bikers, express post. And a bit short on time at the moment."

The Canon nodded; he was very pleasant. "Tell your principal to come and see me. Your employer, that is. Time is the enemy for us all, isn't it? Miss Delacey and I are extremely busy too. We'll bid you good morning."

"Yes," Dowty said.

It was a signal.

Maxwell, suddenly in action, took a twisting grip on Catherine Delacey's hair and stood her erect. Gently then, he laid a hand on each shoulder. "Tell your lover-boy to do his writing," he said.

Catherine Delacey said, "I have a temptation . . ."

"Keep it in your kinky drawers, duckie."

"To spit in your eye, ma heelan' squaddie."

The momentary silence of shock was infinite. The squelch was an explosive flatulent emission. Dowty smiled.

Expertly, a hand under the clothing at each shoulder, Maxwell dropped to the floor, took everything with him. Catherine Delacey was naked but for shoes and suspended stockings.

Maxwell stood and inspected her; walked about her, inspected her again.

"Not bad, am I?" Catherine Delacey said. "With a better face I might have made the 'Bluebells'."

Catherine Delacey could spit: there was a trick in gathering saliva, compressing it behind tight lips and releasing the jet.

It sent Maxwell staggering back into the grip of the arising Harney. Harney's fingers clamped on his throat, broke the flesh. But Catherine Delacey despatched him.

With Harney's knife – an upswing of precision – she dug it beneath his ribs, snuffed him out.

Dowty was crouched, at the moment of springing. The Canon, cloak hanging free, brought his stick in a lightning sabre swing. He shattered Dowty's skull, left him in blood and oozing brain: even his eyes, gelatinous sea creatures, hung from their sockets.

There was perfect stillness: the dead were dead, the Canon and Catherine Delacey frozen in the moment of execution. Harney took his gaze from the beauty of Catherine Delacey's body and focused on the gory floor: he felt humble in the company of such champions.

He watched the Canon's feet as he moved to Catherine Delacey and embraced her for a moment.

Only the wind, Harney thought, was reassurance of a world outside.

"Thank you, Harney," the Canon said. "We're most grateful."

Harney saw Catherine Delacey's blood-soaked clothing on the floor, looked no higher. He cleaned his shoes carefully on the doormat, removed his trousers and jacket. He held them out.

"For you, ma'am."

There was a moment of silence, warmth. "Well, you are a dear man," Catherine Delacey said.

Harney stood, inelegantly in long johns, his flies open, his penis, a frightened creature too, peering out.

Catherine Delacey said, "Button up, Harney."

"Jesus!" Harney said.

"Well, fair is fair," she told him. "You had a look, I had a look. A peek for a peek."

Harney picked up his shoes, took his knife from Maxwell's body, and went out into the world, towards the Mortuary, a strange hobbledehoy figure now, his laughter above the wind a series of great cheering roars.

Catherine Delacey was an untidy Chaplin caught midway in dressing. She looked at the battlefield and its blood. The Canon put his cloak about her.

Sulvan was standing in the open door.

"The filthy dead and their traces," he said. "I'll see to it."

He watched them move away towards the churchyard and the Rectory.


The wind, at the precise moment, slapped like a wave against them and Doll and Flo were flung in the church: they came with a great swarm of leaves that fell between pews, littered the aisles, the arcade, even the sanctuary.

197

The profanity was outrageous, muffled, lost. Together they pushed against the door and snapped it shut.

Breathless.

Doll said, "I ain't sweeping that lot!"

"Let that half-pissed bell-ringer with his turban have a go."

Flo looked at the litter, even flinty pebbles from the pathway. She looked at St Anthony, 'frozen' perhaps by the phenomenal succubus of Mrs Murphy's passion. And the Canon? What strange orbit had he taken in his flight?

Doll was deep in peevish misery; she said, "Come on, come on!" Saturday was early start, finish and go. "I'll be down that road before twelve, like a shot, before he switches on them Angelus bells."

They were wrapped and hooded like snowland fur-trappers, revenant beadsmen flitting in the cloistered arcade. They reached the Mortuary and peeled off the outer layers of wrapping. Doll wheezed.

"Cuppa first."

"And a fag," Flo said: she arranged the mugs, a packet of king-size, fitted her Walkman headphones above butterfly earrings.

"Know something?" Doll said. "It's getting darker out there. Morning, moving for nine, and it's getting dark!" There was only the sound of the wind. She turned and saw diamante Flo and her headphones. "Wasting my bloody puff, ain't I? Talking into space! What is it? . . ."

Flo shushed her.

"Balls!"

"Warning," Flo said with lost interest. "Flood warning. A puff of wind and high tide and you should run for the Archway and Highgate Hill!"

Doll nodded, lit her fag. "Then, 'fresh breezes', they tell you, and you get a hurricane. Warnings!" She blew out smoke. "We've had them all. Health warnings, sex warnings, flood warnings. You dodges sideways for one, the other one gets you. No one listens no more, that's favourite for me."

Flo wore her Walkman now like a primitive torque. "High wind, high tide, serious, he says."

198

"Well, they got all them building blocks and snailshells for stopping floods at Woolwich."

Flo was thoughtful. "Woolwich is up there, we're down here. Wrong side."

Doll brought the kettle. "No warnings on bags of tea yet, is there, love?"

They settled themselves in a cloud of steam; Flo lit her cigarette. Like impermeable topers at a bar, they sat and waited for talk to come but it seemed an empty world.

"God," Doll said.

Flo nodded. "I was going to say that."

"All them leaves out there."

"Fingers to the leaves."

"And the dark."

"Yeah, it's getting dark, funny that, morning-time and it's getting dark."

Doll explained it. "Dust in the atmosphere is what causes it, see? From anywhere. Egypt, Cyprus, Timbuktu. Sucked up one place, comes down another."

"Dirty buggers."

"Who?"

"Them Gyppos."

Doll wasn't sure; she said, "Funny, ain't it, the darkness."

She remembered a vague distant summer day when darkness had come at high noon. She told Flo, "My mother, RIP, said it was the end of the world, took a bus to Roehampton."

Humour was returning in snatches. "And lightning," Flo said. "There's people rush for the bed when there's lightning."

"My fellow don't need lightning for *that*," Doll said.

They were back to their screeching selves again; they smoked, drank their cooling tea.

"You get a smell or something?" Flo raised her snout. "Like something's gone off."

"Or let off," Doll said. "Harney! That pisspot's insides, God, full of booze and gunge, don't bear thinking about."

"After nine. He should be on the creep by now, shouldn't he?" Flo listened.

"Came maybe and left his pong behind."

Flo blew out protective smoke from her nostrils. "And Father Jim running late too. Funny morning."

Funny old world, Doll thought: Roehampton was a 'foreign land' of trees and grass; and at Putney Bridge the swans moved with such dignity; 'blacks' with suitcases came out across Victoria Station them days, from sunshine to pissing rain, workers for wards and trolleys and buses, the shops, the kitchens: good people. The nicks had chalk lines to measure your alcohol; a man could park his banger round the corner at Selfridges, find a boozer and drink wallop till the shopping was done, steer home safe as the Band of Hope. And it had all gone wrong.

"Times has changed," Doll said and blew out smoke.

"You what?" Flo said.

"Just thinking. You know, looking back, like."

"Oh."

"School with the nuns."

"Did their best, I suppose."

"Born here when the bombs had hardly stopped, loving Ma and Da. 'Home', they tell us, is over there in Paddyland."

"I ain't never been."

"Same as that."

Prayer books and rosary beads. Doll thought of ageing parents and their bones up the road in foreign ground, poor bastards, going back . . . going back . . . going back . . . always next year!

"We must go and see the graves one day," she said.

"Last time we couldn't find them, remember?"

Doll remembered. "We got pissed instead."

They were in a harmony of hoots and whinnies once more when the crash of the front door flung open by the wind reached them; the swirl of cold air too; and then the diminution of sound when the door was pushed shut again.

"An arrival," Flo said.

"More leaves," Doll reminded her. "Bloody Epping Forest out there with stained-glass windows."

"'Funland' at Margate, love."

"Mrs Murphy's ten-foot jump . . ."

"The Canon's flying circus . . ."

". . . Francis Xavier's nuts on the danger-list."

Harney was suddenly in the archway, shoes in hand, long johns tucked inside his socks.

Flo looked at the headband of tape on his forehead; his hair, bereft of cheese-cutter, blown into spikes of chaos.

"The Wizard of Oz," she said.

Harney took the bloodied knife from his shoe where he had carried it; he wiped the blood on the coarse fabric of his underwear.

Doll said, "Or a Halal butcher."

"Them buttons," Flo told him, "on your flies, is a bit loose, darling."

"Eh?"

"The buttons on your 'how's your father'."

"A busy passageway," Harney said.

Doll nodded. "It must be to the john. Happens to us all in the end."

Harney looked on them with strange affection, approval, with a gleaming smile created mystery and puzzlement for them. He was beyond the range of barbs or ridicule.

He took a bottle of whisky, laced their teacups to the brim, drank enormously himself.

"Well, it'll kill the smell," Flo said. "It's like someone crapped in here." She looked at the rear flap of Harney's long johns.

Harney put the knife in the Infant's crib, sat on the holy-water butt and suddenly laughed with bright winsome innocence.

"You're pissed," Doll said. "Out of your mind. Where was it?" She looked at his get-up.

"Fancy dress, was it?"

"'Sweeney Todd on his way to the Bog'." Doll took a regal cloak from the Magi and draped him; she stood and examined him. "Backstage at the Palladium now, eh? Suits him too."

"Funny thing," Harney said. "I had a grandfather, a showbiz man."

"A lion-tamer," Flo said.

"Close," Harney said. "There was a cage."

"He used to get in it and look out."

"He put yobboes in it," Harney said. "Always puddin' heads in every parish. Loincloths, red raddle, tomahawks. A notice: 'Don't Give Whisky to the Indians'. A lot of money."

Flo waited.

"He was killed," Harney said.

"Tomahawked?"

"Transvaal 1899. His last words, 'Goodbye, Dolly, I must leave you'."

"His faithful horse?"

"I couldn't tell you," Harney said. "His wife was Angelina. He was a knife-thrower too."

"Poor thing," Doll said.

Harney came with the whisky bottle again but they clamped hands on their cups. "We got work to do, Harney," Doll said. "Work, work, work. Why don't you paint a few Indians and go on the road again, love?"

"They do it themselves now," Harney said.

Flo appraised him, had a moment of sympathy for him. "Where was you, duckie, where was you? Out in the storm in your knickerbockers? Get your death."

"Death," Harney said. "A work of mercy."

He remembered West African steam and sweat: death in the morning, buried at sundown, from stink to maggots.

"I still get that pong," Flo said.

Harney didn't hear. "Up from Takoradi once," he said. "Miles up. Tarzan country. Kicking football with their bare feet, all them blacks, and the keeper hits his head on the goalpost. They had rocks for goalposts, you see. Before dark and mosquitoes, they shouldered his box up the road, kicked football all the way. Singing and drums too. Respect, a work of mercy. The passing of a sportsman."

Doll wondered about madmen and flashers and birds on the game.

"Some people likes death," she said. "Like the Canon and his bird."

"The Canon and *Miss Delacey*." Harney's mood paled a little.

"That's what I said. His bird."

"*Miss Delacey*," Harney said and waited.

"Miss Delacey," Doll said.

A blast of wind slammed against the stone and sealed doorway of the Mortuary, was dichotomised again and again and spent.

Harney cocked a professional ear. "Heavy squall," he said and listened to the lingering moan. "But she's blowing up out there, the big one."

Muted squeaky music from Flo's pendant Walkman faded; Flo listened. "Flood warnings again," she said. "They're closing that thing at Woolwich." There was less boredom now.

"The flood barrier," Doll explained. "They're closing it."

Harney was looking at the ensemble of the Christmas crib, smiling at its beauty; wrapped in his Magi cloak he took his place among the effigies: the Holy Family, the sleeping beasts, the Magi, the shepherds. Joseph seemed suddenly the cloaked bereted Canon, Miss Delacey, the kneeling Mother.

Doll said, "There's a flood tide, Harney. We should be the other side of Woolwich."

Flo, still listening, said, "Marginal floods, that's what they say."

She hung the Walkman on her neck again, pointed to it, told Doll, "Music now. 'Twist Again', that's what they're playing, love."

"'. . . like we did last summer . . .'" Doll was remembering; coping with creaking hips and ankles in a flight back to youth.

Harney listened to what seemed passing gusts and silences. "It'll be a big one when it comes," he said.

"Bad for Father Jimmy's wheeze-up tonight." Doll's distress was dreamy happiness.

And Flo; she said to Harney, "Not a square dancer in sight. A rest for the clodhoppers. Imagine it. Just the little cowboy, the singing sisters and you and Father Jimmy at the doze-ee-doe."

"Nunz v Narcos," Harney said.

"Oh yeah," Doll said. "Something like that."

"Shut up!" Harney told her; he had taken his knife from

the swaddling clothes of the Infant, and joined them. He pointed at the cups. "Finish it! Get it down!"

They were afraid now; they drank.

The wind struck again, sent gravel peppering on the ancient door, moaned a faint tenuous shriek.

"Not natural," Doll said.

Flo nodded. "A freak."

"A freak," Harney said, "is an Act of God." He looked at the clustered figures of the crib again.

Doll put the cups away. "We're off," she said. "That Hall gets a cat's lick, and that's it! We're off! Up the road, past Woolwich, into the world again, you know. It'll be us sitting behind a couple of barley-wines in Roman Road, if you're passing."

Harney drove his knife into the table, flicked the handle with his fingers, left it shivering there.

Doll was gawping, thunderstruck.

"Scream," he said to Flo, "and I'll gut you."

Harney's flushed face seemed to pale and attenuate; he gazed at the stained-glass surround, the carved roof-trusses, the holy-water butt, the ultimate confusion left behind by the leather jackets.

The big jock was laid low now, he thought, and his mate had eyeballs hanging on strings!

He pulled the knife from the table and held it under Flo's chin. Her teeth chattered. He said to Doll, "Bring the Canon and Miss Delacey. The hour of espousement is at hand. They are my friends, chosen ones. This place of sadness will be a place of joy, by God! You have ten minutes! *Bring* them!" Harney said. "Don't *send* them! Or you'll have a barley-wine on Roman Road, on your jack." He pressed the knife against Flo until she whimpered.

"Go ye forth into the highways and as many as ye shall find . . ." He thought suddenly of the desolation all about him.

Flo made an almost soundless whinny.

Doll screeched, "I'm fucking going! I'll bring 'em, I'll bring 'em!" She was running. From the passage she called back to Flo, "I'll come for you, love, I'll come for you!"

204

"Ten minutes!" Harney shouted.

They heard her clatter through the church, felt the chill of wind until she tugged the door shut.

"'Go ye therefore into the highways and as many as ye shall find bid to the marriage.'"

He was smiling again. He sheathed his knife, poured a drink for Flo and watched her gulp it. He drank from the bottle himself.

In a whisper Flo said, "You know I'm married, kind of, don't you?"

Harney said, "I wouldn't marry you if my nuts were on fire."

"Oh God," Flo said; she took the bottle and drank again.

"Now we work," Harney said. "Ten minutes."

To banish disarray and leave beauty in its wake would be a daunting sentence, a month in hard labour, he knew. The litter of the floor was gathered, pushed, swept behind the spirit cases, the tomb of Father Jim and the cowboy: Harney worked with a great ferocious enthusiasm, called out his instructions to Flo. A countdown.

"Five minutes . . ."

"Jesus," Flo prayed; she quickened her pace.

The floor swept, the trestle-table covered in yellowed white runners, stained or frayed, that had once clothed the church altar for the Mass, the naked bulb shining down: an arcane chamber of wizardry stumbled upon.

Harney put a pitted unsteady candelabrum of tallow stumps at each end of the trestle-table.

"Flowers!" he called out, and pointed.

Flo saw on the cluttered shelves a glass case of paper flowers; she peered through the dust at roses, red and white, perhaps a century old: she dusted the glass . . .

"Bring it!"

"What are we having?" Flo whispered again; fear was gathering.

"Bring it!"

She carried it to the table. "It's for a funeral," she said. She cleaned the dust away. "There's a card, see? 'To Mr Peacock from his loving Kitchen Staff'."

"Ass-licking dossers!" Harney said. "Flowers can laugh or cry." He planted it as a centrepiece and arranged it.

"What do you think of it?" he threatened her.

"Oh, nice," she said.

"The whole shebang?" Harney's eyes were gimlet points. "Flowers, candles, holy linen cloths?"

"Artistic, Mr Harney. Artistic."

Harney brought the beer crates from where Doll and Flo had squatted and made himself a dais. He arranged it at an oblique angle to the table.

He was gazing at his watch. "Thirteen seconds," he said.

Flo drank from the bottle.

"Five seconds."

The church door had opened, a charge of wind swelled and died in the cul-de-sac of the Mortuary.


"Oh God," Flo moaned; she looked for her beer crate to flop on.

The door of the church had clanged shut, blessed life-saving steps approached, slow, unhurried. Flo groped about but Harney had appropriated the crates for his dais; and now he stood on it, arms flung to whatever invisible audience he had gathered about him, to apostrophise in silence.

Like the function of some ancient heat-circuit radio, faint words came at first from a distance within Harney and were amplified to a great boom.

"'And it came to pass when Man began to multiply on the earth, and daughters were born unto them, that the Sons of God saw the daughters of Men that were fair; and they took them wives of all they did choose . . .'"

Flo sat on the water-butt, saw dimly the arrival of the Canon and Catherine Delacey in the archway. Doll cowered behind them, watched Harney.

"'. . . And God saw that the wickedness of Man was great in the earth, and that every imagination of the thoughts of his heart was on evil continually. And it repenteth the Lord that He had made Man on earth and it grieved Him at His heart.'"

206

The Canon raised a hand in salutation to Harney coming down from his 'pulpit', beamed his composure. Doll, witch-like from the wind, gibbous, darted across to resuscitate Flo with trembling sweaty hands.

The Canon hid his compassion, said, "There's a gale in the making out there, Harney. Gusts that might whip you off your feet. Listen!" The roof was hammered with a thousand rods. "Sudden cloudbursts of rain. I'll enjoy it, Harney . . . the river . . . the river."

Harney was rapt, a holy tranquillity surrounding him; he no longer trembled, the violent urgency was diminishing.

"White horses on the Thames," the Canon said. "A breath of air, a search for the sky. Grey rain and desolation. The big ships moving like ghosts."

Harney said in a whisper, "Funny, I always enjoyed the winter. Rain and wind and storm. Summer, with yellow newspapers baking on the pavement-slabs, was never in my line."

"Yes." The Canon understood. "Narrow deserted streets go down to the river, Harney. Tottering piles of brick, the falling slates, the tide on the first creep."

Harney saw it all. "Pub signs!" he shouted, "swinging frantic like thuribles, newspapers whipped up, instantly made birds, skimming the vanished rooftops. And the clatter of dustbins."

"Delightful, Harney," Catherine Delacey said; she came and took his hand. "This is an occasion, I believe?"

"An event."

Flo, embraced by Doll, slid the Walkman to her ears again, listened a moment, let the earphones clatter to the floor.

There was silence, even the wind and rain stilled; Harney looked across at the little buzzing metallic earpieces.

"High tide," Doll apologised. "Floods, that's all."

Flo's face was shrunken in fear: beneath her chin, where Harney had held his knife, a tiny pinhead of blood had congealed. Doll touched it gently and pressed and kissed her hand in comfort.

Flo was voiceless; she let a limp hand point to the Walkman.

"Pick it up," Harney said.

Doll picked it up; she said, "We're off. That's it."

"Sit!" dog-trainer Harney told her. "Sit!"

Doll was for battle. "Get your Father Jim here! Get him! He's the Guv'nor!"

"Father Jim," Harney said with sad courtesy, "regrettably will not be with us, nor his Camden Town Maverick of 'country' and 'blue grass'."

"Unfortunate," the Canon said. "Those wires and boxes, things of beauty to him, I suppose, lying in waste out there."

Catherine Delacey said, "A painful experience for him, was it, Harney? Left him in distress?"

"Left him breathless," Harney said. "Without breath."

The conversation was measured; an air of decorum.

"Our neighbour, Mr Sulvan," Harney suddenly remembered.

The Canon said, "He would be charmed, Harney, I'm sure, but would regret a prior engagement. We left him a little while ago."

Harney, of spiked hair, the flowing embroidered cloak, bowed. "He is in good health, I trust."

"The residue of some pressing business needs tidying," the Canon said.

Harney was gracious. For Catherine Delacey, he took Doll's tea mug and poured Empire sherry.

Doll held Flo close to her, watched the mock ceremonial with growing rage; the earphones on her lap suddenly buzzed with urgency. She raised them up.

The transition from rage to fear on Doll's face was a strange metamorphosis: the mouth, ready to release its burst of invective, softened, sagged, gaped; the earphones were held high, waved.

"Dr Sinclair?" Harney asked.

"Racing in the West Country, I'm afraid," the Canon said. . . .

Doll screamed!

The final relief of such pent-up terror was an ear-splitting needle of sound.

"Shut it!" Harney said.

"A volcano!" Doll roared, in full voice again. "Down in the river, Harney, you arsehole, a volcano, an explosion, a bomb, a wave! . . ." Breath ran short; she whispered, "You bloody madman!"

Harney smiled, pondered his own wisdom, nodded to the Canon. "Not surprising with all the crap that's down there."

With a taper he lit the withered stumps of his candelabra. The wind had risen outside, rushing on before a great force.

"A wave!" Doll roared again. "Fucking floods, wind, rain! Listen, you plank! Hear it?"

Harney held up a warning finger.

"Fifty foot, Harney, rising up, coming for us!" Doll was in tears.

"A wave," the Canon pondered, seemed to gaze at some distant place.

"If we are composed," Harney said with just a shadow of menace, "we will arrange for the ceremony."

He gestured to the table, switched off the naked bulb: it was a strange crepuscular candlelit cave.

Doll quavered, "The wave . . ."

Flo was drained, her belligerence down to the lees.

Harney said, "Don't whimper! Shut your little faces!" He took a long satisfying drink.

Doll watched the air-gurgles in the bottle, the shocked throes of Harney's distorted thyroid. Derring-do and spleen returned for a moment, resignation. She said, "Top yourself up, that's it. Go on, have another one, give us maybe the pleasure of seeing you off, Harney, watching some pissed-off old 'reverend' pressing the button to float you into the flames of Paradise."

"More old drunks than doctors about," Harney said. He began his arrangements. "Canon, would you be so kind? And dear Madam Delacey?"

He stood them at the trestle-table, before Mr Peacock's flowers from his loving kitchen staff.

"The bride on the left," he told Catherine Delacey.

"Marriage!" Catherine Delacey beamed; she gave him a

209

gentle peck; midway down she safety-pinned his cloak to obscure carnality.

Doll, jolted from her fear for a moment, said, "Thank God for that!" And then screamed, "The wave, Harney!"

"There's holy water in that barrel," Harney said. "Another hoot and you're in it, headfirst."

He bowed to the Canon.

"Am I the celebrant?" the Canon asked.

"You are the bridegroom," Harney said.

"Ah." The Canon took his place.

Harney looked at them and was pleased: the Canon's kind asceticism, the stark definition of cloak and beret thumbed into the twilight, the gleam of lignum vitae; Catherine Delacey, re-apparelled in green leather greatcoat, her face framed with quiet sanctity, Harney thought, in his sou'wester hat.

"A best man?" the Canon wondered.

Harney brought Joseph from the crib.

"You look quite regal in your robe," Catherine Delacey said, ignored the sometimes visible nether buttons at his crotch and flitting glimpses of the 'beyond'.

Harney passed an exploratory hand along the flies.

"Disgusting," Doll said. "Don't bear thinking about."

"God!" Flo said.

They were caught in a grip of fear and anger; courage was a weak moment of defiance.

"A bridesmaid," Harney said: from the shelves he brought a dusty statuette and positioned it on the table.

"St Rita," Catherine Delacey said. "Known as 'saint of the impossible', dear boy."

Harney placed a Magus at each end of the table. "'Wise Kings' would have queens," he said, "but they can make do with scrubbers in a pinch." He placed Doll and Flo in their roles of consorts.

"You don't look mad," Doll said, "but your brain-box is in a bad way."

Harney was caught up in creative enthusiasm; he paced about his candlelit stage, pondering, viewing his ensemble. There was an air of satisfaction.

For a moment he looked at the depleted crib. "The Virgin Mother and Child," he said gently, "we must leave undisturbed. In the gentle care of shepherds and their flocks."

"Splendid," the Canon said.

Flo, a death's-head, donned her Walkman to listen; or to distance herself from an enveloping phantasm.

"And we are honoured in our celebrant." Catherine Delacey smiled.

"Cap'n of the ship, ma'am," Harney saluted. "Empowered, you might say."

"Thank you, Harney."

Doll, resigned, perhaps mad, said, "You ain't asking the clapped-out cow and Neddy the moke, are you?"

Harney considered it. He put an animal on each flank.

Flo suddenly babbled, sent little squeaks of noise into the darkness, clamped hands against the earphones. "The wave! . . ." she exhaled in a long dying breath, fading to silence.

Harney took the earphones, listened, was pleased with it. ". . . eruption . . . explosion . . . volcano!" He was laughing. "Tar barrels," he said. "All that dodgy crap the bastards put out there."

"I got friends on the river," Flo wept. "Friends in Gravesend."

"I'm sorry, love." Doll sent her condolences.

Harney, back on his dais, shouted, "Places!"

"Sixty foot now . . . sixty-foot wave . . ."

"Places!"

Doll and Flo, a last rally, looked as if they might stampede but Harney unsheathed his knife and, blade upwards, made some ceremonial motion of silent blessing or malediction. "Harney rode the waves from Finisterre to Benin!" he said.

"Sixty foot high . . ."

"We are ready."

The Canon nodded and Doll sidled back between her cow and Wise King.

"We are ready, dear friend," the Canon said.

Harney pointed to the river. "The wedding barge awaits. God will send us a wind."

211

"Send us a wind!" Doll was mouthing without sound. "Send us a wind, you asshole! Another puff and the whole effin' place is down . . ."

Harney was intoning, "'In the six hundredth year of Noah's life, in the second month, the seventeenth day of the month, the same day were all the fountains of the deep broken up, and the windows of Heaven were opened. And the rain was on the earth forty days and forty nights.'"

Flo dried her tears.

"The barge awaits," Harney said.

Doll said, "What barge?"

"Boats don't struggle. They know where they are going. The wedding barge."

"There's only that floating Council khazi down there, full of stinking crap."

The Canon said, "Our message to the future."

Harney prayed again. "A whole world thrown away. Cans, cartons, dead men's clothes. Even a breath-old child in a Sainsbury's bag, and rats swimming ashore at the cast-off . . ."

The Canon gazed in wonder, Miss Delacey in compassion.

". . . bare bones of a hundred Sunday joints," Harney said, "discarded roasted hearts, yellow with lard . . ."

Softly the Canon said, "There isn't much time, Harney."

Harney came to them, placed hand on hand, covered them with his own. "I am minister of the mysterious, grand wizard of wedlock, joining together what no Father Jims may put asunder. Go forth to meet the storm." Harney drove his knife into the table.

Doll and Flo fled, screaming, through the church and the howl of wind. The open church doors hammered and thrashed behind them, leaves came through the canal of the passageway and swirled on the mortuary floor, and upwards, dowsed a flickering candle here and there.

Harney was kneeling now, on his dais, arms crossed and clutching his shoulders, motionless, an image, only the faintest of distant smiles: a glimmer of his ecstasy.

"Madman," Doll had screeched in her flight.

Hardly, the Canon thought.

212

"He is a priest," Catherine Delacey said.

"Yes."

She arranged Harney's regal cloak, touched his nerveless face. He seemed at peace in his deadhouse. She kissed him.

"He has a journey to make," the Canon said.


They went, the Canon and Catherine Delacey, into the maelstrom of the open church, the roar of wind, leaves swirling, rising, diving like bats at first dark. The doors of Father Jim's confessionals swung and clattered for penitents and confessors, a lectern was toppled from its plinth, altar-cloths spun like wraiths, were in flight, grovelled on the aged flagstones, were in flight again. The plaster saints gazed at it all.

They reached the tower, the tower porch, hugging tight like scrummagers, gripping the cloistered arcade, the ironwork of holy cherubs and sainted faces.

The porch was a whirlpool to catch the savage rushes, turn them, send them abroad again. The winding stone staircase ascended the tower: its well was a great orifice for the wind to ram, and withdraw and ram again. It pushed and sucked at them in their climb, stabbed at them through lancet windows.

At the topmost landing there were oaken steps to the belfry floor. The Canon climbed and raised up the carved studded trapdoor, held the weight erect by its brass ring, and Catherine Delacey came aboard. Against the rush of wind, the trapdoor seemed to fall and seat itself with a yawning weightlessness.

They lay silent awhile, spent. The Canon stood, kept himself upright by the huge oak spans that had held the Dory triplet of bells. At the four louvred belfry windows Father Jim's amplifiers stood now, to relay his peals and triumphal hymns at the press of Harney's thumb on some remote bedside switch. Wind still swept through but was weakened, buffed and distorted by the louvred slats.

213

Darkness was already in the sky; but darkness had crept up too, in a black wall, on the eastern skyline. A rising black wall. An edge of mourning. The wave.

The movement was discernible now; it encroached on distant lights, left darkness behind it. Out beyond the four mounted amplifiers, beyond the louvres, street and vehicle lights of a thousand square miles made a prodigious aura, a ghostly sunburst in morning darkness; on the ground, from skyline to skyline – an immeasurable trinket-box of tangled glittering chains and gaudery – people must be in flight from impasse to impasse.

Down below, the churchyard trees and shrubs dug their roots in the holy ground, crouched from the gale. The Hall, the Rectory, in darkness, stood impassive. A single light burned at Sulvan's. The Canon's eyes streamed against a relentless bellows, but the window-slats curved it, diverted it, sent it high into the spire lights . . .

*. . . He saw Lucy Dory-Catchpole's grave. In that same immemorial summer-day aura she embraced her handsome soldier-poet, rested in his arms. She turned and looked to the belfry, the Canon, smiled from her youthfulness he had never known. Then they were fading into the storm, leaving darkness and the remembrance spikes of granite bled of glitter . . .*

The swell of water, hardly a mile distant, sent a hoarse crackle of destruction ahead of it. It raced towards them. They stood clasped together.

"A minute perhaps," the Canon said.

"There's a light."

"Sulvan's. An empty house," the Canon said.

The night-time darkness was fading into an absolute. Harney had come out from the gaping church doors below them, and was moving across the whistling desert. They saw him stagger with his load, stumble and fall in the sweep; he crouched and fought the dogged battle.

Along the gravel path to the gateway and Sulvan's grave, he paused to drink and totter, dragged his canvas-wrapped corpses towards the river.

"Father Jim and his cowboy," the Canon said. "May they have rest."

"And Harney?"

"A job done."

The mountain of water had arrived: the Hall disappeared under its swell, the church roof, Sulvan's, his jetty. Harney and his parcelled dead were deep down on a black careering voyage. Its peak, a vast plateau of dead and debris, lapped the belfry louvres as it sped. The Dory tower ploughed against it, a mitred regal head of stone, indestructible; and Harney's electronic bells, triggered by whatever magic freak of circuitry, pealed out, "Hail Queen of Heaven . . . the morning star . . ."

The decibels struck, stunned, were lethal. The Canon kicked, clawed at the outputs, dislodged them. The silence was like death.

They watched the great gathering avalanche pass them; it would race over the river's tongues of headland, over riverside hinterland, over the 'stepping-stones' at Woolwich, until the first great barrier loomed: the medieval Tower and its latter-day metal bridge.

They heard the thunderous clap as it struck, that would send it rearing skywards, a hundred feet, and then plunged on, monstrous now, to strike London Bridge, climbing, climbing, peaking on the groynes of the world's great square mile: a billion billion tons falling on treasures and trinkets.

The fading corona of gold was the toppling of glass cathedrals reaching for God, uprooted. The rumble and crunch of destruction drifted back. The dome of light was quenched.

The Canon said, "Now, there's the ebb."

From the riverbanks behind them, facing them, the torrents poured back to the mainstream with its corpseload of destruction.

They stood in silence, watched morning light creep back, midday, the afternoon, until the first shadows of early evening were close.

From the streets, the drowned houses, the hinterlands, north and south, the spent divided force flowed back. The river was a smooth millrace rushing home.

The church rose up again from the flood, the Hall, the Rectory, Sulvan's. Ada's cabin had crumbled and vanished. The world was painted in slime.

They looked out to where Sulvan stood, motionless, a deathless sentinel on his jetty.

"We are substantial ghosts," the Canon said.

# J. M. O'NEILL
# OPEN CUT

Hennessy lived in London: grafted, struggled and eked out his days in a London respectable people are careful never to see. A construction-site world of 'kerbside sweat, open-cut trenches, timbered shafts'. A bleak, desolate world of whisky-dulled pain, casual brutality and corruption.

But Hennessy planned a change to his station in life. An abrupt and violent change.

'Fascinating'

*Yorkshire Post*

'An original and assured first novel . . . it is convincingly alive'
*Books & Bookmen*

# DUFFY IS DEAD

Duffy was dead. Taken suddenly on the Holloway Road outside the bank. They'd rung Calnan at twenty-to-bloody-four in the morning. Him standing, string-vested, shivering and barefooted in the unswept, beer-damp debris of the bar. Reaching for a drink, a brandy, and another, knowing there'd be arrangements to be made and he'd be the man obligated to do it.

Never close to Duffy alive, Calnan had no reason then to think of Duffy dead as an agent of great change, or of a quiet burial as making a considerable upheaval in his life.

'The atmosphere is indescribable but absolutely right: as if the world of Samuel Beckett had crossed with that of George V. Higgins . . . an uncannily exacting and accomplished novelist'
*The Observer*

# JOHN MACDOWELL
# CARA MASSIMINA

Morris Duckworth, an impoverished and bored teacher in Verona, sees his path to financial salvation through marriage to Massimina, a seventeen-year-old student. However, her wealthy mother objects to the match so the couple elope. But Morris, still bent on pecuniary advantage and hankering after a little excitement, presents their escape as a kidnapping, and his bizarre odyssey spirals into a nightmare of deception and violence.

'An unusually classy thriller, true to life and not to be missed'
*Julian Symons in The Independent*

'A sharp and witty thriller, expertly paced, frequently horrific and often very funny'
*Shaun Whiteside in The Times Literary Supplement*

'Stylish and funny, the novel keeps us wondering to the end whether MacDowell will let Morris get away with it'
*Andrew Billen in The Observer*

'Comparable to Highsmith at her best . . . the convincing characters, the excellent plot manipulation and the tense atmosphere mark MacDowell as a writer with real talent'
*Maria Lexton in Time Out*

'John MacDowell presents the real, virginal, boastful, cracked Morris lurking behind his own justifications as matters turn lethal and ugly. Clever, blandly humorous and utterly immoral'
*John Coleman in The Sunday Times*

sceptre